National and international bestselling author Joya Ryan is the author of the Shattered series, which includes *Break Me Slowly*, *Possess Me Slowly* and *Capture Me Slowly*. She has also written the Sweet Torment series, which includes *Breathe You In* and *Only You*. Passionate about both cooking and dancing (despite not being too skilled at the latter), she loves spending time at home. She resides in California with her husband and her two sons.

Visit Joya Ryan online:
www.JoyaRyan.com
www.twitter.com/JoyaRyanAuthor

By Joya Ryan:

Yours Tonight
Yours Completely
Yours Forever

Yours
Tonight

JOYA RYAN

piatkus

PIATKUS

First published in the US in 2015
First published in Great Britain in 2015 by Piatkus

3 5 7 9 10 8 6 4 2

A CIP catalogue record for this book
is available from the British Library.

ISBN 978-0-349-40716-6

Typeset in Adobe Garamond by M Rules
Printed and bound in Great Britain by
Clays Ltd, St Ives plc

Papers used by Piatkus are from well-managed forests
and other responsible sources.

MIX
Paper from
responsible sources
FSC
www.fsc.org   FSC® C104740

Piatkus
An imprint of
Little, Brown Book Group
Carmelite House
50 Victoria Embankment
London EC4Y 0DZ

An Hachette UK Company
www.hachette.co.uk

www.piatkus.co.uk

Chapter 1

'Maybe if we left and I got these pants off you, I'd be more convinced.'

Okay, that had to be one of the better – worst – lines I'd heard tonight. And, like all the other lines, it wasn't directed at me.

'I think I'll have to show you my tattoo after all then,' the woman responded. The way she spoke was so confident. Like she was in control of herself and her sexuality, and the man coming on to her was eating it up.

The woman also looked happy.

Not scared in the least.

I took a deep breath, ignoring the flash of envy shooting through my veins, and looked around again.

Waiting.

Tattoo woman and her guy didn't seem to care that they were all but invading my table in order to better climb all over each other. Mine was a small table wedged against the corner of a packed bar ... a table for two.

And yet, I sat alone.

I had been there for almost an hour, and was now convinced my 'blind date' wasn't coming. Pulling out my phone, I called my best friend Harper; she was the one who had the great idea to set me up in the first place.

'Hey, Lana,' she answered.

'Hey, so Rick never showed up.'

'What? He didn't? I'm sorry. He was an idiot.'

'Then why did you set me up with him?'

'Because you need to get out more. Date. Be social. It's summer, you should be enjoying your freedom.'

Ah, yes, freedom. Too bad all I could think about was the fall and starting grad school in my sleepy town of Golden, a safe twenty miles outside of Denver. Harper was on this kick that I needed to 'live life,' to which I politely pointed out that going for my masters in statistics was a plenty thrilling endeavor.

Tattoo girl bumped my table with her butt again, only this time it was because she and Mr Smooth Talker were getting even closer.

'I think I've reached my fun quota for tonight,' I said, wishing I had driven myself into the city, instead of having Harper drop me off tonight. 'Can you come get me now?'

'Yeah, I'm at the office. I just need to finish up a few things. I can be there in an hour.'

I laughed a little. 'And you tell me to have fun? You're the one still working on a Friday night.'

'What was that?' she teased. 'You don't need a ride home?'

'Yes, I do. I'll wait. Thank you.'

I glanced around. An hour. Not my ideal scene, but, surely, I'd survive.

I hung up and scrolled through my text messages. My heart skipped when I saw my dad had finally texted me back about my suggestion for lunch tomorrow. But that skip didn't last long, since it was a polite way to say:

Sorry, Pumpkin, can't tomorrow. Next week?

At least he used a colon and parenthesis after the rejection to soften the blow. Text jargon or not, it was a smile from my father, so I'd take it.

Running a few fingers through my brunette curls, I tried to smooth away a little of the anxiety creeping up. One hour. Two words that were growing a little daunting. I pulled out my phone one more time and texted my dad back.

I know it's a little late, but can I come over and hang out for an hour until Harper can pick me up? I'm kind of stranded in the city.

And send. My dad only lived a mile away. Twenty minute walk, max. Though his wife wasn't my biggest fan, it was better than sitting alone in a busy bar. Maybe not better, but the lesser of two evils. My phone dinged and excitement raced. That was quick!

I smiled and read:

Sorry, Pumpkin, busy night tonight.

My smile faded, and I put my phone on the table and sat back in my seat. Looking down at my simple summer dress, I felt the same thing I'd felt a thousand times growing up, while I waited around for my dad to swoop in and save the day:

Invisible.

When the couple bumped me again, apparently I wasn't the only one they annoyed. A guy standing next to them started yelling. Before I comprehended what was going on, a fist was thrown, and the two men were in a fight. One of them knocked against my table so hard it spilled my water all over me, and I gasped in fear and put my arms over my face like an 'X.'

3

My nerves went into overdrive from the shock of what had just happened. Mentally chanting to myself to calm down, I slowly lowered my arms and saw a large man in a white T-shirt throwing himself between the two fighting men and, along with the bouncer, kicking them toward the exit.

They're gone, I told myself, trying to get a handle on my breathing. The water had hit me straight on, and covered my stomach and lap. I did my best to blot the wetness with my napkin, shaking my head. I shouldn't have even come tonight. I should have stayed home, like usual.

Two more months and I'd start grad school in Golden and not have to come back to the city for any reason, other than my part-time job working at my dad's financial service company. A job I was doing so well at that I had been bumped up to thirty hours a week, now that summer was here. If I kept up this pace, logged my hours at his company, and succeeded at grad school, he'd hire me on as an account lead. Finally, he'd give me the chance to build toward the dream he'd hammered into me since I was a kid. Family business. Sure, it was a small, struggling business he'd started back when I was a kid, but when he married Anita, she and her money put my dad in the black. I may be the dirty, poor step-child, but I was still his, and whether Anita liked it or not, I was determined to be a person he'd be proud of.

People were already over the fight and back to enjoying themselves. At least their eyes weren't on me anymore, but I was soaked and now getting cold.

'Excuse me?' A deep, raspy voice said. I looked up to find a tall, chiseled man with the darkest eyes I'd ever seen, staring down at me. 'Are you alright?'

'I, ah . . .' I looked down at the front of my damp dress and blotted again. It was no use. The thin fabric was clinging to my thighs, making me very uncomfortable.

4

'Here,' he said, shrugging out of his jacket and placing it on my shoulders. It smelled of spice and leather. I tried to work a breath out, but it was no use. Between the sudden heat of his jacket enveloping me and the sight of his obviously broad chest and hard torso, I found it difficult to make my mouth move.

I didn't know if it was the rush of the fight I'd witnessed followed by the cold water, but whatever it was, my body was confused and prickling with heat while flushing with goose bumps.

'Are you sure you're okay?' he asked, his onyx gaze roaming over my entire body.

When he began to roll up the sleeves of his white button-up shirt, I watched transfixed. His forearms flexed a little as he moved to the other cuff. The way his long fingers worked the material, exposing tan skin as he went, made me wonder how the simple act of rolling up his sleeves could be sexy.

Trailing my gaze up, I took in every edge of his face. With a five o'clock shadow that matched his black hair, he looked exotic. Powerful. What must it be like to be a man like him? A person with so much confidence it radiated in every tiny movement. What would someone have to do to obtain that kind of essence?

Without knowing the answer to that, I'd likely sign up. Because whatever Kool-Aid this guy drank, I wanted some. Bad.

Harper told me once that prey could recognize predators and, while most run, some go into shock from the predator's power. I think she had been on her third shot of tequila and was only half listening to the *Animal Planet* episode that was on, but it made some sense.

True or not. I felt like prey, transfixed by a predator. And I didn't have the good sense to flee just yet.

'You don't have to lend me your jacket,' I said, kind of wishing I hadn't. But manners were manners. 'I'll be fine.' I caught a

5

heavy whiff of his scent again, and it instantly swarmed my senses, warming me from the inside out.

'Please, I insist.' His words were kind, but there was a definitive tone that made me not want to challenge him. The man had to be a couple inches over six foot, and the large jacket covered me well, reinstating a bit of security.

'Are you sure you didn't get hit or injured?' He tilted his head and examined me. The low light of the bar made shadows dance across his face, like some mythical underworld god.

I smiled a little because while he might look fierce, his concern was sweet. Actually, he was the only one who'd asked. Everyone else just stared. Then I realized why he must be asking. I hadn't gasped, I had yipped like a spooked puppy.

'I was just surprised, but I'm really okay. Wasn't even touched. Well,' I glanced down the front of me again, 'aside from a little water.'

He did that body scanning thing with his eyes again, leaving a trail of hot shivers along my skin.

'Good, I'm glad.'

I went to thank him one more time, but something near the entrance caught my attention. My eyes went to the door and I froze ... it couldn't be. Oh, God, it was ... *him*.

He was here. Walking into the same bar I was currently sitting in. My throat closed up and the sudden urge to bolt, to vomit, to scream, overwhelmed me. An unfortunate reaction, but one I'd had many times whenever I encountered my step-brother. I'd seen him thousands of times over the years, and yet, it never got easier. I just learned how to remain silent and pretend I wasn't terrified.

That I was okay.

'Brock.' I whispered.

What the hell was he doing in Denver? He worked for my father too, and was supposed to be overseeing the New York branch. Which meant he hadn't been around in six months. Six months of blessed peace that allowed me to actually work at my father's company.

He took another step into the bar. I watched his beady eyes scan the room as he adjusted his tie. He was only six years older than me, but his dull brown hair had flecks of gray, and his chest puffed out a little extra to make up for the fact that he was five-nine on a good day. Since he was still in his suit, he'd likely come from the office, but which one?

Everything else in the world blurred, because all I could think about was getting away. Gripping the table with one hand, I tensed to move, to leave, but he was right at the entrance, and there was no way I could get out without him seeing me. Granted, the way he kept looking around, he'd likely notice me any moment.

My blood pumped faster and a kick of anxiety laced with a heavy dose of fear surged until all I could hear was my pulse beating. I couldn't escape.

I looked around, wishing I had a wall, something to hide behind. But I didn't. Just like I didn't that night ten years ago when he came into my bedroom.

When Brock shifted his stance in my direction, my nerves short-circuited. He was going to see me. Huddling the best I could, I tried to make myself smaller. I wished I could disappear. I wished for the thousandth time that I could just be someone else. Somebody braver.

Somebody who mattered.

But, once again, I was alone. Like a laser beam, his gaze was drawn closer . . . closer . . .

'Hey, hey,' the man who gave me his coat whispered. He'd obviously read my body language, and the fact that I was bouncing in my seat, yet not making a move to stand. 'It's okay, those guys are gone,' he said, referring to the men who had been fighting.

It was a reasonable assumption on his part that I was having some kind of post-traumatic freak out moment. Which was half true, just the wrong moment.

He sat right next to me and turned his body so that I faced him head on, and his back was toward the crowd and the bar.

A wall.

'I . . .' I couldn't get words out. Because I didn't know what to say. I didn't want him to go. Between his broad shoulders and strong chest, he effectively kept me hidden from Brock.

He just sat there, one arm on the table, the other gripping the back of my seat, boxing me in and shielding me with his entire body.

'Y-yes, I'm fine.' It was what I always said. What I had rehearsed over and over as a girl. Even at thirteen, I knew that if I didn't pretend that I wasn't broken, I would really break and I'd have no one to help put me back together.

I looked into the stranger's eyes. They were like smoldering obsidian. He was so intense and in control. I should have felt threatened, but I didn't. There was an intensity, sure, but also a gentle understanding and heat that warmed me instantly . . . made me feel safe. And, suddenly, I didn't want to lie . . . not to him.

'No, actually, I'm not fine. I saw someone I don't want to see.'

'Man from your past, I take it?'

'Something like that,' I said, not wanting to go into detail. 'How did you know?'

'You went pale. Before, you were almost on the brink of a smile, then your whole body tensed. Something obviously terrified you.'

My heart sank when I realized that my fear was obvious to a

8

total stranger. Embarrassing even. A true sign of weakness. One thing I hated being, but worried I would never overcome.

I glanced at my hands in my lap.

'Hey,' he whispered and tapped his finger under my chin, making my gaze meet his. 'No one can see you.' He flexed his shoulders just enough to reassure me that he did, in fact, provide the perfect barrier.

Every syllable that left his mouth was coated in power. The exact thing I lacked. From the way he sat, to how he moved, it was obvious this man was all things alpha and in control. And prey or not, I was caught. And I liked it.

I peeked around his shoulder. I didn't see Brock, but the bar was dark and with the low lights and mass amounts of people, he could be lurking anywhere.

Or maybe he'd left.

I could only hope that was the case, because I still had an hour to kill.

'What's your name?'

'Lana,' I said, finding it difficult to breathe with him so close. But for a totally different reason than fear.

'Thank you for—' I motioned at his chest, 'being my wall.'

He smiled back and – *wow*! Talk about an earth-shattering sight. All those straight white teeth and the small crinkle by his eyes made his face light up.

'I'm happy to be your wall.' He leaned in a little. 'Anytime.'

My legs instantly ached and my chest pounded with such a hot need it sent tingles along my breasts and straight to my nipples. Which was shocking. Mostly because I had never 'needed' much before.

Not in this way.

My body was very aware of him. Right down to every last goose bump he brought to my skin.

'What's your name?' I asked.

'Jack.'

I repeated his name and he glanced at my mouth. Suddenly, it was hard to swallow. He was still, and a calming, controlled essence rolled off of him.

He glanced behind his shoulder real quick. 'Would you like me to stay seated like this?'

'No, it's fine.' I was about to tell him that I didn't see Brock anymore, but that would start a conversation that I wasn't interested in having – ever.

He adjusted slightly, but kept his full attention pointed in my direction. Such a thing was new, and I couldn't help but fidget a little, swaying my shoulders, threading and unthreading my fingers.

'Am I bothering you?' he asked, glancing at my hands.

'No,' I shot out quickly, because he wasn't. His stare on me was like an acute laser beam, but for some reason, I didn't want it to go away. I wanted to be seen, by him at least. 'I just don't usually meet guys in bars. Much less . . .'

Much less what? The more I babbled, the more I realized I had no clue what I was doing. Dating was a bad idea for me, despite what Harper thought.

'Lana?'

My gaze snapped back to Jack.

He tilted his head, examining my face with a softness in his. 'Care to continue your thought?'

'Not really.'

He laughed. Jack didn't look like the kind of man who laughed much. Not because he was scary, but an intense, professional, controlled aura definitely surrounded him. That fact that I just made him snicker a little, felt good. Like I'd accomplished something.

'Well, now you have me very intrigued.'

I shrugged and tried the best I could to explain away my obvious awkwardness. 'I'm not very smooth with this—' I motioned between us – 'type of interaction.'

He raised a brow. 'Oh? And what kind of interaction are we having?'

I swallowed hard. 'The kind that makes me nervous.'

He leaned away. 'I see. I didn't mean to make you nervous.'

'It's a different kind of nervous than a regular nervous,' I said quickly, not liking that he was backing away.

His dark brows sliced down. 'You're losing me on your logic.'

I licked my lips, an action he seemed to zero in on, and tried again. 'I'm not great with words, I tend to blurt things out. Quantifying things is easier than qualifying them.'

'You must work with numbers?'

I nodded. 'I just got my degree in statistics.'

'Impressive.' He scooted a little closer, and I didn't shy away. Instead, straightening my shoulders, I allowed the advance. I was even excited about how it made me feel. 'I've found that playing to your strengths allows for practice of your weaknesses.'

It was my turn to frown. 'Now you're losing me.'

'Let's keep it simple with words and quantify. That's what you're more comfortable with, correct?'

I nodded.

'You say I make you nervous?' He ran a finger along my folded hands. A shiver raced at the contact. 'On a scale of one to ten, how nervous does this make you feel?'

'Five,' I breathed. Probably pathetic, since it was a mere touch of hands. But my hands were in my lap, which meant his hands were near my lap. My skin zinged with anticipation, not only from the proximity of this man, but by the fact that I hadn't been touched in a lot longer than I'd care to admit.

'And is it a hot or cold nervous?'

That made me pause. I'd never thought of it that way. The nervousness I felt most of the time when I was out of my comfort zone, much like I'd been feeling sitting alone, waiting for Brock to zero in on me made me cold. Very cold. But when Jack sat down, the first thing I felt was ...

'Hot.'

His eyes bored into mine and he removed his hand. 'So that was a Five: Hot.'

I smiled and nodded. 'Sounds like the makings of a flow chart.'

'That would require more data.'

Suddenly, I was very interested in what kind of data we would collect.

'I brought you a fresh bourbon,' the bartender said, interrupting to set a glass in front of Jack.

'Thank you, Angel,' he said. The extremely beautiful female bartender stood, giving Jack a little smile.

I swallowed hard, realizing right then that she was the kind of woman he must date. And I was nowhere near the five-ten, painfully pretty, rail thin goddess who was slinging drinks and, from the looks of it, warding off wandering hands regularly.

Plus, he called her angel. It was a sign of familiarity.

I'd learned a long time ago that endearments usually came with strings. They were said when someone was prepping to brush you off, or needed something. My father called me 'Pumpkin' every once in a while, but he was the head of a financial service company and didn't need much from me.

Brock, however, was my father's pride and joy and backed him up accordingly. While it wasn't technically an endearment, my father called Brock 'son.' Even when I was a kid and told my father what happened, Brock had denied everything, and my dad chose to believe him instead of me. I pretended that maybe it was because he couldn't handle the truth, and believing Brock was easier and less painful information to deal with. But, deep down, I feared he was really trying to avoid a scandal.

I shook my head. Tonight was not the night to think of this. No night was, actually. The past several years had been spent with me burying such thoughts. Jack was my focus . . . what I kept my eyes on to drown out the rest of the world around me.

But he must have a history with the bartender. They may even be seeing each other now. And if a mere hand touch made me a Five: Hot, I was obviously way out of my league when it came to the likes of Jack, or his tastes and what it would take to make *him* hot.

Not that I was considering that.

'Could you also bring us another water and,' he glanced at me, 'a pineapple vodka and soda?'

The bartender looked at me with annoyance. 'Sure.' She hustled away and Jack readjusted so that his gaze was solely back on me. Funny how I craved it already. Like his attention was some kind of rare, priceless charm. Of course, such a rarity would also be considered unlikely to obtain. A fact I should keep in mind.

'Pineapple and soda?' I asked.

'I figured you'd have your water, and if you wanted something else, it was available.'

'Thank you.' A drink did sound good.

The bartender was surprisingly quick returning with the drinks. She set them in front of me, her cleavage pressing into Jack's space was obvious. But he never glanced at her. Just said a simple thank you and she walked away with a bit of a stomp.

I looked between Jack and the distant-growing bartender and took a sip of my drink. Forget the water, I needed something stronger. Maybe some liquid courage.

'Something you wish to say?' he asked, taking a drink of his own.

'Why would you ask that?'

'Because you're glaring at Angel.'

My eyes widened. 'Wait, her name is Angel?'

Jack nodded.

'Oh.' A smile of relief came out, but I tried to disguise it with another long swallow of my fruity drink. 'I thought you were calling her an endearment. Like you two had a history or dated or maybe are dating now. Not that it's any of my business.'

Crap. Babbling again. Stupid words. I shut them down by finishing my drink. The alcohol hummed through me just enough to slow my brain and calm my nerves.

'The idea seems to make you,' he looked at me over the rim of his glass, swallowing down his drink, then gave a sly smile, 'nervous.'

'More like annoyed,' I muttered, then clamped my mouth shut and embarrassment flooded.

'Really? My possible history or present interactions with Angel annoy you?'

'I'm sorry. This is inappropriate of me. I don't even know you and have no right to feel—'

'You have every right to feel however you want, whenever you want,' he cut me off quickly with seriousness in his tone. 'I just wish you'd follow through on those feelings.'

'Excuse me?'

'If you feel something, want something, want to know something, then follow your gut or ask. Don't simper.'

My mouth hung open. He was direct, I'd give him that. And whether it was the alcohol or how he'd gone from protector to challenger, a fire sparked inside me, rising to the challenge.

'Alright,' I said and raised my chin. 'It's obvious the bartender has a thing for you. It annoyed me because it was a blatant display.'

'That's it? So you prefer to play coy?'

'No, I don't play anything. I just . . .'

Sit there.

Waiting to be stood up. Waiting for my dad to save the day. Just . . . waiting.

But that wasn't what I wanted to get into. Because it reminded me that the reality was, I wasn't the bartender, or tattoo girl. I was in a damp sundress staring down a man that fascinated me and made my blood heat. A welcome notion after being bored, lonely, and cold for far too long.

I was tired of waiting.

'You're avoiding again, Lana,' he said, his tone a little rough. 'Perhaps my conversational skills are lacking?'

'Nothing about you is lacking.' That time I slapped a palm over my mouth.

He grinned. 'I like your honesty. You should say what's on your mind more often.'

'I don't know if that's a good idea.'

'I disagree,' he said calmly and set his drink down. 'You may not intend to play anything,' he said, using my exact words from earlier, 'but you do.' He leaned in a little and whispered in my ear. 'So, let's play.'

I swallowed hard. 'W-what's the game?'

'Honesty. Let's start simple. I'll ask something, you answer. Quickly and honestly. No thinking.' I opened my mouth to protest, but he cut me off with his first question. 'Am I still making you nervous?'

'Not like before.' Quick and honest. Easy enough.

The look on his face made me think I'd just answered wrong.

'That's a shame.' Taking one fingertip, he ran it along the condensation of my drink, then slowly slid it up my knee.

I jolted a little.

15

'Give me a number, Lana.'

'S-six,' I said with a small stutter.

'Hot or cold?'

'Hot.' It was instant, no thought needed, because my body was the one talking. His finger may be cold, but the way it grazed my skin left a heated trail.

'Good. The number I can work with. The cold I can't.'

His words hit a spot deep in my chest. Like he cared. Understood me in a weird way that allowed me to feel in control and calm, while on fire at the same time. The number was a way to keep track of my limits. But the cold? He couldn't work with that? It spoke to the kind of man he was: one that wasn't interested in scaring a woman.

Pushing limits maybe, but not scaring.

I knew this deep down. Though he was still an unknown rogue-type of hero out of nowhere, he wasn't cruel. Cruel men I could sense. Not Jack. He was hard and intense and dark, but not in a way that frightened me. Instead, he had a way about him that rose my curiosity and my blood pressure.

'You said there was a man here, someone from your past you didn't care to see. Is he still here?'

I peered around again. Though I couldn't see Brock, I had a feeling he was still here. Lurking.

A violent tremor rushed through me, and I went for another drink of my vodka, only to find it was empty.

'I'm not certain.' Without thinking beyond the desire for another dose of liquid courage, I took Jack's bourbon and finished it.

'Careful,' he said.

I winced because it burned, but somehow dulled the ache in my chest that had become a permanent fixture. Just as vital as my heart and lungs, so was the emptiness. The hole that fed on

16

insecurity and grew slowly every day. It was also why I didn't date much.

To be honest, I'd had one college boyfriend, and I didn't think my attempts at sex with Andy counted, since I always started panicking every time he tried. Brock had ruined me, and a few less than stellar moments of 'intimacy' attempts with Andy later, I decided it wasn't worth it.

I looked at Jack.

Not worth it?

Then why was my body screaming? Why was I responding to him in a way I never had with anyone else? It was as if someone had come and flicked a light switch, turning everything I never knew existed, like lust, on. Was this how the tattoo girl felt? How a normal woman felt?

I wanted to explore that, but had no idea what to do. How to feel. How to act. It took one encounter and a matter of moments to feel comfortable around Jack. Something that never happened when I met new people. Hell, it never happened after years of knowing someone.

'I'm going to get another,' I said, my voice a bit shaky. I reached for my wallet, but Jack laid his hand on top of mine.

'I'll get you another one.'

All he did was glance toward the bar, lift his chin, and magically, drinks were being brought over to us in record time. When Angel sat down another pineapple vodka and bourbon, she deliberately looked at Jack and said, 'I get off work at two.' Then winked as she strutted away. A quick surge of jealousy shot through me.

'Sounds like a good offer,' I said, taking a sip of my fresh drink.

'I must have missed it, because I heard no offer.'

I laughed. 'I know you're not that dense. She was just—'

'I'm aware of what she was doing.' He shifted so his knee barely

17

parted mine. The feel of obviously expensive denim scratched my skin in a way that sent a surge of need straight to my core. 'But I'm busy at the moment.' A small smile tugged his way-too-perfect lips. 'I seem to find myself engaged in a game I'm not ready to quit.'

I took a deep breath, trying to hold on to any kind of boldness I had. 'All games end eventually.'

'True.'

'And there's always a winner and loser.'

He nodded.

Trying to hone in on his energy, and thanking God the alcohol was helping, it was my turn to lean in just an inch … that spark in me flickering a bit stronger.

'Statistically speaking, smart money would be placed on a sure thing,' I said and glanced at Angel behind the bar, then back to Jack. 'Because I'm not interested in being on the losing end of anyone's game.'

Respect, accompanied with dark expression, flashed over his face.

'Here I thought I was the one losing myself.'

His tone was deep and soft and packed a punch straight to the stomach that had me thinking this man was interested in me. Beyond interested. And I was beyond ready to take him up on it. But there was too much unsaid, too much unknown to make that possible.

'What do I make you?' When he frowned, I clarified. 'We've established that you make me nervous. What do I make you?'

'Captivated.'

Air caught in my throat. His response was quick. If this was the game I entered, playing by his rules, then I could only hope he was being honest.

In the spirit of saying what was on my mind, I decided to try it. What had Jack told me? If I had a question, ask?

18

The way he was looking at me, brows furrowed in concentration and dark eyes staring at my face, making me feel more seen and alive than I ever had, made me desperate to know:

'What are you thinking about right now?'

Without breaking that penetrating gaze he said, 'What you taste like.'

My lips parted, and that was when I caught a glimpse of Brock, hovering near the opposite corner of the bar.

Brock's gaze met mine, and for a horrifying moment, time hung and I felt everything good and warm melt away and spiral into a ball of panic in my stomach.

I couldn't handle it. Not tonight. Not under the same roof with *him*.

'I need to go,' I said, clutching my phone and fumbling for my purse.

Jack stayed seated and did that 'protecting body shield' thing again, but was obviously surprised by my change in mood.

'Okay,' he said calmly. 'Why don't I see you home safely?'

I shook my head. 'My friend is coming to pick me up in about a half hour.' A half hour was too long to stay there, waiting for Brock to approach me. Especially now that he'd seen me. I had to get out. Now.

Jack stood up, and then I did. Well, tried to stand. Between the drinks hitting me fast and my nerves, I stumbled a little. My hands landed on Jack's chest. I looked up at him and he held the underside of my wrists as I righted my stance.

'Why don't you drink some water first?' he offered.

'No, thank you, but I have to leave.' With that, I bolted for the exit.

Chapter 2

I'd gotten three strides down the street when I heard my name called. I knew the voice. It froze me in my path like an anvil of terror had just been dropped on my head. I turned and saw him.

'Hello, Brock.'

'What are you doing rushing off like that, little Lana?' He took another step toward me. 'I get the impression that you were trying to avoid me.'

'I was,' I mumbled.

He tsked at me. 'Dad wouldn't like us fighting.'

I sneered at him. The only thing that momentarily squashed my fear was when he referred to my father as his.

'I thought you were in New York.'

'I was, but I'm back now.' Another step closer, so I took two back. 'You didn't hear the good news? Dad promoted me to VP.'

My mouth parted just enough so I could feel the breath sweep from my body, carrying my horror with it. 'No.'

He nodded.

Another step forward.

Another two back.

'Aren't you going to congratulate me? I'll be overseeing the Denver branch. Working side by side with the old man.'

I shook my head. It was my first summer finally getting to work there with my dad. And we were only in the first few weeks!

'But I heard you got a grunt position at the company. I think that's sweet. Don't worry, I'll be a nice boss.'

Bile rose in my throat and I tensed to run, but my feet were like ice.

'There a problem here?' Jack said, walking out.

Brock spun to face him. Jack immediately positioned himself between me and Brock, inches from my disgusting step-brother, staring him down. It was then I realized how tall Jack was. At six-two, he towered over Brock.

'Oh, good evening,' Brock said to Jack in a professional tone, which shocked me. 'Aren't you——?'

'Why don't we go have a chat over there?' Jack cut him off with so much sharpness in his voice I thought I saw Brock wince. But he complied, and both men walked back toward the bar entrance. Before they were out of earshot, Jack looked over his shoulder and said, 'Stay there, Lana. I'll be right back.'

I nodded and crossed my arms, trying to keep the chill away. But the cold was coming from within. Jack and Brock spoke for a moment, then Brock went back inside, and Jack came toward me.

'Is that who was bothering you?' Jack asked.

I swallowed and he eyed me, awaiting my answer.

'That was my step-brother.' It took all the practice I had to pull off my straight face and calm my nerves so that I could diffuse this situation without him thinking the worst. 'We don't see eye to eye on things.'

Jack looked at me for a long moment. Whether he bought my story or not, he thankfully didn't push it.

'You said you were waiting for a ride, I don't want you waiting outside,' he said. 'Why don't you come back to my place, it's just right up the street.'

I frowned. We were in the middle of downtown, and the only

21

homes nearby were a few brick mansions and luxury high-rise apartments. Which meant, if he did actually live close, he was wealthy enough to afford such a place. Still, even though he seemed trustworthy enough, and I felt some sort of connection to him, it wasn't a good idea.

'Thanks, but I'll be fine.' However, my body was on the brink of shaking from the surge of adrenaline.

'You don't look fine.' His voice seared to the core of me and I was helpless not to meet his gaze. 'You are very smart to be cautious. We are still strangers, after all. But having you wait in the dark, outside on the streets of Denver, is not acceptable to me. Especially when you have that scared look.'

I folded my lips together. I didn't want to have that look. Hell, I didn't want to have that feeling. But, I didn't want to be where Brock was. Especially now that the second drink was settling in my belly and buzzing through my head.

'How about this? Pull up your friend's number on your phone.'

Though I didn't know where he was going with this, I did. Then Jack gently grabbed my cell phone from my hand. He fiddled with a few buttons, then took a photo of himself.

'You want to capture this moment with a lone selfie?' I asked.

He handed me back my phone. There was a picture of him, and his address was in the body of a text message to Harper.

'Send that to your friend, so she knows where to pick you up and what I look like.'

I smiled a little. 'Smart.'

'Safe,' he clarified.

I met his eyes again, and there it was ... that intensity. It hummed through me more than the alcohol. Those dark depths were drinking in everything I was, like he could see straight to the soul of me and ease everything tense in my muscles. I couldn't help but shiver.

I sent the text to Harper, then nodded. 'Thank you for letting me wait at your house.'

He looked pleased and came to stand beside me. I felt oddly safe, taken care of, and was even enjoying my time with him, all things considered. Tonight had been bizarre, but not all bad.

Thanks to Jack's presence, my mind and body were spinning, totally at odds and cranked up from crashing adrenaline. I didn't know if the sudden rush of emotions I was getting was normal. A thought slapped me out of nowhere:

What would it be like if Jack touched me?

The idea hit me harder than the cool summer night air of Colorado as we walked the couple of blocks to Jack's house. Technically, he'd already touched me a little. That small interaction was a taste of a much bigger drug I was seeking: Heat.

It was addicting. Especially since, with one encounter, Brock could chase away all that wonderful calm I'd just felt. Calm that Jack helped me feel. If a small touch did that, spurred that kind of fire and strength and want . . . what would more do to me?

Whether it was the alcohol or the sheer oddity of the situation, surely a notion like that was not one to be thinking about. Especially for someone like me, someone who didn't even like the idea of dating.

We got to a beautiful home nestled in downtown with a massive porch and entryway. The house was huge and had just enough elegant details and lines that it looked like a work of art.

'This is your house?' I asked.

He nodded.

'It's amazing.'

'You haven't even seen the inside,' he said, walking up the steps and unlocking the front door. Inside or not, it was still amazing.

'How old is it?'

'It was built in 1898.' He held out his hand and I took it.

23

He led me through the door, and I stopped in awe. Partly from the home looking so classic and breathtaking, and partly because Jack's touch sent heat through me. The fantasy of what it would be like to feel more of his skin overtook my mind again. Squeezing my eyes shut, I tried to dislodge the thought.

It'd never happen.

Couldn't.

Shouldn't.

Maybe it was because, for a twenty-three-year-old woman, I wasn't very sexually experienced. Or maybe it was because I had a past littered with less than pleasant memories. Whatever the reason, my body chose tonight to turn on and entertain the idea of something more.

A kiss maybe?

Whatever may or may not be, in that moment, I felt alive. And for the first time in a long time, more warm than cold. More relaxed than frigid. More confident than scared.

My eyes shot open in time with the tap of his shoes against the hardwood floors as he walked further into his home. I looked at Jack, standing amongst the finest craftsmanship I'd ever seen and wanted to sigh . . . or bolt.

No, not bolt. I wanted to stay. Despite tonight tilting between being scary and exciting, I was already in over my head. But I didn't care. Being afraid was exhausting. And nothing about this man caused me fear. In fact, he brought out a slew of other emotions I didn't really know existed.

'Would you like to come in further?' he asked, as I hovered at the entrance in the foyer.

I took a few more steps and looked around the beautiful house. It was cozy. Buttery walls with rich leather furniture lined the living room. Wrap-around windows gave an impressive view of the city surrounding us, and hardwood floors expanded as far as I could see. Dark reds, browns and creams made up the color palette. It was truly warm and inviting. The staircase looked like an antique itself, and had intricate designs carved throughout the wood.

'Make yourself at home,' Jack said. He disappeared for a moment, walking around the corner, quickly returning with a cup of water.

'Thank you.' The instant I drank down the cool liquid, I felt a bit better. But I still needed a minute, some air maybe. Because I didn't know what to do or what to think. Why did I want to pull Jack to me right then and see what his kiss was like?

'You look flushed,' he said, his tone so raspy it made me want to tell him why.

'I was just thinking of something,' I whispered, my gaze zeroing in on his mouth.

'Oh?' He took one step closer. 'Care to share your thoughts?'

I licked my lips ... ready to share more than just the thoughts. He'd said earlier he wondered what I tasted like. I was wondering the same about him.

'Is it easy for you? Telling the truth?' I asked.

'Generally.'

'How? Not that I lie, but I just don't know how you can say what you say.'

'You mean voice what I want?'

'Yes.' It was then it hit me. I wanted that. To be able to say what I wanted. Put a voice to my fears. My desires. My everything. To have someone actually listen.

'It's a matter of worth over value,' he said. 'Any given thing has a value. I just decide what it's worth to me to keep that value.' He took a step forward. 'For example, you have a value. My silence wasn't worth you walking away.'

A heavy ache settled in my ribs. This man thought I had value and was worth hanging on to? For how long? Did it matter?

25

'It makes the truth easy,' he continued, his smooth voice rolling over me like freshly melted caramel. 'To tell you I think of your taste is easy to admit. Especially if it means you'll look at me like that.'

'Like what?' I whispered.

'Like you just may let me find out.'

I opened my mouth to tell him yes, when my phone buzzed. I grabbed it and saw a text from Harper. She'd made good time and was fifteen minutes early, waiting for me out front.

'My ride is here,' I whispered.

Jack nodded once. 'I'll walk you out.'

He took my glass and set it on the coffee table. I grabbed my purse, feeling hot and bothered, and like I had just missed a moment I desperately wanted to get a second chance at.

He led me back to the front door, but instead of opening it, he maneuvered me so that my back was against it and he faced me. His dark eyes zeroed in on mine and I knew right then, that yes, I was small prey in the sights of a predator. A sexy, tanned-skinned predator.

'Tonight was surprising,' I stated like a moron. But I felt like it needed saying, since Jack was closing in on me, his black gaze on my mouth.

'I agree, and I want to hear what you were about to say.'

I tried to take another step back, but there was nowhere to go. The cool door pressed against my back, and I felt the indentations of yet more masterfully carved wood.

'I was going to say ... well, do something ... I shouldn't—' Shit! I couldn't say what I needed to. What made sense. But what made sense didn't seem to match up with what my body wanted. And that was Jack.

'You shouldn't what, Lana?' His voice was like gravel, zinging through the air and hitting every part of my skin, making me shiver and ache.

26

'I shouldn't want you,' I whispered.

The faintest grin tugged at his mouth, and it was heart-stopping because there was something sinful about it.

'I disagree completely.'

He closed the distance and seized my lips with his. Hard and rough. One hand cupped the side of my face, and he pressed his thumb down on my chin, causing my mouth to open.

He didn't wait. Didn't ask. He just took.

Thrusting his tongue inside, he consumed me. The heat and intensity of his body pressed against mine, his erection digging into my stomach made me want to arch my hips into him.

It should have frightened me. The feel of him. So close. So hard. But it didn't. He must have read my mind, or my body, because he gripped the back of my knee with his free hand and yanked me closer.

A moan escaped, because his actions caused my dress to bunch at my hips, his hard cock now rubbing against my center.

Flashes of pleasure crackled from my core to my breasts and everywhere in between. He didn't stop. Didn't let up. Just took me. And I felt his power – wanted to drink it down like a potion, in hopes that maybe I would walk away with some myself.

Weaving his tongue in and out like a lusty dance, taking and demanding, I realized he wasn't kissing me. He was consuming me. As if I were edible and made of sugar, he licked, sucked, and bit. Owning my mouth and my body, like he knew exactly how to move and how to work me over so that I felt . . .

In control.

Which was confusing, because I felt totally dominated by him at the same time. Not in a way that terrified me, but in a way that snapped every ounce of will I had to the forefront and pushed away the uncertainty.

All I felt with Jack was a heady dose of confidence, power, and desperation. An elixir he had locked up and in one kiss, I was already addicted.

He growled my name and tore his mouth from mine to nip my earlobe, then sucked on the pulse beating wildly in my throat.

The hand on the back of my knee slid a little higher. Gripping my leg, he dug his thumb into my inner thigh, so close to the place I was craving him most. A violent jolt of wet need rushed, and I pressed closer against him. Desperate to ease the ache I never realized could hurt so much.

When his mouth traveled lower, the stubble on his strong jaw scraped my collarbone. Sparks rushed to my nipples, as if they were standing up and begging for attention. I was on fire, melting from the heat of him. The heat that was purely Jack.

I groaned, my mind spiraling out of control. In that moment, I'd never felt more consumed. More guarded. It was the same feeling I had the second Jack sat down:

Safe.

He was the wall I'd been searching for.

He brought something out in me. Something that wanted to grasp on to the world and take it, not let it rule me. Not be afraid. Not cower. Not wait.

I was tired of cowering and I was tired of waiting.

I kissed him with everything I felt. All the hurt and anger of my life up until this point, I unleashed on to him. A relative stranger. A man I met in a bar. A man that in the short time I knew him, made me feel more seen and safer than any other man I'd ever encountered.

'Jack,' I breathed his name and bit his bottom lip a little when I went back in for another searing kiss. My grip on him tightened.

'That's it,' he said against my mouth. 'Not so shy right now, are you?'

His teeth grazed my lips. When had I started clawing at him?

His hips were grinding against me, but he leaned back enough to look me in the eyes. Our noses touching while we breathed for each other. Still cupping my face, he ran his thumb along my lips which felt swollen and tingly.

'Give me a number.'

On heavy exhales, I said, 'Eight.'

'Hot or cold?'

'Very hot,' I whispered.

'Good.'

He let my leg drop and I stood on two feet once more, trembling a little from the intensity of what just happened.

Tucking a lock of hair behind my ear, he backed away. His dark eyes were wild, like lightning behind midnight skies.

'I hated what I saw on your face tonight. The look of fear. I don't know what exactly is going on, but you should never feel that way.'

I took a deep breath and admitted one thing I hadn't said out loud ever. 'I don't want to be afraid anymore.'

A muscle ticked in his jaw, and he looked like he was about ready to say something. He reached out and ...

Opened the door behind me.

The summer breeze met my skin, and beyond the large porch and down the steps, was Harper parked on the curb, waiting in her car.

I walked out, then turned to look at Jack. 'So much happened tonight. I don't know what to do or what to say.' I was also certain that if what just happened was an eight, I may not be able to handle a ten. Yet, I desperately wanted to find out. 'Do I give you my number?'

'You can.'

I looked him over in confusion. 'Do you have a pen?'

'No. You can just tell it to me. I'll remember.'

He grinned and ran a hand through his hair, smoothing away the mess I had made of it. The action caused his shirt to pull tight over his torso, giving sight to a hard chest and rippling abs that made my mouth water again.

I rattled off my cell number and he nodded.

'I look forward to seeing you again,' he said.

It didn't sound like a threat or a promise, but a threat *and* a promise. With the scent of pine on the breeze, I crossed my arms and walked away. Already missing the heat.

Chapter 3

'What are you doing here, Lana?' my father asked, opening the door to his million dollar, eco-friendly home with surprise on his face. Though it was in the same city as Jack's house, everything about my father's place had clean lines, no color, and felt sterile.

Since my encounter with Jack last night, I hadn't been able to sleep. But the more I thought about Brock, about his new 'promotion,' the more I needed clarification.

'I know it's early, but I needed to speak with you in person.'

His gray brows knit. 'Okay.'

He let me in, but kept me near the front door, as if to push me out suddenly if the moment arose. And I knew what moment that would be, and her name was Anita, my step-mother. Though I didn't see her often, it was more than I interacted with my own mother, unfortunately.

When my parents divorced, it was as though my mom divorced me too. She moved to Florida with her new husband to 'get a fresh start on life.' Aside from holiday and birthday calls, I didn't talk to her much at all.

'I saw Brock. He said he's working with you in Denver now.'

My father crossed his arms and nodded, but his eyes stayed on the floor. 'Yeah, that's right.'

'Dad?' I tried to get him to look at me, but all I got was a glance. 'I thought we were working together this summer. I can't work with Brock, you know that.'

'You need to get over your issues with him.'

The words hit me hard, but they weren't the first time I'd heard them. Still, it didn't make the sting any less potent. My father and step-mother didn't acknowledge the past regarding Brock and I. My father always told me to 'get over my issues,' but never gave weight to my claims. And I never spoke of it. I'd never called Brock out since the night he hurt me. Years later, we all still danced around the truth.

'I can't be under the same roof as him. Much less have him be someone I report to.'

'Then maybe the Case-VanBuren firm isn't where you should be working.'

My stomach tightened. 'I need this job, you know that. I have grad school to pay for.' I had a partial academic scholarship that covered tuition, but all other expenses were on me.

He looked over his shoulder, then leaned in and whispered, 'I can try to get some money to you. Off the books.' He winked, as if that made it all better. But I knew this game.

My father and I didn't come from money. He'd been a struggling real estate agent when he met Anita. Case Investments at that time was a young business, and it had been drowning. She was the one with the money and the name, an effective leash she kept around my father's neck.

Case Investments turned into Case-VanBuren. My father might be president, but Brock was VP, and would take over, despite my father having started the company on his own before he met Anita.

'I won't take her money. Not now, not the other times you've offered it. I can support myself. I've been doing it for a while. But I need a job to do that.'

'You have one,' he said harshly. 'Just keep your head down, and you won't even notice Brock.'

Yeah, right. But this went deeper than Brock being in Denver. 'Why is he even here? He was running the New York branch. Why bring him in?'

'Because Denver has lost a major client. Brock can bring more of them in. New York is fine, but Denver needs some help.'

'I can help! That's why you hired me. I can bring a client in.'

'Brock has the track record, and you're not even an associate. You're . . .' he waved his hand, and I finished the sentence for him.

'I'm just in a grunt position.'

He didn't deny it, because he knew as well as I did what I was and how he viewed me.

'Look, Brock is staying.'

'Dad—' but the rest didn't come, because it didn't matter. Just like that night, when I'd gone to my father and told him what had happened, he chose Brock over me. I wasn't going to wait any longer for him to save the day. I wasn't going to put myself in a position that sickened me.

'You have a job if you want it, but I won't discuss Brock with you anymore.'

I shook my head. 'Then I can't work for you.'

'That's your choice. Not mine.'

I clenched my jaw, because my choice had been taken away ten years ago. And it was that one moment that changed everything.

I steeled myself against the tears, like I always did. I'd figure it out. Would have to. My father didn't see me as an asset. I'd just have to convince him otherwise. Brock didn't have his master's degree. It was the one area I could trump him in. Someday. Maybe, someday, my father would see my value.

Jack's words flashed in my mind. Everything had a value and worth. Looked like I needed to up my profit margin.

'I didn't know we were expecting another for brunch,' Anita said, her heels clicking as she walked toward us.

'Lana's not staying,' my father replied quickly. 'Just came to say hello.'

'Oh, shame you can't stay. Brock will be here. You two could catch up.' The cynicism in her voice was enough to make me want to retch. It was no secret she hated me. Even though I hadn't said a word about Brock since the night he hurt me, I still had to face her, face everyone, alone in the truth.

'Darling, can you check the quiche?' Anita said, and my father didn't even say goodbye. Just scurried off like a lap dog, leaving me to stare down evil incarnate. 'Lana, I know Brock's promotion must be hard for you, but surely you two can find a way to get along. This sibling rivalry must end. Understand?'

I bit the inside of my cheek. I understood. I'd understood for a decade now. Like a fool, I'd come here thinking my father would be on my side in this. Whether they painted the past with words like 'sibling rivalry' or 'issues,' the fact that Brock hurt me remained unknowledgeable. And so, the dance continued.

A part of me thought of my father as a victim along with me. Maybe it was easier for me to bear it that way. He never used to be like this. Of course, that was when I was very young, before he met Anita. No matter what, I loved him. Once, he had loved me back. He had thought of me as his little girl and fought for me after my mother divorced him.

But that was a long time ago. Funny how feelings could be beaten out of you and replaced with hate, anger, and fear.

'You have a good day,' I said in a slow, fluid tone. No way would I let her see me tremble, see my mind work, or see a shudder of fear race over my spine every time I saw her face or heard her son's name.

She smiled, the crow's feet around her eyes squinting.

'You too, Lana. Good luck with the job hunt.'

I turned and walked out of the house. At least I wouldn't have Brock controlling me.

For all the games I didn't play, why did I feel like I just lost once again?

I slammed my laptop shut. No emails, no messages, and not a single response about any job I'd applied for over the past week.

'Still no luck with the job hunt?' Harper asked.

'Nothing yet.'

I'd quit my father's firm when I walked out of his home last weekend. Seven days had passed, and not a single call or email back. Not from potential employers, or from Jack, for that matter.

'I bet everything is slow because it's the Fourth of July weekend. Lots of people take time off before and after. Maybe you'll hear something next week?'

I appreciated Harper's attempt to look on the bright side. The holiday probably played a part. 'I don't think I can last another week unemployed.' Even if I got hired, or an interview, the process and paperwork took time. It then took more time to get the first paycheck.

'I was hoping to start a job this coming week.' Things weren't looking hopeful for that, and even less hopeful for Jack calling. I was trying not to dwell on that too much, though it was clear by now that he had no interest in seeing me again.

'We'll figure something out,' Harper said, curling up on the couch. Her tone was soft, and she glanced away like she had a trick up her sleeve. Unless she started paying me to be her roommate, I was in trouble.

35

'In the meantime,' she said, grabbing her cell phone and scrolling through it. 'Tell me more about last weekend. You met a hottie and stared down your father and the evil bitch, but you never gave details.'

'Not many details to give.' I poured myself a cup of coffee.

It was still technically the morning, and I hadn't had my caffeine fix yet. This week had given me lots of time to think. I'd made the right decision in leaving the firm, and the only time I had to go into Denver was to apply for jobs. Working there over the summer was one thing, but I liked that Golden was a small, cheery town and had an amazing grad school. It was more my speed than the city.

Going to work at my dad's company had always been a goal of mine. The path in getting there was the tricky part. Especially since he kept adding to the list of things I needed to do in order to make 'associate.' Things Brock never had to do.

'How about you dish about the fun stuff? Like, was this hottie a good kisser?' Harper asked, flicking the blinds with her finger, peering at the quiet fire station across the street.

I sat in the oversized chair opposite from her and pulled my knees to my chest. 'Yes.'

She frowned at me. 'That's it? That's all you're saying?'

Between the hard realities I was swallowing about Brock being back, tied with the fact that I had met a man I didn't immediately cower from, not to mention that kiss – which was more than good – my thoughts were a whirlwind. I had replayed that amazing moment with Jack about a thousand times, and had a hard time wrapping my brain around much of anything else.

There was something about him.

But I hadn't heard from him, and while I wasn't an expert in dating, I was pretty sure a week with no word was a brush off.

'You've dated a lot,' I said slowly, and Harper turned her attention back on me.

She tied her red hair into a messy knot on the top of her head and raised a brow. 'Yes, I have.'

I glanced at the coffee cup in my hands. 'Have you ever thought about a guy, in a serious way, after you just met him?'

She smiled. 'Well, look at you. I could barely get you to agree to one date, and now you're talking about one night stands?'

'It's not like that. Well, kind of . . .' I shook my head. 'Not the one night stand part. Jack kissed me, but I wanted him to. And now all I can think about is—'

'Jumping his bones?' Harper winked.

'I've never thought of a man this way. He makes me want things. Physical things.' The sexual tension my body felt when I was with him was new and exciting. And I wasn't ready to give that up.

'Wanting sex is a good thing. It's a normal thing.' Harper drawled out the last part, and I met her stare. 'Thanks to that asshole step-brother of yours, you associate it with fear and pain.'

She paused a moment, as if the words hurt her throat to say. Harper was my best friend, and I knew she loved me and cared. She also hated what Brock had done to me. She was the only person in the world who believed me.

'I know you attempted a relationship with Andy a couple years ago, and you two never really sealed the deal.'

'I tried,' I whispered quietly.

'I know you did, hun. But to get past all the shitty memories, it takes something stronger. It takes passion. Sounds like this guy from last week made you back burner the bad things, and focus on the good.'

37

I thought about that for a moment. Jack did make me feel good. Safe. Hot. He made me want sex ... want physical things I've always shied away from. Maybe Harper was right. Maybe it was the passion. But passion was a feeling I had zero experience with.

'Back up for a second though, you never told me how you ended up at this guy's place last weekend.'

'Brock showed up at the bar.'

Harper's face fell, then twisted into a pissed-off glare. 'That fucker. Are you okay? What did he say to you?'

I shook my head. 'Nothing at first. He didn't even know I was there, actually. Thanks to Jack.'

'Knight in shining armor kind of thing?'

'Something like that. He read me, and it felt like he could sense my anxiety, and somehow just ... ' I glanced at the ceiling and smiled, 'gave me a piece of power.'

'Wow,' Harper said. 'Sounds intense.'

I laughed, because if there was one word to describe Jack, that would be it.

'It also sounds like a pretty successful evening of making new friends. You seem a little ballsier since then.'

'I'll try to take that as a compliment,' I said, taking a sip of my own coffee.

'You should. Because the fact is, your dad is a letdown, but you faced him. And you're talking about sex for the first time in ... ever, which makes me think that either you underwent an invasion of the body snatchers kind of thing and you're not really Lana, or—'

'Or I'm losing my mind?'

'No, you're standing up for yourself and finally admitting to what you want.'

'I want to stop being afraid. I want to stop feeling weak.' It felt good to say it to Harper, and she nodded.

38

'I want that for you too. So, anything that can give you power and happiness sounds like a good idea to me.' She looked at her cell again and appeared to be scrolling for something.

Jack sounded like a good idea to me too. In the short time we were together, he affected me in a way that spurred desire. Desire for more of him, more confidence. Just more.

My dad raised me. Well, I kind of raised myself, since he was working a lot. When he married Brock's mom, things went downhill. I was never able to catch my dad's eye, yet I still tried. Even to this day. But I truly believed that he must love me. Because the alternative was too much to bear.

I took a long swallow of warm coffee, and it did little to ease that throbbing ache of uncertainty buried in my chest.

I hated talking or thinking about things like my past or my dad. It was too much stress, too much heartache to hold on to. Then, it hit me.

'I have to let one of them go.'

'Huh? What do you mean?' Harper asked.

'Brock or my dad. I need to let one of them go. I can't keep holding on to all the badness. I can't keep fighting both of them.' I was either fighting for my dad's love or against the idea of ever being around Brock. I had to move on from one of them if I was going to attempt to be a stronger person.

'Jesus,' I whispered, and looked at Harper. 'Brock is technically the only person I've ever been with.'

Tears collected, but I didn't want them to fall. The horror of that fact made me realize that he still had control over me. Had succeeded in wrecking me.

'No, you weren't *with* Brock. He raped you.'

The word was so sharp, it felt like it punctured my lung. I stayed away from using that word because it made it more real.

'I'm tired of holding on to that. I want to move on. I want

39

good experiences, not a single bad one to keep weighing me down.'

Harper nodded. 'I think that's a great idea. So, you're going to let go of Brock?'

It sounded easier said than done, but yes, that was my goal. It didn't mean he didn't disgust me, maybe scare me a little. It certainly didn't mean it changed a damn thing, and I would be around him. But I would try to finally move on from the inner turmoil he left behind.

'I'm going to try,' I said. 'But I'm holding on to my dad.'

I wasn't ready to let him go. I wasn't ready to accept that our relationship couldn't be salvaged. Stupid or not, I loved my father, and wanted to fight for this happy ending that may never come.

Harper's expression was soft but serious. 'Okay, but at some point, you need to be prepared to let go of this idea that your dad is going to, all of a sudden, be great and be there for you. He's not. He never has been.'

But that went against every hope I had.

'If I could just ...' I took a deep breath because my chest constricted. 'If he could just see me, believe in me, then maybe—'

'Things will be different? The past will somehow be different?' Harper finished, shaking her head. 'It won't, Lan. Even now, you're killing yourself to prove your worth to him, all while going to grad school next year so you can graduate, and then what? He'll hire you on at his firm?'

'Yes,' I said. Because that was the plan. If I worked hard, aced everything from statistical analysis to finance, maybe then he'd see I could be an asset.

'But he already fired you,' she said gently.

'No, I technically quit. By the time I'm done with grad school,

40

hopefully Brock will be back in New York.' And my grand plan could be reinstated. 'I just need a job in the meantime.'

Harper stalled a moment, chewing her lip, as if thinking over something serious. Finally, she motioned to her cell phone. 'My friend Shannon runs a temp agency, and she was saying a while back how she's hiring people to do payroll for some resort. I think they hire pretty fast over there. I was just looking up her contact information.'

'That would be great. Can I get her number from you?'

'Of course.' Then Harper's expression was one I'd seen a few times before, whenever this topic got brought up. Pity. And I hated it because it added to the growing mountain of weakness I was battling.

'Don't look at me like that,' I said in my best casual voice.

'I just worry about you. You say things that make me hurt for you.'

'Please, don't.' The last thing I needed or wanted was pity. Besides, 'All I said was that I wanted my dad to believe in me. That's a pretty standard request for a daughter.'

'I think you're mixed up about what you think you want from your dad.'

I frowned. 'What do you mean?'

'I don't think you want him to believe in you, I think you want him to *believe* you.'

Bile lined my throat, so sour and deep it made water threaten to spill over my lashes.

What happened with Brock was the one taboo, the secret scandal no one talked about, but we all knew was there. It was the one time in my life I ran crying to my father, reaching for his comfort, his promise that he'd protect me, save me, but it never came.

Instead, he told the thirteen year old me that Brock could

41

never have done such a thing and I was being dramatic. Made it up in my mind. Never to be talked about again.

My eyes stung thinking about the discussion. Realizing I was alone in that moment.

Afraid.

I got up off the chair and put my coffee on the counter. I told myself last night that I was done waiting for him to swoop in. I was also done with a lot more than that.

'I'm done being afraid.' I wanted more. Wanted to be more. Wanted that powerful heat that started with a look, a kiss, and surged through my veins, leaving me feeling hot and strong. I got a taste of that last week.

I needed the *heat*. Craved it.

Which meant I had to make a move to get it.

'Good for you!' she smiled. 'In the spirit of taking life by the balls, why don't you come with me to the party across the street tonight?'

'At the firehouse?'

'Technically, it's not at the firehouse. It's at the park next to it. But, yeah, I was invited, and you can be my plus one.'

Something had been going on with Harper lately. Apparently, she had it bad for some firefighter. Not surprising. Every once in a while we'd steal a glimpse of them cleaning the trucks or running drills. Every time I tried asking about it, she just shrugged it off and changed the subject.

'I don't know about that.'

'Why?' Harper asked. 'You have plans with Mr Intensity?'

'No, I don't. I don't even have his number.'

Harper looked confused. 'Well, you gave him yours, right?'

'Sort of.'

'How do you *sort of* give your number? Did you switch to roman numerals halfway through or something?'

42

'No. I told it to him. He said he'd remember it, but he didn't write it down.'

Harper sat back on the couch and avoided eye contact. The last thing he'd said to me was that we'd see each other again. That wasn't looking likely. I knew where he lived, but there was no way I'd just pop up there like a stalker.

If he wanted me, he would have called by now, right? Maybe I'd misjudged our connection. Maybe it was more one-sided than I'd thought.

My big balloon of semi-confidence was deflating.

'Okay.' Harper clapped and stood. 'We're not going to over-think this. This city guy sounds great. No reason to freak out. Just let things play out like they should. Which includes you going to a party with me tonight full of hot firemen.'

I let out a rough breath.

'Come on.' Harper shimmied closer, half dancing. 'You know you want to go. It'll be fun. No thinking about anything except the drink in your hand and testing out this new Lana that isn't afraid.'

I raised a brow. That did sound nice. No thinking. No fear. They were firemen, for goodness sakes. Good guys.

'Unless you want to mope around here, trying to cyberstalk the guy from last weekend?'

I laughed. I didn't even know Jack's last name. Besides, cyber-stalking wasn't my style.

I didn't know what to do next, whether I'd ever see Jack again, but the way he looked at me, and the way he spoke to me with that sinful promise in his voice, I could only hope. In the mean-time, I had reality to face and a best friend who needed a wing girl. Time to step up.

'When does the party start?'

43

Chapter 4

It was almost dusk, and I was standing in the middle of the large park, complete with a barbeque, a couple of picnic tables full of food, ping pong, which turned into beer pong an hour ago, and a makeshift bar. Harper was near the open field area, flirting with two different firemen. The fire station wasn't far away. I could see the big trucks parked out front in the driveway. Good thing, since most of its crew seemed to be here.

'I hope someone is actually on duty,' I said to myself, finishing my second drink of vodka and something from a red plastic cup.

'There always is, Kitten,' a deep voice came from behind me. I turned to find a tall, broad wall of muscle with bright blue eyes staring down at me.

I almost choked.

'Do you usually sneak up on people?' I asked, realizing that two drinks seemed to be the right amount for my courage to show up. The man had a dark blue Golden Fire T-shirt on, paired with jeans and a whole lot of muscle.

'Do you usually talk to yourself?'

I glanced at my empty cup. Great, just great. Captain America thought me a crazy person. It had been too long of a day to feel any more embarrassed, though. I'd promised Harper and myself, that tonight, I'd attempt to have a good time.

44

'Yes, sometimes I do. When I can't find suitable company to occupy me otherwise.'

He raised a brow and chuckled. Man, he was built. I could see the rivets of his six — no — eight-pack through his thin tee. An intricate tattoo peeked out from his right sleeve and took up his entire bicep, all the way to the crease of his elbow.

'Suitable company, huh?' he said, reaching behind him and grabbing a bottle of water off one of the tables. He untwisted it and poured some into my plastic cup. 'What qualifies as suitable in your mind?'

'For starters,' I paused, because he drank down some water from the bottle he'd just split with me, and watching his mouth and throat work made me fantasize momentarily about being that bottle.

Jesus! What had Jack done to me and my brain? Because I had one thing on my mind, and it involved mouths and skin and so many other parts.

'Um, someone with manners is always a plus,' I said quickly.

'Ah, then we'll be great friends. Look,' he tilted his chin at my cup, 'I got you a drink. Pretty gentlemanly.'

'Depends on your motives behind it.'

'What makes you think I have motives?'

I shrugged and took a sip. 'You never know.'

'Ah, yes, the water motives.' He glanced at my cup and leaned in to lower his voice. 'It's all part of my plan. Ply you with all the water you can drink, and get you hydrated enough to admit your darkest secrets. Then, and only then, will I bring in the ice cubes and go for the fantasies.'

'That's some plan.' Here I was trying to forget last weekend, or at least keep my mind off of it, and this guy with disarming charm and an easy smile that seemed so genuine and a little dangerous, made my body aware that it had undergone a switch recently.

One that made my body hot and now had me thinking of ice cubes.

'Are you thinking about which fantasy to tell me now? Because I'm all ears,' he said, pouring a bit more water into my cup.

He looked at me for a long moment. He was easily over six foot, about Jack's height. Maybe a bit taller. He towered over me with muscle and yummy-smelling cologne and a naughty expression paired with a lazy smile. He was charming. He knew it. I knew it. But tonight wasn't the night, and I wasn't that girl.

'So, you're on duty?' I asked. Probably one of the reasons I felt okay around this guy. He had to be somewhat responsible. There was also a sexy swagger that must come department issued. Because running into fire required adrenaline and danger. But in the spirit of testing out this 'new Lana,' I went with casual conversation.

'Yes, I am on call.'

I nodded and looked around. Everyone was having a good time. The women were all beautiful, like Harper. My best friend was actually beyond beautiful. She had fiery hair with creamy skin and big gray eyes. I had borrowed a pair of her heels, and a skirt. But she was so much taller, with ungodly long legs, that her 'mini skirt' hit just above my knees. Still, all I felt like was the same plain person, only hoisted up another few inches.

I was an idiot to think a few drinks and hours would change the outcome of this past week.

'What am I doing here?' I mumbled.

'Uh-oh, talking to yourself again? I'm standing right here? Shit, I must be losing my edge. Is it the stubble? I'm told some women don't like it,' the firefighter teased.

I couldn't help but smile a little. 'The stubble is good.'

'Hey,' Harper came over and pulled me close, not caring about the firefighter next to me. 'So, who's your target?'

'Target?' I asked.

'Yeah, the guy you're going to go for?' After agreeing to come to this party, Harper decided that I should try to 'check out my options.' Though I still thought of Jack, it was difficult to convince myself that I would see him again.

'I um . . .' I glanced at the firefighter, and he just looked at me with a raised brow, curious to hear my answer himself. 'I wasn't going to *go* for anyone.'

'Yeah, that's smart,' the firefighter said. 'You never know what *motives* they may have. Like water motives.'

Harper turned and looked at him. 'What are you talking about, Callum?'

'Just having a conversation with your friend here about suitable company, that's all.'

'Uh-huh.'

Harper knew more firemen then I'd thought. And Callum didn't seem to be her favorite. Which was crazy to me because, between the dimples, navy blues, and easygoing attitude, I was having a hard time *not* looking at him.

'Callum?' I asked him, verifying his name.

'I like the way you say that.'

Harper rolled her eyes, ignoring Cal's obvious flirtation with me. Which had me buzzing and a little giddy. 'So, who's it going to be?'

'Ah, hello,' Callum said.

'She can't handle you, Cal,' Harper whispered to him.

'Excuse me?' I stepped away to look at both of them. 'What is that supposed to mean?'

Harper reached out and took my hand. 'Nothing bad. Just that you're kind of shy and recently breaking out of your shell. Which is great, and I'm so happy you came with me tonight, but Cal is—'

47

'Standing right here,' he interrupted.

'Don't you have a cat to save from a tree or something?' Harper said.

'I've got my sights set on a kitten right now, actually.' He winked at me. 'Besides, you're the one, Harper, who has two of my buddies head over ass for you, and it's cutting into bro time with their bitching and whining. I don't think you're one to dish on who can handle what.' He looked at me, and holy crap, what had I missed? Apparently, there was more going on with this secret crush of Harper's than I'd thought. A crush that involved two firemen?

With his ocean eyes piercing mine, Cal said, 'Don't support and discredit your friend here. She may be a bit shy, but she's got claws. I can tell.' Though he spoke to Harper, he kept his gaze on mine.

Now I wasn't sure if both of them were mildly insulting me, or did Cal just stand up for me? Either way, I was not going to wallow or pout, and I certainly wasn't going to have my best friend think me weak and shy. I had made a promise to move on, at least in some areas of my life.

'I do have claws, damn it.'

'That a girl,' Cal winked.

I was tired of being walked over. Dismissed. Losing at this game of life.

'Time for the races! Find a partner,' a guy called out.

Most of the men in the area 'whooped' and attached themselves to a female. Harper's name was being called out from across the table area by what I assumed was one of her admirers.

'I didn't mean anything bad. I love you, and I want you to keep this strength you've found and be happy.'

'I know,' I said, and I did. But I didn't want to give into this feeling of unease any longer. It could be consuming if I let it be.

48

'What do you say?' Cal asked. 'Want to be my partner?'

Though I didn't know what 'the races' consisted of, how bad could it be? I was trying to branch out, after all. I was in a safe place. And there was something about Cal, a recklessness, yet a responsibility in him that was intriguing. I thought of Jack. Thought of the game we played and how honesty could be helpful. Yet another game it was looking like I lost.

Though it may have been a one night encounter, he'd taught me something: honesty could be a valuable thing.

'First, I'm going to ask you a question, and you say the first thing on your mind.'

'Okay,' Cal agreed.

'What are you thinking about right now?'

He grinned. 'My stubble against your thighs.'

My eyes shot wide. I didn't know what to say to his admission. It spurred some interesting thoughts. Like, what it would feel like, his strong jaw trailing up my thighs, the tickle of that light brown stubble scratching as he got closer to my—

He grabbed my hand and tugged me toward the open field at the back of the park. Men were lining up, getting ready to race, and their female counterparts were standing in front of them.

'Just stand like that,' he said, ushering me to face him. He was only two inches away, and staring at me.

'What kind of race is this?'

'The firefighting kind.'

'Go!' a yell rang out.

With that, Cal bent and hoisted me up, tossing me over his shoulder like a sack of potatoes. I screamed, then laughed, as he ran down the open meadow to God knows where, while he carried me. Thankfully, his strong forearm was clamping my skirt down, so I wasn't flashing everyone. I bounced around and held on tightly to his belt, trying not to overstep and actually touch his ass, his seemingly perfect ass.

I realized the side of his face was, in fact, against my outer thigh. Not the picture I'd originally thought of, but it made sense now.

'Switch!' the voice rang out.

At the command, Cal spun me around, like I weighed nothing, and held me like he would a damsel in distress. With one arm under my knees, the other was tight around my back. He carried me, my shins swinging, as he bounded toward the finish line.

My arms wrapped around the back of his neck, and I clung to him. His nose tickled my ear, and a shot of warmth raced through me.

I laughed and held on tight. The finish line was in sight. So close . . .

'Winner!' the voice rang out.

I looked up at Cal, and he smiled down at me, breathing hard.

'Did we win?'

He nodded. 'Fuck, yeah, we did.'

There were groans and cheers and people talking. Everyone started heading back toward the garage, delivering a few slaps to Cal's back as they went. But Cal stood there, hanging on to me.

Tears lined my eyes, and I hated that my emotions were getting the better of me.

'Ah, no, did I hurt you?' his voice was so soft, so concerned. I shook my head.

'No, it's not that.' A small laughed escaped, and I looked at him. 'We won.'

He nodded. 'Usually, that makes people happy.'

'It does.'

50

'Then why do you look so sad?'

I shook my head and met his eyes. 'Because it's been a long time. Do you ever just really need a win?'

An intense blue heat radiated from his gaze and his brow furrowed. Not in pity, but like he understood. 'Yeah.'

I glanced at the falling night sky. The last seven days had been a roller-coaster that left me feeling like I was in a free-fall, with no idea where I stood with anyone or what my true value was. It was a battle against every insecurity, every fear, and every nightmare. Everything good I wanted to cling to seemed to be disappearing. My job, my father, Jack.

It was a meaningless race, but Cal had hung on to me, ran with me, and we'd won.

He seemed to understand that, deep down, I just needed a moment of victory over something, because never coming out on top could start to weigh on a person. But in that moment, I was weightless, because Cal was still holding me. Not just me, but all my baggage, and for a brief moment in time, I let him.

The crickets' song was stronger now that everyone was out of earshot. Cal and I were left in the open field beneath the stars of Colorado.

'What's your name?' he whispered. His face getting closer.

'Lana. We've had a whole conversation and race, and you're just now asking?'

He nodded, a serious expression lacing his face.

'Why?'

'Because I wanted to know first.'

'First?'

He didn't answer, instead he snared my lips and pulled me closer into his body.

My eyes shot wide with surprise. My instinct was instantly at war with itself. Push him away or pull him close?

51

He was big and warm, and I felt like nothing could touch me. While his hold was tight, his kiss was soft. Gently tracing my lower lip with his tongue, making me open for more. The decision was reached: I pulled him close and gave in.

Delving his tongue deep, he slowly worked my mouth with his. Taking every ounce of this moment, every second, to his advantage. As if searing every move and taste to memory. My entire body hummed with need. With confusion. With lust.

I was wrapped up in strength, yet desperate to find my own.

He hissed, then smiled against my mouth.

'I told you so . . .' He bit my lower lip. 'You have claws – you should bare them more often.'

I relaxed my grip, realizing my nails were digging into the base of his neck, beneath his shirt.

'I'm so sorry,' I said, running my fingertips over the welts I'd left. 'I didn't realize.'

'Don't be sorry about being passionate. It's a good thing.'

There was that word again: passionate. It was showing up more often, and making me forget the bad and want more of the good.

I'd never considered myself a passionate person, but his words hit me, just like Jack's and Harper's had. Wanting someone, wanting sex, wanting more, was a good thing? For so long, it had been associated with terror. But in the last week, my world had tipped on its axis.

I was nowhere near the strong woman I wanted to be, with healthy experiences, but maybe I was getting closer. Maybe I could try.

Cal leaned in once more. Just as his lips touched mine, the firehouse alarm went off, and Cal's cellphone beeped. With a mumbled curse, he set me down and cupped my face.

'That's my call.'

I nodded.

He looked like he would say more. But he just smiled and went with, 'Good to meet you.'

Good to meet you? The only surprise was that he didn't high five me before running off, like he hadn't just kissed me like crazy.

Standing in the middle of the field with sirens going off up and down the street, I watched Cal run away.

'What was that?' Harper asked, clasping my arm and walking across the street back to our little yellow house.

'I was just going to ask you the same thing. Why haven't you told me about all the *friends* you made at the firehouse?' I glanced over my shoulder at the glowing station. The trucks were gone, and on them, Golden's crew, including Cal.

Harper shrugged, and our heels clicked as we made it to the sidewalk and up the steps to our front porch.

'You had school, then worked in Denver for your dad.'

'Not anymore,' I said.

'Yeah, but you've been busy.'

'Not too busy for you.' I looked at my best friend. The normally brassy, ball-busting redhead seemed to be carrying the weight of several things, and I'd had no idea. 'I'm sorry if I've been wrapped up in my own crap and been a terrible friend.'

'You're not,' she said, and fished her keys out, unlocking the door. 'You're a great friend, and I just want you to be happy. You've come a long way already. Last weekend, when I picked you up, you were practically buzzing with a permanent smile. Then, you confronted your dad for the first time, and quit the shitty situation and job he put you in. I want you to keep whatever this newfound awesomeness is.'

We walked through the door, the same feeling I'd felt thousands of times crashing down.

Weakness. I hadn't told her that Jack not calling bummed me out more than I let on. Hadn't told her that tonight I felt like an outsider that didn't fit in. That was, until Cal started chatting me up, only to kiss me, and then rush off. Yeah, he had a fire to get to. But it was the few seconds before that.

Too bad that passion, while it was a new feeling I was experiencing, tended to linger.

It was laughable how easily my mood could change, my heart could break, with a single conversation with my father or a glare from my step-mother. My confusion could skyrocket at a single encounter with a firefighter or my need to be touched, to be consumed, could ignite with one kiss from a dark-eyed man built of raw intensity and power.

'I'm working on it,' I said. 'I quit my job, and I meant it when I said I was done shying away from life. You're right, I need experiences. Good ones.' I just didn't know exactly how to do that, or where to acquire the tools to tackle that kind of undertaking.

Harper nodded, tossed her keys on the side table, and kicked her heels off. 'And I want to help with that. I just don't think Cal is that guy.'

I frowned. 'I'm not looking for *that* guy.' Though, after last week and up until this morning, I thought Jack was the only guy that made me feel those kind of emotions. Of course, Cal caught me off guard in a surprising way. Not bad. He wasn't intense like Jack, definitely not bad. 'I wasn't aware you even knew Cal or his friends. Were you two together or something?'

'Cal and I? God, no. He gives me crap because ...' Harper finished her sentence with a shaking of her head rather than words.

'What's going on, Harper? You're always talking about helping me. But I want to know what's happening with you. I care, you know.'

54

She nodded. 'I know. I've gotten myself into a small predicament that I don't know how to solve.' She waved her hand, and the strain of conversation away. 'But it's nothing I can't handle, and I don't want to talk about that anyway. I want to talk about you.'

I tried to protest, but she just continued. 'Look, the way I see it, whatever gave you that smile and strength last week is something worth hanging on to.'

'You said it yourself, I don't have Jack's number.' That didn't mean I didn't crave his heat. Stupid, considering I'd just met the man and was drawn to him.

'He brought out something in you.'

'I need to find myself, by myself.'

Harper huffed. 'You're right. *You* need to take back your life for you. And that's what *you* are doing. You made that decision. But Jack helped those kickass emotions you needed rise to the surface to do that. I'm not saying he's your hero, but he may be the catalyst for your shift in strength. No matter what, it still comes from you. Don't forget that. In the meantime, there's no sense in letting go of something good. You can always stop by his place.'

I didn't want to argue with her, but I didn't want to just show up at Jack's house. Facing rejection from him was something I didn't want to gamble with. Besides, it was just a kiss, right?

'I think I need to focus on how I'm going to pay rent,' I said, changing the subject, and putting the Jack, Cal, trifecta of passion and my uncommon behavior on hold.

'Agreed. I'll call Sharon on Monday, and I bet by the week's end, she'll place you in a job.'

'Thanks.'

'I still don't recommend hanging out with Cal.' Clearly, Harper wasn't done with this subject, despite my best efforts.

'He's not so bad.' He actually made me feel good. Looked at me like he understood the broken part, and with all his strength, could smother it away.

'He's a runner, Lan. Actually, he's a runner and a jumper.'

'What do you mean?'

'Cal works wild fires over the summer. He's one of the adrenaline junkies who go behind fire lines and sometimes right in it.'

'Wow.'

Harper nodded. 'He's charming, and there's a bad boy vibe there, I get it. But—'

'You don't think I can handle him.'

'I don't know any real details,' Harper said, a little softer. 'But Cal has been through some crazy shit. I guess he had it rough as a kid? I don't know for sure, but, for whatever reason, he doesn't do commitment.'

'I'm not seeking out marriage or anything.'

'I know. But Cal is used to women who know the drill.'

'What drill is that?'

'A one-nighter, no strings kind of drill. You have a pretty raw heart and fresh emotions, Lan. God love you for it, but I don't want you to get hurt anymore. I just think baby steps are a good thing. You have the whole summer ahead of you, and in one week, you've kissed two men.'

'They kissed me.'

'That's right, they did!' She nudged my shoulder. 'But a lot has gone down.'

That was true. I was all over the place with emotions and between Jack's hot kiss – rough and wild against his front door – then Cal and his strong hold and soft sweep of his lips, I was on the brink of a meltdown. In the end, neither man owed me a thing. Nor I them.

We were all relative strangers, but the ache throbbed a little harder when I thought of how close I'd been to something good. I was standing on the edge of it, staring into Jack's dark eyes, I could have fallen into the abyss of intensity. That was looking less and less likely. Besides, Harper was right. I didn't know 'the drill.' Both Jack and Cal were experienced and could easily crush the little confidence I had.

'Maybe slowing down is a good idea,' I said. At least when it came to men. I needed to focus on getting this job, and saving this summer for school. That was the priority. If the men wanted something from me, or to talk, or whatever, they'd find me. Right?

'I don't know about you, but I'm exhausted.'

I nodded. 'Me too.'

Walking down the hall, I went to my room and sat down, determined not to think of Jack, of how he tapped into a side of me I'd thought lost forever. Strength. That strength in me directly led to my handling of Cal. Everything felt woven together.

No, I wouldn't think of how Jack's hands felt on my skin.

I also wouldn't think of Cal, or his smile.

Chapter 5

Mondays always seemed to spike my adrenaline. It was a new week. A chance to start fresh. Especially this particular Monday, because I was half a day into my new job of crunching numbers for the staff of one of the many Reign Resorts.

And we had a meeting to go to in five minutes.

Harper had been right about the temp agency hiring quickly. I called Sharon first thing last Monday, and it only took her a few days to find me a job and do the paperwork.

I still hadn't heard from Jack, and with another week passed since I kissed Cal, hadn't heard from him either. But seeing as how we didn't exchange any info, that was no surprise. I did go to the fire station a few days ago to touch base with Cal. I found out he'd been sent to go help with a big wildfire in Montana.

The team he was on was an intense one, and it meant I wouldn't be seeing him any time soon. At least the majority of the summer, his co-worker said.

No note.

No goodbye.

Once again, I was kissed and left to figure out what it meant. Which, apparently, was nothing.

I pinched the bridge of my nose and cursed my brain for the spiral. I was trying to be stronger. Trying to be more confident. Yeah, trying and failing.

At least I had a job I could focus on.

I typed a few more numbers on my ten key and balanced my spreadsheet. Coming to a stopping point, I grabbed a dollar from my purse, then locked it away and wound around the endless lanes of cubicles to the break room.

I needed caffeine, and the vending machine was calling my name. People were already bustling toward the large conference room. Of course, it took two tries for the machine to accept my dollar.

'You coming?' Devin said, as he stood in the doorway of the break room, blocking my only way out.

'Yeah.'

He snickered and openly stared at my chest.

I swallowed back disgust. The man was gross at best. It took only a few minutes in his presence this morning to realize he was a walking sexual harassment suit waiting to happen. But he was also my floor manager. The guy I reported to. Gripping my soda can, I took a few small steps in his direction, hoping he'd take the hint and move.

When he didn't, an icky taste rose in my throat and I glanced at my feet.

'We better get in there,' I said.

I felt his gaze linger on me for a minute, then he sighed. 'Yeah, we better.'

He opened his stance to let me pass, and I hustled through quickly, hating that I had to brush against him as I went by.

I walked into the boardroom and people were already crowded in. The chairs that were set out were filled, and only a little standing room in the back was left. I stayed as close to the door and as far away from Devin and his overwhelming aftershave smell as I could get.

I was just about to ask Edith, the woman who sat on the other

59

side of my cubicle, and the only other person I'd gotten a chance to know aside from Devin, what this meeting was about when my question was answered.

'Good afternoon, everyone.'

I'd recognize that deep raspy voice anywhere. My gaze snapped to the front of the room where Jack stood in a three piece black suit, looking every bit the sexy man I remembered from two weeks ago. So much so that it made *my* heart throb to a point I was certain everyone around me could hear it.

'What is he doing here?' I whispered to Edith. She was smoothing her hair and smiling like crazy. She was close to my age, and I realized what had made her so happy: Jack. His charm or hotness seemed to know no bounds.

'Edith?' I tried again. She reluctantly pulled her stare from Jack and frowned at me like I'd robbed her of a toy.

'What?'

'What is he doing here?' I asked again in a whisper.

Now, she looked shocked, then patted my shoulder. 'Sweetie, that's Jack Powell. He owns the resorts.' She glanced at him and sighed. 'Hottest boss I've ever had. He almost never stops by.'

My mouth dropped. Owns the resorts? 'As in ... Reign Resorts? The company we work for? Jack *owns* it?' She nodded and looked at me like I'd lost my mind. Which I must have, because this was, 'Unbelievable.'

'I wanted to stop by today to tell you all you've been doing a great job with the payroll for the Rocky Mountain Resort. As you may have noticed, extra staff has been hired to oversee the Pacific Resort as well.' His dark eyes glanced around the room until they landed on me. 'Please help the new hires feel welcome, and keep up the good work.'

When he walked out of the room, all the confidence he radiated followed him. The world around me seemed to close in until

I was dying to have just a moment with him – to share in the same space, the same breath.

He's my catalyst.

And that feeling was too overwhelming to ignore. And so was this situation. If Jack Powell was my boss, that was going to be a problem. Because I couldn't handle him having power over me in that way. All of my bright ideas of being a bold woman didn't extend to my boss.

So, I scooted out of the meeting, and followed him.

'Jack?' I said, just as he exited the building into the midday summer sun.

The streets were relatively calm, considering the work day was still in session, but when the wind blew a slight breeze, I caught a whiff of that same spice and man that I had the night we met.

'Lana,' he said, not surprised to see me at all.

'This isn't a coincidence, is it?' I asked. 'Me working here?'

He didn't say a word. Didn't shrug. Didn't give any kind of answer or emotion away.

Instead, he turned and started walking, glancing back at me as if expecting me to follow. I did.

'I was pleased to see you today,' he said.

'Are you leaving without answering me?' I kept stride beside him, rounding the corner of the building.

'My office is a few blocks away.'

'I didn't know you owned the resorts.'

'Does that make a difference now?' His tone was a little sharp, so I went with honesty.

'Yes, it does.'

'Why?'

'Because I . . . ' I tried to get a handle on my thoughts, which were scattering a million miles a minute. I had admitted the truth

61

to him once. That I wanted him. And he did have a powerful persona, and it was one of things I liked most about him. But, in a work environment? No, not a good idea.

'I don't think I can work for you.'

That made him stop and face me. His dark eyes skated over my entire body. My simple black dress was sleeveless and hit just above my knees. It was sleek, but professional. The way his eyes ran the length of me made me feel anything but professional though.

'You said you'd see me again,' I blurted out, hating that my social skills, especially with men, were lacking. But this situation was too easy to ignore, especially since he was one of the only things I'd been thinking about. 'I didn't think it would be like this. Did you know I was being hired? Somehow set this up?'

The moment the words left my mouth, I felt like an idiot. Harper had been the one to mention this job to me. There was no way – aside from Jack being part magical – he had anything to do with that.

'I met you in a bar, Lana.'

I nodded. Again, hating how stupid I felt.

'After our encounter,' his gaze paused on my mouth and a shiver broke over my spine, 'I did look into who you were, and the fact that you applied for the payroll position came up, but you'd already passed through the hiring process.'

'I see.'

He took a step toward me. His eyes locked on my face. I glided back just a foot.

'Still running from me?'

'No,' I gasped, because it was the last thing I wanted to do. It was just instinct.

A man came toward me, I took a step back. Simple.

62

I didn't want to do that with Jack. I hadn't before. But I was so off kilter with seeing him like this. Out of nowhere.

He was different. At least, I thought he was. Then I hadn't heard from him. Same as Cal. 'Kiss and ditch' was becoming my motto, and somehow, it left me feeling like the bad guy. It also took a toll on the faith I'd had in Jack.

No. I didn't have any ties to either Jack or Cal. If I had, I wouldn't have kissed Cal, rather, let him kiss me. Just like now, I had no ties to Cal. He was gone. Kisses weren't contracts, no matter how hot.

Too bad I kept thinking about Jack's front door, and the way it felt against my back. The way he felt against my front. He'd read and tapped into my emotions and somehow let me feel in control. All the while exercising his own intensity over me.

'Now, about this notion that you can't work for me?' He took another step and I could already feel the heat radiating from him. It was everything I could do not to get swept up in him again. 'I want to clarify that I'm the owner of the resorts, but I don't plan on interfering with your job.'

I bit my bottom lip, thinking it over. Surely, the owner of the entire resort company had better things to do than to monitor one small payroll branch. Edith had just said he didn't stop by much.

Yet, he was still here. And if I were totally honest, my pride hurt a little. I was getting the sense that I was easily discarded. I just wanted to work in peace, save for grad school, and not be reminded what a sad sack I was.

'I still don't think it's a good idea,' I said, trying for an authoritative tone.

He took another step, his expression like stone. Reaching out, he traced his fingertip along my cheek bone. 'I don't hear much confidence in your voice.'

That's because there was none. Not about this. When it came to Jack, I didn't know what was rational or normal. He made me feel things that made a professional relationship difficult. If he wanted me, I wanted him to see me. Not because I worked for him. Not because he had some arbitrary title like 'my bosses boss' kind of hierarchy, but because he simply wanted me.

Which he didn't. Because, if he did, I would have heard from him before now. If he'd been thinking about me the way I had been him, then he would have reached out.

My eyes met his. The building shaded us just enough to hide us from the few passersby on the street only ten yards away.

'I'm happy I got to see you again,' I admitted. It was the only truth I could say with confidence.

His eyes were like two smoking volcanos – dangerous, smoldering. 'Are you?'

I nodded.

'And have you seen anyone else?' His tone was steady. Not accusing or angry. Simply asking. My mind flashed to the night I met Cal.

'That's none of your business.'

'So, you have.'

'I didn't say that.'

'You don't deny it.'

'You didn't call!' I finally said, feeling defeated. 'I haven't heard from you. I didn't know what to think.'

'I told you I'd see you again.'

I shook my head, and a humorous laugh escaped. Looking at him, it was clear. He knew the game, hell, he probably invented it, when it came to women. I wasn't the kind that could keep up. Harper was right, I wasn't a 'drill' kind of girl. No pun intended.

'You're right, you did say that. You also made no promises or shed any clarity on what to expect. So, yes, I kissed someone. But that—'

'Just kissed?' he asked sharply, like he had a right to be jealous.

'Yes, just kissed. What about you, huh?' I crossed my arms. Maybe Jack brought out the fire in me, maybe I was just irritated and frustrated, and staring down his perfect face and dark eyes was too much to handle all at once.

'I've kissed no one since you.'

I swallowed hard. 'Oh. So, you don't have a girlfriend?' Something I should have asked before, but right now, it just seemed like I needed all the clarity I could get. Plus, it gave me more info.

'No.'

I glanced at the ground and threaded my fingers.

Jack flicked the bottom of my chin with his finger, forcing my gaze up. 'You do that when you're nervous. Keep your eyes on me when you speak. Do you understand?'

I nodded.

'Good.' His knuckles trailed the length of my jaw, then down my neck. 'Give me a number.'

I swallowed, wanting to arch into his touch. I had to keep some pride, so I said. 'I'm not that nervous . . .'

'Quantify,' he said sharply.

'Three: Hot.'

He nodded. 'Don't look away. Even when you're unsure. Say what you need to say.'

A dose of courage surged. He was right. I squared my shoulders. 'Everything else aside, I was hoping I could see more of you, but that was before today.'

'Before you realized I owned the resorts?'

'Yes.'

A sexy smile tugged at his lips for a split second. Lips I knew firsthand to be sinful.

65

'Why don't you come by my home tomorrow on your lunch break, and we'll discuss this before you make any rash decisions.'

'Your home?'

'Yes, I have an office and take several meetings there. It's where I'll be tomorrow. However,' he pulled a card from his pocket. 'Here is my corporate office information. A clear statement of my intentions to pursue per your request. Because I like this idea of seeing more of each other.' He cupped the underside of my chin in one hand and brought me close enough that I felt his lips move against mine when he whispered, 'Now, don't go kissing anyone else. Do you understand?'

I nodded, not knowing what else to do.

He closed the fraction between our mouths and branded a searing kiss on me. So quick and consuming, it almost knocked me off my feet. One deep thrust of his tongue had me moaning and teetering on my heels, because as soon as he advanced, he retreated, leaving me breathless and dazed.

He wiped his thumb over my bottom lip – the lip he'd just sucked on – turned, and walked away.

66

Chapter 6

Of course Jack would have an office in his incredible home. I had an hour for lunch. While his corporate headquarters were in some building downtown as well, I made the short trek to his home, which wasn't that far.

'Ten minute walk,' I said to myself, doing some mental math, as I reached the front door of his home. Depending on how long it took to actually get face time with him, a safe estimate meant I'd give him thirty minutes. That allowed for plenty of time to walk back and eat lunch, take a deep breath, and re-focus on work.

The re-focusing part was going to be tricky.

I had no idea of Jack's agenda, but being around him frazzled me enough to consume my thoughts. I had replayed every word, smile, and stare, and finally come to a decision. Yes, he may be a super sexy sparkplug that made me feel and want things – like his body and attention – but I couldn't be with him. He would technically have power over me professionally.

I glanced at my watch, then rang the bell.

'Half hour,' I reminded myself. I'd stick to my plan. State plainly that distance was best while I worked at the payroll office.

'Miss Case?' A woman asked, opening the door. Her presence shocked me. Didn't people who worked from home typically wear sweatpants and order in Chinese?

'Miss Case?' the woman asked again, because I stared like a buffoon. Finally, I shook off my surprise and glanced around. Yep, right house.

'Sorry, yes, I'm Lana Case. I though Jack was . . . here?'

She was pretty. Young. Her short bob and bangs were perfectly coiffed. Suddenly, the dress I'd picked this morning felt like a shabby clearance rack item. Which it was. Not that anyone would know. Typically I wouldn't care, but the woman before me looked like she wore only the finest designer skirts and heels.

'I'm Nina, Mr Powell's assistant. He is here and expecting you.'

Wasn't that great. His assistant knew me and hung out at his house. I suppose there weren't a lot of single brunettes coming to see him. Or maybe there were and this was part of the 'drill'? I hadn't said a time I'd show up, and he hadn't given me one. With the power of technology, texting, email, even a phone call, Jack made it hard to understand not only his motives, but timeframes and expectations. Especially since he'd used none of the above to contact me thus far.

Something I was going to clear up.

Just like I practiced last night. Sure, I may have looked like a freak, pacing in my room and talking to myself. Going over talking points and why my decision that Jack and I maintain a professional relationship was smart.

When Nina led me up the staircase, and wove down the hallway, we came to a large wooden door with a brass knob. She opened the door, and when I saw Jack standing at the other end of the large office, hands in his pockets, looking perfect in matching black pants, vest, and tie with a crisp white button up, those talking points went right out the large window he was looking out.

He didn't say anything and neither did his assistant. She shut the door behind me, the knob bumping my ass and pushing me forward, as if the damn thing were shoving me closer.

'Good afternoon,' he said, facing me. Between the black suit and wicked gleam in his dark eyes, every inch of his skin looked tan and mouthwatering. Apparently, I had been way off on home offices and working in sweat pants, because Jack dominated this domain. All hardwood floors, with a massive desk that looked fit for the King of England, circa the sixteen-hundreds. Large built-in book shelves that matched the desk took up an entire wall, while two other doors were on the opposite side, and large windows framed the center back wall.

'Hi.'

He took a step toward me. 'You look beautiful.' That dark gaze raked over my body. 'I'm glad you wore a dress.'

'Why?' The thin-strapped summer dress was flowy and pink, but was still within the dress code for work. When he didn't answer my question, I cleared my throat and attempted to recite my logical decision I'd come to yesterday, because standing there and staring at him wasn't helping anything. Unless my skin collecting goose bumps counted as helping. Besides, Jack liked it when I spoke plainly. Actually, he had helped me start doing that.

'I like my job,' half-truth. My job was okay. But it was a means to an end, and it was a paycheck, one I needed to live and save for grad school. 'I'd like to continue working without distraction.'

He looked at me like I'd just issued a challenge. 'You think I'm a distraction?'

He pulled his hands out of his pockets. I was instantly trans-fixed by the buttons of his vest running down his stomach. It made me wonder how long it would take to unbutton each one. What hard muscle lay beneath? Surely, two seconds per button, which would cut into the original half hour I'd allotted to tell him why we should keep a distance. Distance and undressing him were counter ideas.

69

'You're definitely a distraction,' I said, still doing mental calculations on how long the pants, shirt, and tie would take to shuck.

'I see. And what is it I distract you from?'

'My job,' I said quickly.

'Bullshit.' His response was fast and cut quick, shocking me. 'I know this is an interim job for the summer for you. And I've told you I won't interfere. So, tell me the truth.'

'I am,' I said. Time to recite: 'Since you own the resorts, you have a professional power over me. If we entered into any kind of non-professional relationship and it went sour, you could fire me at any point.'

'I could also just fire you now for no reason whatsoever.'

I frowned, then tried to swallow back a little unease. 'I guess that's true.'

'You said professional power over you,' he restated my words. 'What if I'm not interested in that? What if I want a different kind of power over you?'

I frowned. 'What other kind is there?'

'Every other kind.'

I stared at him for a long moment. He was serious, unmoving stone. Something I was learning he did well. Opening my mouth to say something turned into a quick fail. Because no words came out. Was this a game? Did he want me? What did 'power over me' mean exactly? While all these question were buzzing in my brain, he continued.

'Enough of this professional relationship excuse. It's a weak argument. Especially now that we've determined firing you is not on my list of desires, and holds no bounds anyway to now or later. So, what is it that you're really struggling with?'

'You,' I snapped, my eyes meeting him. 'I'm struggling with *you.*'

'How so?'

'You make me feel things, and distract me, and—'

'What things?'

'Excuse me?'

'What things do I make you feel?' He stepped until his Italian leather shoes met my cute wedges, and I could smell his rich scent and feel his heat. God, I've missed that heat. And I'd only had it the one night.

'Different,' I whispered.

The night I'd met him, he made me feel safe. Protected. He put me at ease while challenging me. Just like now. And I wanted to rise to that challenge and grab hold of the strength pumping through my veins. 'You make me feel different.'

'That's a vague word. Care to give me another?'

I shook my head, because any other word I could come up with didn't sound appropriate. Words like hot, bothered, and downright lusty.

'Alright, then I'll have to, once again, decipher your half answers.'

He took my hand and yanked me toward his desk. 'Jack, I came here to—'

'I know why you came. Now sit.'

I looked behind me. 'You want me to sit on your desk?'

'Yes.'

He cupped my hips and hopped me up, instantly wedging himself between my parted thighs. I gasped and went to wiggle away, pulling on my dress to cover my legs better. He gripped my wrists, and with them in his fists, rested them on either side of me. Trapped.

With the cool glossy wood of his desk beneath my palms and thighs, a zing of fire shot through me, and the feel of him so close only made me want more.

71

His mouth hovered over mine, as he looked at my face.

'I make you feel different,' he repeated, that mouth now trailing to my ear. 'How about nervous? Do I still make you nervous?'

I nodded.

'Hot?' he asked.

I nodded again. He trailed his nose along my neck and my eyes slid shut. Whatever plan I'd had coming in here was failing.

'You are an anomaly to me, Lana. You have to be handled delicately.'

With my eyes closed, I frowned. 'I'm not weak.'

'I didn't say that. I was referring to the pursuit. I have to be careful. Not scare you off. I've seen fear in your eyes, and I want you to understand that is not my goal.'

'I'm not afraid of you.' Not in the way I was of most men. Not in the way Brock scared me.

The only thing I felt with Jack was confusion. Because my body was screaming for him, my mind racing, and my chest pounding. It was all new: wanting someone. But I did want him. So much. 'Not calling me made me think you weren't interested.'

'I was out of the country. I have a lot of resorts to handle.'

And didn't that make me feel like an idiot. I hadn't considered any details like his job or life beyond the making-out moment. Up until yesterday, when he showed up as my boss, I didn't have any idea about him beyond how he dominated a kiss. But he did have a life. And now my lack of experience in matters of men, dating, and expectations in general, especially when it involved physical interactions, was getting the better of me.

'You said you didn't want to scare me off,' I said, trying to change the subject. 'What's so scary about you?'

72

He grinned, but there was a sinister glow to it. 'Several things. What I want and how I take it can be ... abrupt.'

Hence, me sitting on his desk, dress hiked up my thighs and him between them. Still, I had to know: 'What is it you want?'

'You.' He gently nipped my jaw.

I gasped, but tried to keep as calm as possible. He was so quick with his words. Like he knew exactly what to say. Could he really want me? In the way I wanted him? The warning in Jack's voice, when he spoke of taking what he wanted, made me wonder if I could, in fact, handle him. Only one way to find out.

'H-how would you take what you wanted?'

'Thoroughly and repeatedly.'

His admission hit my mouth, and I wanted it to be true. He was direct, painted a picture of what exactly those two words meant, and how he'd carry them out.

'But, again, I have to be careful with you.' He released my wrists and trailed his hand up to my neck and cupped it. 'You may not be weak, but you haven't realized your full strength yet. I want to help with that.'

'Why?'

'Because of how you make me feel.'

'What way is that?'

He wrapped his free arm around my lower back and pulled me into him. My legs parted further, my dress scrunched higher, and his hard cock rubbed against my panties.

'Different,' he said, using my own word against me. He slowly moved, hitting a spot between my legs that stirred heat. It started in my core and began building.

'You want me to elaborate on my feelings, yet you won't?'

He thrust hard, sliding that steel rod along my center. Reaching between us, he moved my panties aside. He didn't touch me,

73

though. What was more surprising was that I let him. The only thing I felt was needy. My skin was slowly scorching and desperate for more of anything he'd offer. Because nothing had ever felt this amazing.

He moved his hips in a way that put his cock between my folds, directly pressing on my clit. A surge of pleasure rushed over my entire body. My skin tingled and my hands reached out and wrapped around him. He thrust slowly, up, then down, running his erection the entire length of my core. Though his pants were a barrier, I felt him perfectly. The soft, crisp fabric against my heated flesh only added to the realization of how close and yet how far away we were.

'I want to get back to how I make you feel. You said hot?'

I nodded.

'What about wet?'

'Yes.'

'Did you think of me? This week? Last week? Whenever it was you kissed another man?' He thrust harder this time.

A jolt of lust pricked from the little bundle of nerves he was rubbing against to the base of my neck and everything in between.

I bit my lip, but nodded. 'Yes. But—'

'Do you feel weak around me?' He did a twisting movement, circling over and over that same spot. That blessed spot that made me ache and claw for more. Because the prickling beneath my skin was rising with every move he made.

'You make me feel weak in a different way. In some ways, I feel stronger with you.'

'Good. That's the beauty of power. Having it and wielding it. It's beneficial for both parties.'

'You said you wanted to wield power over me?'

'Yes.' That was straight to the point and he punctuated it with another thrust.

I moaned, and my head would have fallen back if he wasn't keeping a tight grip on my nape. I should be shying away, but didn't. I stayed there, my thighs surrounding him.

He was the only man I'd ever let touch me like this. Any other try in the past never got this far, and ended with me warding off tears and terror. Not now. Everything about Jack was different. Like he understood what I needed. What I wanted. I didn't know how he knew, but at the end of the day, at least he was being honest. The least I could do was be the same.

'I don't like men having power over me. Ever.'

He looked into my eyes. 'It requires trust.'

'Another thing I don't typically give men.'

'But you gave me some. Let me take you to my home. A part of you trusted me, and is trusting me now.'

That was true. I did. It came from the same place that had an instant connection with Cal. They shared a common denominator that allowed me to feel . . . safe.

That word rattled my skull because it was a wonderful feeling, just one I didn't have much acquaintance with. Involving myself with Jack would be going so far beyond my knowledge and comfort zone, I didn't know where to start. But I knew, looking in his eyes, it was serious.

'I want to earn more of your trust,' he rasped. His grip tightened as he moved against me. Like trying to get deeper, closer, but there was nowhere further to go. He set the boundary.

'Why?' My breaths were coming faster, pleasure building. 'Look at you. You don't have to work for a woman.'

I dropped my glance from his eyes to his chest. Those damn buttons daunting me. I wanted to rip them open, but shook off the desire and clung tighter to his back. I didn't want to go into specifics, but he should know a hint of the truth.

'I'm not experienced in this way.' I rocked my hips a little,

75

meeting his motion, and a low hum broke from his chest. 'I don't think that I'm the type of woman you're looking for.'

With his palm still on my neck, he raised my face, making me meet his eyes.

'I disagree.' He moved his hips again, hitting my sweet spot over and over until breathing was impossible. 'You may not be experienced, but you have the desire. I can feel it – smell it – on you.' His lips were against mine when he said, 'Whatever the reason it is that your passion has been smothered is a fucking shame. You have to know yourself before you can have strength and full confidence.'

'And you'll help me know myself?'

'Yes.'

'And for that, you want power. Over me?' I moaned again, because the ecstasy was climbing higher. 'Power like you have over me right now?'

'Is this so bad?' He shoved me even closer, his arm around me like a clamp.

No, it wasn't. But it was apparent who was in control. And it was Jack. To have as little or as much of me as he wanted. And I sat there, praying he'd take more.

'I want you to trust that I know what *I'm* doing and we'll both come out better from our encounters. But in the end, you always have the power. And that comes with one word: No. The moment you say it, I'll stop. Anything and everything.'

That idea was a heavy one. He respected a single word, and it was up to me when and if I wanted to say it. I didn't. In fact, I wanted to say yes. But several things were still weighing on me. Things I needed clarity on.

'I didn't feel better after this past week. I felt confused. Felt bad.' Not a smart thing to admit, since I was already in a vulnerable state. I ran my lips along his. Desperate for a taste.

He groaned, and it was the one sign I'd gotten that he was perhaps just as affected as I was. In control or not, he felt something too.

'I understand now that you don't do space without explanation,' he rasped. 'And you understand that I had a prior engagement that took me overseas. But neither of those occurrences deters from the fact that I want you.'

I thought back to the night I met him. He was right, a piece of me trusted him. Was this my moment? To explore trust and be a woman who had confidence? To refuse to be wrecked by my past? Wanting these things was different than taking action to get them. But I'd be naïve to think I was the kind of woman who had a clue as to the extent of what Jack wanted sexually.

'I want you too,' I admitted. 'So much. But I'm nervous.'

'I know. We can work with that. Just because I take pleasure in power and control,' he gave one final thrust, then slowly slid to his knees, 'doesn't mean you won't get to obtain the same.'

I looked down at him, half hating that he'd left me when my body was so close to euphoria, the other half realizing what he was doing. He'd purposefully put me in a position to feel above him, to feel confident.

This whole time, he kept a barrier between us because he sensed my limits. Maybe he didn't want to test them just yet? All the while being a force tightening around me like gravity. He was controlled, enough to understand what I needed. Which should scare me a little, but there he was, just like the night I met him, tapping into a deep need within me. And that need was finally coming alive.

On his knees before me, he ran his palms up my calves.

I shivered and fought the urge to squirm away. Even if I wanted to, I couldn't, because his wide shoulders prevented my knees from closing. My body shot to code red when his lips landed on my inner thigh.

'Wait,' I breathed. 'No one has ... don't look ...'

Despite my best efforts, I started to fidget. No one had ever looked at me down there before. This was the most exposed, most intimate, I'd ever been with anyone. There was nothing quick or clinical about this. It was slow, hard, raw, and consuming. But it was new. And the nerves got the better of me.

'Shhh, Lana. Look at me.'

I swallowed hard, and realized my eyes were squeezed shut.

'Look at me,' he said again.

With a deep breath, I opened my eyes and looked down at him. My God, he was beautiful. Just the brief moment of darkness behind shut eyelids was enough to make me miss his face already.

'Good. Now keep your eyes on me. I'm not going to touch you, I'm going to look.'

My brows shot up, but I kept my gaze on him. I watched his stare go from my face, to between my legs. Exhales were heavy and growing in pace. But he just looked. It was then I realized his typically stony expression was full of lust.

He look up at my face once more. 'You're beautiful.'

I took a deep breath and nodded. We'd passed a milestone. I didn't think I even got a full sentence out, yet he picked up on just how inexperienced I was, and went slow. I wanted to hug him. To thank him. To kiss him for days and days.

'Now I've seen you, I'm telling you to never be embarrassed of showing me again.'

Though his words were sharp, his tone was soft.

'O-okay.'

'Good, now ...' He reached out, took one of my hands and placed it on top of his head. 'We're going to go one step further.'

He licked up my thigh. 'I'm in control, and you get to hold on.' Those dark eyes looked up at me. 'Yet, I'm the one on my knees. Do you feel weak right now? Feel like I have so much power you can't escape?'

'No, I don't feel weak,' I whispered. And I didn't. Not in the least. I was ready to do, to give, whatever he wanted. This was all a carefully executed plan of dominance and submission. One thing was clear: Jack was a pro. It was a conflicting notion of power and exchange. He said the only thing that made sense: 'Trust me.'

I nodded, my hand closing and fisting his hair as he pushed my dress up higher until it bunched at my hips, leaving me in nothing but my disarranged panties.

'You know why I love lace?' he rasped, as his lips hovered just over my center.

'W-why?'

With a flick of his wrist, he ripped the thin material and removed the tatters in one fast swoop.

'That's why.'

A tremor raced over me, and I looked down to find him staring again.

'So pretty,' he said, running his finger along my slit. 'Innocent.'

I swallowed hard, because while I wasn't technically a virgin, my experiences were minimal, and not what was deemed an act of sex or love making. This time would be different. It already was. And it didn't matter how far we went, Jack took me past any bad feelings or horrid memories and kept my focus on him.

I liked that he saw an innocence in me. It allowed me to pretend for a moment I wasn't completely ruined. Because he seemed to see strength in me. Maybe I could be both. Maybe he could help me feel both.

Keeping my fist fastened in his hair, he looked up at me. 'Has a man ever made you come?'

79

'No.'

His gaze fell back to the juncture between my parted thighs and the look on his face made me gulp: determination. He slid both hands up my legs, around my hips and clutched my ass, bring me dangerously close to the edge of his desk.

I placed one hand on the surface to steady myself.

'You can either hold on to me, yourself, or lay back. Do you understand?'

I looked at my hands. One on his head, the other on his desk. I moved it quickly and placed it with the other on top of his head. The only thing keeping me from falling was his grip on me.

Seeming to read my mind, he smirked. 'Don't worry about falling. If you do, I'm right here. I'll happily catch you.' His voice was so raspy, the sound alone melted me another degree.

His fingers dug into my cheeks and he yanked me into his mouth.

'Oh, God!' My whole body tensed, and like he promised, he caught me.

He tugged me further off the edge of the desk and his tongue speared my opening. His whole mouth covered me, the heat of his breath fanning over my entire core. His upper lip brushed my clit, while he impaled me with his tongue, deep and hard.

'Jack, I ... I can't hold on ...'

The feel of his wicked mouth working me over, delving, licking, eating ... it was too much. I released the hold I had on his head and laid back. My shoulders met his desk, while I heard the sound of crinkling papers and random items falling to the floor. I hardly noticed, and cared even less.

Nothing had ever felt so wildly consuming. So intimate. His hands stayed on my ass, lifting me like he would a cup of water ready to drink it down. And that's exactly what he was doing.

My back arched, my breasts straining against the top of my dress, felt almost pained from lack of touch. My nipples were whining for attention. A single brush of fingers or a quick pluck ... anything to ease the ache. My entire body wanted his mouth and hands on it.

Lifting my hand, I went to grab my breast, then stopped. That would be inappropriate. My mind was racing, my body heating. Jack just worked faster, diving in and out of me, then flicking my clit so hard and perfectly that my lungs hurt from trying to breathe, and my thighs trembled.

I was close. So unbearably close that I could hardly take it. My breasts had never ached so badly, never wanted to be touched so desperately. I went to touch them again, then stopped. What was wrong with me!

Jack growled. Keeping his grip on my ass, he rose and leaned over me. Using his teeth, he tugged down the top of my dress enough to expose one nipple, which he quickly sucked hard, making me scream in pleasure. That was what I'd needed, but I also needed the magic he was preforming between my legs. I wanted all of it. All of him.

'Do what feels right,' he growled, releasing my nipple and settling back between my legs. When his tongue flicked my clit, I groaned and gave in to his command.

I cupped my breasts in my hands, pinching my nipples, realizing I liked the sting it left behind. One was wet from Jack's mouth, and it only intensified that sensation.

'Good, baby,' he rasped and bit my inner thigh. 'Now, let go. Let this pretty pussy of yours come.'

Let go ...

Something I'd never done. Always too scared, too cold, too in my head, instead of in the moment. That wasn't the case this time. All I felt was the moment and Jack's mouth on me.

81

He ran his tongue along my slit, then delved deep, and that was all it took. Clutching my breasts, a throaty moan ripped from my chest as I came hard. Little spasms, like hummingbird's wings flapping beneath my skin, made me shake and convulse. Jack just kept going. Licking and sucking at me, until every one of my muscles were tense and reaching for the stars from this one amazing climax.

My dress was left in disarray around me as Jack rose to stand, pushing me back on the desk just enough so that I could lay there a moment without needing his support. All I could do was stay still and catch my breath.

Jack took a few steps back, but kept that dark gaze on me.

He licked his bottom lip, and a devilish grin laced his handsome face. He just stared with a look of lusty pride on his face. When I sat up, he watched every move. I didn't know what to say, or what happened next, so I fixed my dress quickly to cover me. I saw my panties in tatters on the floor, and finally looked at Jack.

His eyes were on fire, his body poised to pounce and devour.

A predator.

He was breathing heavy too.

'Look.' I pointed at his torso and pants. There were a few damp spots of cream looking – 'Oh, no … oh God …' Mortification rose so quickly when I realized those stains were from me. When he'd thrust against me. When he rose up my body to suck at my breast. I was on him, ruining his expensive suit. 'I'm sorry. I'm so sorry. I'm going.' I fumbled off the desk, to my feet and prepared to run. Jack caught my arm.

'What did I say about being embarrassed?'

'This is different. I ruined your clothes with my …' I couldn't even say the word. I didn't know how to deal with this. I had dirtied him. Did that make what we did dirty?

'Stop,' he said harshly.

Cupping my face in his hands, he kissed me. I could taste myself on his lips, something he didn't seem to mind.

'Stop thinking,' he said against my mouth. 'There's nothing to be sorry about. Feeling you come, tasting it, is the highlight of my fucking year. Do not shame yourself or make this moment to be anything other than what it was.'

'What was this moment?' I asked breathlessly.

'Fucking perfect.' He kissed me hard once more, then released me. Glancing at the clock, he said, 'Looks like your lunch break is almost up. Wouldn't want to show up late and get the boss upset.'

He was joking. I could barely tell, because Jack didn't joke really. But everything about this situation was so far from what I'd expected or imagined. I didn't know what to say or do. So I simply nodded and turned towards the door.

'Um, what about you?' I motioned at his suit, and God help me, I about offered to pay for dry cleaning, but that somehow sounded bad in my mind, so it'd be even worse out loud.

'Simple fix,' he said, leaning over his now messy desk to grab a remote control and pressed a button on it. One of the doors opened automatically. It was a closet with perfectly pressed suits hanging in it.

He put the remote down and simply stared at me.

'Okay then,' I whispered, and opened the office door.

'Lana,' he called. I looked over my shoulder to see him run his thumb along his lower lip, then taste it. 'Have a good afternoon.'

I swallowed hard. 'Y-you too.'

With that, I shut the door behind me and walked my shaking legs down the stairs.

Chapter 7

'At least it's a different table,' I said, looking around the bar I'd been stood up at over two weeks ago. It was where my co-workers went for happy hour during the week, and this time, I was invited.

After yesterday in Jack's office, I could really use a drink. Harper had come home after I was asleep, and I left early this morning. I was dying to talk to her, but she seemed to be working late hours, and I didn't want to wake her.

So, I had spent that last twenty-eight hours, yes, I was counting, since my last encounter with Jack, trapped in my own mind, and wondering what to do next.

'Lana, want to sit by me?' Edith asked, as a few of my co-workers shoved into a booth.

Edith was nice and, by all accounts, normal. She was one year older than me and had been working for Reign Resorts for a year. She was friendly, and when she wasn't talking about her ambitions to move up and work in the actual resort, as opposed to behind the scenes, she was chatting about how hot Jack Powell was, or the most recent scandal she'd read about in the tabloids.

I sat on the end next to Edith. I was the only 'new hire,' and everyone was chatting and seemed to know each other fairly well.

'Thanks for inviting me,' I said to Edith.

'Of course.' She was the one person who had been nice and

gone out of her way to get to know me. 'So, you going to dish about the other day when you ran out after Mr Powell left?'

Edith was also a bit of a gossip. I didn't want anyone to know about my relationship – if I could even call it that – with Jack. Especially co-workers. It would look bad if I was seeing the owner of the resorts, in any capacity.

'I just needed some fresh air,' I said, and looked at the happy hour menu. It was laminated and sticky, and the first thing I read sounded perfect. Especially if it got Edith's questioning glare off of me.

'Why don't I get the first round? Margaritas sound good?' I announced, and everyone seemed happy with that. Couldn't really go wrong with four-dollar margaritas.

'I like you already,' said Walter, the mid-forties man who worked two rows down. 'I'll get the next round.'

Nodding, I walked to the bar, the chattering of the table getting fainter the further away I got. My anxiety was a bit on the high side, with trying an outing with new 'friends.' It was better than remaining a social outcast, though. Besides, broadening my horizons with people was part of me attempting to gain control of my life.

When I reached the bar, the tall model wasn't working, thank goodness, and while the place was relatively bustling with people, it wasn't overcrowded like a weekend night. It was still early, after all. Getting off work at four was nice. But all I kept thinking about was the other day in Jack's office.

'Hi,' I said to the bartender, an average man with a nice smile, who had to be in his late twenties.

'Hi, there.' His smile turned a little brighter as he glanced at my chest, then back to my face. 'What can I get you?'

'Four margaritas, please. Blended.'

He winked. 'Coming right up.'

I pulled a twenty out of my purse, and rested my forearms on the counter while he went to work making the drinks at the other end of the bar.

I glanced around. The place looked different in the daylight. Rustic, yet modern. Eclectic décor like old framed posters and a signed Colorado Rockies jersey hung on the walls.

'You really have no idea, do you?'

'Jesus!' I gasped and saw Jack standing next to me. With his hands in the pockets of his expensive navy suit, he leaned his side against the bar and looked at me. That dark gaze heating my blood like a Bunsen burner.

'There I go, scaring you again.'

'You don't scare me,' I said. 'You surprise me.'

I looked back at the table where everyone was sitting. They were chatting and didn't seem to be paying attention to me or Jack. Likely didn't even know he'd come in.

'And, no,' I answered his earlier question. 'I didn't have any idea that you were standing right there.'

I chanced a quick glance at him, because anything too long and I'd get caught up. He sat on a bar stool and faced me. The way he moved was so fluid and commanding, he was like some cosmic force.

'You're like Bruce Wayne or something. Lurking discreetly,' I said.

'That's not what I'm talking about. Though the Bruce Wayne reference is mildly flattering.' His voice was low, deep, and just loud enough for me to hear but still keep our conversation private. Like all his attention and every syllable was meant for my ears alone, and the thought made me both hot and happy.

Keeping Jack's focus was a prize to be won. It was an understanding I'd realized from the moment I met him. It was also something I craved. Something I'd do a lot to keep.

'Then, what are you talking about?'

He glanced at the bartender. 'All these men in here have their eyes on you.'

'That's not true.' I said instantly, looking around. People were having conversations, holding eye contact with the ones they came with. Certainly not on me.

'You don't have to stare to notice someone. It's a quick glance, a small linger of the eyes,' he said this while those dark pools of obsidian did a little lingering of their own, down the front of me, then back to my face in a lazy sweep.

'Why would they look at me?' I turned a little to face him more fully.

'Because you radiate a kind of need that calls to a man. The kind that makes them wonder how they can be the one to give you what you want, which you are silently begging for.'

'They don't look at me the way you do,' I said softly.

He grinned. I loved it when he did that. 'They better not. Because I was not only looking, but recalling.' His gaze trailed lower, to my breasts, then thighs. Thighs that were swaying a little and brushing against the inside of his. It was then I realized I was the one gravitating toward him and standing between his bent knees.

'I know what's beneath that dress. They don't.' He leaned just a fraction closer. 'I know what you taste like. The sexy sounds you make when I lick your sweet pussy. The look of you well satisfied and sprawled out on my desk.'

His hand lifted to adjust his tie, but as he went, he skimmed the back of his knuckles against my stomach, between the valley of my breasts and to my neck before leaving my skin. 'You ruined that desk, you know? I can't get a thing done. Every time I look at it, all I see is you.'

I swallowed hard. 'First, I ruin your suit, then your desk.

Perhaps I should start taking accounting on that so you don't lose any profit.'

'Oh, I profit greatly.'

'Is that part of the power you were talking about?'

'It's part of who I am.'

'So, being with me gives you the power and control that you need?'

'Yes.'

I wanted more explanation and he knew it. But he wasn't giving it up. Like he just said, it was part of who he was. Digging deeper into the why would be tough. For all of Jack's honesty, he was careful with a lot of himself. It was because of that prized control that he didn't give too much of himself away. Just enough to drive me crazy and want more.

But there was one thing I felt the need to ask. 'Why me?'

He straightened and looked down at me. 'Because, like I said before, you give off a need of your own. And I want to be the man you give it to.'

'So, I'm a challenge?'

'Yes.'

That stung. So much that I had to run my hand over my cheek, because it felt so heated I wasn't sure if I was blushing from confusion or if his words had found a way to physically slap me. I faced the bar.

'You're upset,' he stated.

'No kidding!' I snapped, keeping him in my peripheral. 'I'm not some conquest. Not some little toy you can play with, mold, save, whatever.'

Whatever his end goal was, I wasn't it. Because it sounded like he was interested merely in the chase.

'You're confusing challenge and conquest. Do I not challenge you? Don't you see me as something a little forbidden? Weren't

88

you going to tell me to fuck off yesterday when you entered my office? You had a whole speech prepared on the topic.'

My heart stunted and I faced him with shock. Blood rushed to my ears and I felt like I'd been caught doing something wrong.

'Yes, I was going to tell you this was a bad idea.'

'But you didn't. Because you want me. Just as I want you.'

'I don't view you as a challenge, though.'

He cocked his head. 'Think about that before you say it. I'd hate to make a liar out of you.' With his elbow resting casually on the bar, he leaned in and whispered, 'And, in my world, liars get punished.'

With that, he pinched my nipple quickly and I stifled the smallest squeak of shock and awe. My body was not only turned on, but revved up. For a fight. For sex. I didn't understand how he did this to me.

I thought about what he'd said, if I was lying about seeing him as a challenge. Maybe I did. Was I not just mentally debating on how to go about extracting more information from him? Wanting to know him, but realizing that digging into a man like Jack Powell would be a . . . *Challenge*.

He read my face and a victorious expression masked his. He knew he was right. And I now knew it too.

'Not all challenges have to have a negative connotation, Lana.' He brushed that same finger he'd just pinched me with quickly over my now-throbbing and hard nipple. 'One challenge we could play out would be to see how many different ways I can make you come.'

'You can't say things like that.' I glanced around. My body was nearly shaking from the heat and literal plucks of lust being delivered.

'I can say whatever I want. Especially when it involves you and the truth.'

'Just because you ...' I waved my hand, getting a little nervous, 'know what I look like, or whatever, doesn't mean I give off this essence or need. And it certainly doesn't mean other people are looking.'

'I'm correct in this.' He nodded his head at the bartender, who was behind him. The bartender, who was almost done mixing the margaritas, was staring at me with a lusty smile. I was just about to ask Jack how he could have known, but it was useless. In one conversation, he'd proven himself right about so many things, including me.

'Well, I don't care if he looks or anyone else does,' I said, straightening my posture, determined to not give off this perception that I needed some random man.

Jack tucked a lock of hair behind my ear and slid a little closer. 'I like that you don't care. Because if I saw a flicker of interest for another man on your face, I may have a problem.' There was a playfulness in his eyes that made me smile.

How did he do that? Go from intense to grinning in point two seconds?

However he did it would be something I'd hopefully figure out in time. Because the *challenge* that was Jack Powell was one I was very interested in. And being caught in his sights made it feel like I was a prize to him.

'Don't be mistaken. Just because you don't care or try to ignore what you are, doesn't mean it goes away. You have a layer of unease and innocence, but the light in you is bright. Every man in here knows you're ripe, ready to be fucked, and wanting to be.'

'I ... I have done no such thing to—'

'You do it. Everything about the way you move to the small smile you give, to the sweet little way you absently run your fingers over your neck. You're telling me that you want to be touched. Crave it. Have passion, but have suppressed it.'

90

He was right. I did want to be touched. To be seen. But not by just anyone.

'Shy?' I offered. 'Maybe I'm shy.'

'We'll break you of that.'

The way he said that made every nerve ending flicker like lightning crashing through my veins. It was a turn on. Made me want to find out just how he could bring me out of the shell I'd been living in.

'Four margaritas,' the bartender said, setting them in front of me. 'Oh, hi, sir, did you want a drink too? Bourbon neat?'

Holy cow, did everyone know Jack?

He gave a single nod and the bartender hustled to return with his drink.

'I better get back to the group,' I said.

Jack glanced over his shoulder at the booth of co-workers I was referring to. 'Company outing, huh?'

'It's the first time I've been invited anywhere.'

'And you don't want me to join?'

'I don't want people to get the wrong idea,' I said quickly.

'What idea?'

'That we're …'

'Fucking?'

I opened my mouth and snapped it shut. 'Don't worry. No one can have that idea since it hasn't technically happened yet.' He leaned in and whispered in my ear, 'Unless you fucking my tongue counts.'

'I … I didn't …'

'There's that shy thing again.' He took a drink of his bourbon. 'Go have fun with your co-workers. Wouldn't want to embarrass you.'

I couldn't tell if he was messing with me or being supportive. Jack Powell said and did whatever he damn well pleased. My

91

reaction was his fuel. That was becoming increasingly clear with each interaction. He was methodical. He pushed my limits of propriety and made me fidgety for the fun of it. Which was better than feeling frigid.

We'll break you of that . . .

That one statement churned in my mind until it stuck in every thought, every fantasy, like butter against my skull. He didn't allow me to have enough time to refute, or even reply to half of his naughty notions. Didn't allow me to overthink it. Didn't allow me to disagree. And yet, one theme was present when dealing with Jack: What he'd *allow*.

He was in control.

What he allowed me to feel was carefully orchestrated. He picked every word to paint a vivid picture, and watched my reactions. He was learning me. Like plugging in different numbers into an equation and seeing the value he'd get.

It'd be wise to start using my own equation and figuring this man out. Especially since everything in my body was desperate to take him up on his offer.

Yet he said 'we.' Like I would have a part in finding myself. As if he understood, once again, what I needed.

I wanted to ask if I'd see him tonight. Ask if we could have dinner. Ask if we could pick up where we left off in his office and make some unofficial things official. Ask if he'd talk to me in the dirty way he'd just been doing a little more.

But all I got out was, 'Will you . . .'

Jack waited for me to finish, but a husky voice from behind me did instead.

'Yes. To anything you want, the answer is yes.'

I turned to find Callum.

Leaving the drinks on the counter, I stared at the firefighter, and wondered if he always had this kind of timing.

'Careful, Kitten.' He nudged my chin with his finger, effectively snapping my mouth shut. I wasn't even aware it had hung open. 'Guy might get the wrong idea.'

With a wink and a sexy smile that made my already humming body blare out of control, I gaped at him. Did I have a sign on my head that said, PLEASE SAY NAUGHTY THINGS TO ME today or something?

'Are you okay?' I asked. It was the only thing that made sense, since last I saw him was a week ago, and he was rushing off to the fire. 'With the fire, I mean, and the going into it. Is everything okay?'

His navy eyes held a charming twinkle as his brow furrowed. 'Checking up on me?'

'I went to the station several days ago and a guy told me you were gone.'

'He was,' Jack said, the loud screech of his bar stool sliding across the floor as he stood.

And there *I* stood, between two tall, hard men.

'Do you two know each other?' I glanced between Jack and Cal, both of whom were wearing expressions I couldn't determine.

'He's my best friend,' Cal said. 'More like a brother, except for the biological part.'

And my jaw was on the floor again.

It took one look of Jack's dark eyes darting between Cal and me, and he'd figured it out.

'This is the man you kissed, isn't it?'

'Kissing and telling now?' Cal asked, smiling at me. He then stood a little taller and stared at Jack, as if some kind of pride had washed over him. The two matched each other in alpha manliness and strength, but that strength was built differently.

On the brink of panic mode, I tried to explain. 'I didn't tell him we kissed, well I sort of did.' I looked at Cal. 'But when we kissed, Jack and I weren't together, not at the time at least – or now—'

'*Now*,' he said, cutting off my rambling, 'is what I care to discuss. And *now* this woman *is* mine.'

Cal raised a brow. 'Is she?'

I looked at Jack and whispered. 'We're together?'

'We certainly seemed together yesterday in my home.' His tone was even and steady – and Cal didn't miss the insinuation.

'We're going on first-come, first-serve I take it?' Cal said to Jack. 'Because I want her. I was pretty clear about that the other weekend. Especially since you were nowhere to be seen when her lush little mouth was on mine.'

A low rumble broke in Jack's throat, and he looked directly at me. 'Did you kiss him? Or did he kiss you?'

My blood pressure was rising like a fricking African sunrise. Hot and steady and ready to burn me up. 'I, ah ...' I looked between Cal and Jack. The truth hadn't failed so far, so I went with that.

'He kissed me,' I whispered. 'But I kissed him back.'

Cal smiled and rolled on his toes. 'She claws a little too,' he said to Jack.

This was not the time or place for ... whatever was happening right now. The two men didn't seem to be fighting. They didn't look to hate each other. It was like they were brothers messing with one another. I just didn't want to be the new shiny toy they were bickering over. Mostly because I had no clue where Cal stood in all this. He had said he wanted me? He had made that clear?

Not really, buddy.

'It doesn't matter how your little kiss happened,' Jack said with a slow steady tone. He adjusted his cuffs and said, 'Because it *is* first-come, first-serve. Especially since I made her come first.' I gasped, Cal growled, and Jack continued. 'I was out of town the past couple weeks, and expectations weren't yet set. They are now.'

'We were both there,' Cal said.

Jack just held his stare. I, however, finally found my voice.

'Both where?' I asked. But neither of them looked at me. I never thought telepathy existed until that moment. Because whatever was silently being said between Jack and Cal was intense.

'What about when you disappear "out of town" again?' Cal challenged Jack, ignoring my question. My mind and confusion leapt into overdrive.

'You're not one to talk about disappearing, Callum.'

Cal took a step toward Jack, which meant it was also toward me, crowding me between their two massive frames. While part of me was overwhelmed, and trying hard to figure how I'd gotten in this mess, I didn't feel scared. I felt ... protected. As if being between them was like having my own personal walls to shield me.

Just like the first night when Jack had swooped in and blocked out the world for me when I needed it most.

Wait.

Cal had said they were *both there*. Did he mean that first night at the bar? When the fight broke out and water spilled all over me, was Cal there too?

'Hey,' I shouted, only it came out a whisper. They both looked at me, then back at each other. As if reading my face was all they needed, and they didn't bother saying another word.

'Outside,' Cal said quickly, and Jack nodded. I, however, stood there like a moron, while the two men walked out. There was just enough information thrown out to confuse the hell out of me and wonder if this was a coincidence. That would be a naïve notion, and I mentally calculated the actual statistics of this kind of issue. One woman kissed two men who happen to be best friends? The numbers were fuzzy, the probability of such a 'random' occurrence was not high.

I stood on my toes and looked through the big front window. They were talking. Not fighting, not brawling, but talking. Jack has his arms crossed. He was nodding, but a look of death was on his face. Cal was saying something obviously heartfelt, but I had no clue what it was.

'Holy crap!' Edith said, coming up to me and taking two of the margaritas, which were now starting to slushify, and not in a good way. 'Are those two guys fighting over you? And is that . . .' With a pink straw in her mouth, she sucked down a big gulp of margarita and looked out at the same men I was. 'Is that Jack Powell?'

'No,' I said with a nervous laugh. 'I mean yes, that's Jack, but no, they aren't fighting over me.'

My stomach hurt because they were best friends, basically brothers, Cal had said. How had I ended up kissing them both? Luck wasn't a factor here, lack of luck was. And I was back to feeling like I wasn't privy to all the information. Something I'd rectify as soon as they walked back in.

Part of me was glad I didn't have to say more. Didn't have to 'choose' in that moment. Not that it would come to that. Jack and I needed to have a big conversation about 'me being his.' What did that even mean?

Everything was so crazy, so out of my element, I didn't know where to start or what to think. Other than that I wanted Jack, very much. The lingering memory of Cal's lips and strong arms wouldn't dissipate though.

'Let's get these to the table,' I said to Edith. She nodded and I carried two while she carried the others.

'That took a while,' Walter said. 'And was that Jack Powell?'

'Yeah,' Edith said with excitement, and smoothed down her work slacks as if preparing for an encounter with him.

Both Jack and Callum walked back through, just as I set the drinks down at the table. They both looked at me. Cal walked to the bar, while Jack put on his best executive face and approached the group.

'Good afternoon.'

'Hello, Mr Powell,' Edith said in a voice reserved for a nine-hundred number. Yeah, she definitely had a thing for the boss, and the last thing I needed was for this to look like anything gossip-worthy.

'I'm sorry to interrupt, but I need to borrow Miss Case for a moment.' When I stared at him, silently cursing and begging him to not make any kind of move that would imply a scandal between us, he finished with, 'I have a question about an accounting error.'

'Oh, of course!' Edith said happily. Whether she was happy that she thought I may be in trouble, or happy that she didn't obviously think anything was going on between Jack and I was indeterminable.

I excused myself from the group and went with Jack to where Cal sat at the bar.

'Hey,' he said, like it was the first time seeing me. Odd. 'Sorry I interrupted. I came here to meet with my best friend for a going away drink. But,' Cal glanced at Jack, 'I think we'll move the party to a different bar.'

Jack nodded in agreement.

'Wait. What on earth is going on? A going away drink? Where are you going?' I asked.

'I'm heading to a fire in Wyoming. They need more ground support. Be gone most of the summer.' Again, he glanced at Jack. But not with fear. It was like they were silently speaking to each other again. I had no idea how to handle what had just happened. But Cal was leaving. For the summer.

The only thing that felt right to say was, 'Please, be safe.'

Cal nodded and rose to face me. He swooped me up in a hug. The kind that consumed my entire body, and I was engulfed with his warmth. He smelled the same as that night. Felt the same. With my head against his chest, one hand tunneled in my hair as he embraced me tighter.

'I will be back,' he whispered in my ear, then released me, but didn't look me in the eye. He merely turned and started walking out. 'I'll meet you there,' he said to Jack over his shoulder.

I didn't know where 'there' was, but as I watched Cal walk out as easily as he'd walked in, I realized he was a big ball of adventure – closer to wind than man. I could feel him, like I could feel the breeze, swooping in briefly, only to continue on past me.

Harper had warned me about men like this. Warned me about Cal. A man like him couldn't be contained. I glanced at Jack, and realized that while he may appear steady and calm, he wasn't any more obtainable than Cal. Just like a steady tree could still be ruffled, even uprooted, by a strong breeze.

Whatever history was between these two men ran deep. And I stood on the outside, looking into what felt like a puzzle I wasn't allowed to take part in piecing together.

As Cal was heading to the door, he looked over his shoulder. His charming smile was back in place, but there was a sadness in his eyes that flickered so quickly I almost missed it.

'Chin up, Kitten. It's summer. Time to enjoy it.'

Callum turned and walked out of the bar, leaving me with Jack, and a table full of co-workers at the other end of the room. I was confused, relieved, disappointed, and happy all at the same time.

Whatever was said between them outside, some kind of understanding was reached. An understanding that certainly involved me, yet a conversation I was left out of. Cal's words lingered: *We were both there . . .*

I faced Jack. 'I think it's you and I that need to have a talk.'

'I agree,' he said, drinking down the rest of his bourbon. 'Come to my place at seven. There are a few things I'd like discuss with you.'

And if that wasn't an order or some kind of Jedi voodoo where he became the enforcer and me the enforcee, I didn't know what it was.

All I knew was that, when it came to Jack, one thing was clearer than ever: He got what he wanted. Always.

Chapter 8

I knocked on the front door of Jack's house. It had been a couple of hours since I saw him at the bar. The brisk walk to his place was enough to get my blood pumping, and let the less-shy side of me shine through.

That was what I was supposed to be practicing, after all. Plus, the more I thought about it, the more frustrated I became. Whatever that stunt was that those two pulled back at the bar was not only unusual, but lacking in any kind of explanation.

'What on earth was that?' I asked, when the door opened, and I walked into Jack's house and straight into the living room.

Jack took an easy step in my direction, following me, leaving several feet of polished hardwood floor between us. With the wet bar at his back, and the massive couch off to the side in the living room, I had a momentary lapse in judgment while thinking of what my bare skin would feel like against that leather sofa.

'What was what?' he repeated my question. 'You'll have to be more specific. You know I hate vagueness.'

Irritation was already flooding me, and tequila or not, I wasn't drunk. Just coming off a buzz, and not the alcohol-induced kind. One that involved two men, an odd meeting, and lots of questions. Jack's condescension only poked my temper. A temper that hadn't made an appearance in a long time.

Sure, I may be damaged. I may have some issues and fears, but I didn't fear him in a way that made me cower. I feared him in a way that made me bold.

And that boldness was deciding, just then, to breathe.

'Specific?' I repeated, and took a step toward him.

He went behind the wet bar, pulled out two tumblers and poured a light brown liquid into them, facing me the whole time.

'What I *specifically* mean?' I asked, the sharp edge in my voice caught him, and he straightened, holding his glass and looking me in the eyes. 'Let's start with how you and Cal *specifically* walked outside, only to walk back in after a brief discussion, and he ended up leaving.'

'What would you like to me say that I haven't already?'

I frowned and he took a drink. 'Ah, I'd like you tell me what was said outside and why Cal left.'

'Did you wish him to stay?'

'No,' I said quickly, then rolled my eyes at his trick. 'I mean, I didn't mind him staying. I was already nervous with you there.'

'So, Cal makes you nervous too?' Now it was Jack who held sharpness in his voice, and he pulled it off way better than I did, because I actually flinched.

'That's not the point.'

'It is now.'

I wanted to scream at the man, but held on to the tiny bit of composure I had. If I was going to get any answers from him, I needed to speak carefully and intently. The words spoken to me were always purposefully picked out and used as tools. He said them, then judged my reaction. It was my turn now, and the game was: Pushing Jack's Buttons. It was the only way to figure out this mess.

'No,' I said in a raspy voice. 'Cal doesn't make me nervous. He brings out an entirely different emotion.' I took another step toward him, intentionally swishing my hips in a more provocative manner. His eyes zeroed in on the motion and that dark gaze turned to a glare.

'And what emotion might that be?'

Oh! Did he just growl a little?

'I want to know what was said outside,' I challenged.

He set his glass down hard enough to make a cracking sound. 'And I want to know what Callum makes you feel.'

I held his stare for a long moment. Jack was a powerful man. Respected. If I wanted his respect back, I'd have to tell the truth.

'He makes me feel hopeful.' When he frowned hard, I finished with, 'He makes me feel like life doesn't have to be so hard. It can be fun and easy.'

'Yes. That is Callum.' Jack glanced down so quickly I almost missed it. He had told me on more than one occasion that I do that when I'm insecure. But there was no way the intense, steely millionaire could be anything but confident. 'So, Callum makes you feel hopeful, and I make you feel nervous.' He smirked, but there was no humor. 'Statistically speaking, smart money would be placed on a sure thing.'

I gasped. Not because he threw my own words I'd once said to him back at me, but at the dark tone that laced each word.

'You think hope is a sure thing verses nerves?' I shook my head. 'Hope is the most dangerous thing to believe in.'

His jaw clenched, those endless night eyes eating me up with everything unsaid between us.

'Then again, believing in this kind of heat,' I gestured at him, 'these nerves, or whatever you want to call them, is unrealistic as well. Eventually, heat dwindles, just like hope, does it not?'

When he didn't answer, but simply stared at me, I shook my head. I was done playing, because I already felt like the loser.

'You know what? Think what you want. I didn't know you two were friends. Just like I didn't know what your intentions were with me until today.' I tilted my head. 'Cal said you were both there. Did he mean that night at the bar when I met you? Was he there too?'

'Yes.'

A piece clicked into place. I may not have known they were friends, but this was obviously no shock to them. Something was boiling beneath the surface of this whole situation, and I felt like the rabbit in the pot. I may not be socially experienced in a lot of ways, but I knew when I was being left out of something.

'Why won't you explain this situation to me?' I asked.

'There's no situation.'

'So I'm to accept the fact that you and Cal are friends, and I just happened to kiss both of you?'

'That *is* what happened. What more explanation do you want from me? I wasn't even there when you were with Cal. I didn't push you toward him. He didn't seek you out. Things played out how they did.'

A flare of doubt pierced my mind. Cal didn't seek me out exactly. I had gone to the party.

'This just seems very convenient,' I whispered.

He scoffed. 'I'd say it's very inconvenient, actually.'

He was beyond good at talking in circles. So I'd use what he said to try to gain some ground in this conversation. The main issue right now was Jack and I and where we stood.

'You want me,' I stated. 'Remember, you said that, no, pro-claimed that in front of Cal and the damn bar, to which I got to spend the following two hours warding off questions from the office gossip about you and I and the "tall guy in the T-shirt who walked out." Funny thing, I couldn't explain it, even if I wanted to, because you say nothing!'

103

'I say plenty. Perhaps you aren't hearing it.' He grabbed the second tumbler of liquor.

I opened my mouth ready to scream, yell, curse him, then kiss him, and maybe claw at him a little, when it hit me.

He said he wanted me. Proclaimed it . . .

My chin trembled as my focus went back to his face. His painfully beautiful face that held so much hidden behind those black eyes. I was digging into an issue he clearly didn't want to discuss. Cal and Jack were obviously close. The best I could determine was that I was a wrench thrown in by accident.

'I want *you*,' I said softly, and took another step. 'My chest actually hurt the day after I met *you*.'

That got him to walk around the bar and take two long strides toward me.

'You want trust? So do I. What happened today? I want to know, so I can understand. Not so I can go running after Cal. Something was said, he left—'

'That's what he does,' Jack said. 'He has a job. It requires him to go at a moment's notice.'

Somehow, I almost thought Jack had meant something else about Cal leaving. Harper had said a similar statement about Cal being a flight risk.

'I kissed him.' My eyes met his. He knew this, but this word play was getting to me. The brink I was teetering on was a narrow one. Deep in my gut, I had a feeling I could lose Jack, or keep him, for however long he'd have me . . . it just depended on these next few moments.

'I realize that.' He handed me the glass of liquor. I cupped the smooth tumbler in my hand. 'What I'm more interested in is if this hope he makes you feel is something that I can't work around. I don't share. Not a single part of you, including your desires. When you're on my time, that's what you are: mine.'

His admission cut straight to the bones of me. He was honest, in such an intense way it was like a warning. He took the notion of want to a new level, and I wanted to be his. So much so that, yes, once again, it made my chest hurt. Truth was, I didn't want to share Jack either.

'I understand,' I said, with as much confidence as I could muster.

His dark eyes stayed on mine, silently asking me to continue. Instead, I took a moment and downed my liquor. This was going to take the kind of courage I didn't quite have yet.

'Nothing like this has ever happened me. Cal may have been at the bar too, but I didn't see him. I met you, then him. I was confused.'

'Like you said before, there were no commitments. I'm offering one now.'

I nodded. 'Why do I feel the need to explain myself? Like I've done something wrong or wasn't loyal.'

A flash of softness hit his expression. 'You are a painfully loyal person, Lana.'

'How could you know that?'

'Because of how you move. How you interact with people. You keep your promises, and I saw the look in your eyes when Cal walked in. It was an unexpected and difficult situation to be instantly put in. But you gravitated toward me, yet kept him in your view. As if you didn't want to upset either of us.'

I shook my head. 'I don't. I keep telling you, I'm not *that* girl. I barely know how to handle a single man.' And that was being generous. Jack was the majority of my intimate experiences.

'Let me absolve you of any guilt or questions you have.' He took the empty glass out of my hand. 'What happened before my office is not your fault. You did nothing wrong. But from here on out, we move forward.'

I nodded. 'How?'

'Simple.' Though the gleam in his eyes was anything but. 'You agree to be with me and give me what I want, which is you. To fuck, to hold, to pleasure. I won't be gentle or soft or relaxed. I will expect you to obey and respond to me. I want your trust and I want your body and you will enjoy it. If you desire anything, you come to me. Just like I will come to you. You will likely be nervous.'

He paused, and his grin shifted, because we both knew what 'nervous' meant when it came to him. It meant hot.

'Understand one thing: I will push your limits, but I will never hurt you.'

He raised his chin, waiting for my response, which was nowhere to be found. I was too busy processing everything he'd just said. Everything he'd said at the bar. Everything he'd done in his office.

Yes, he made me feel nervous, strong, scared, and so pathetically needy I couldn't walk away. Didn't want to. He wasn't a soft man. I didn't need his admission to know that. But he was observant. In tune with me on a level that was like nothing I'd ever felt. He seemed to know what I needed to be comfortable. From giving me his jacket the first night I met him, to handling my body in a way that didn't make me think of pain or past tainted memories.

He was in control, and would remain so. That was clear. It was also clear that there were reasons for that. Reasons I wanted to know, but that would take time. Figuring out earlier that he was learning me with every interaction would help with my goal: knowing him.

I wanted to know Jack. I was getting glimpses, but I really wanted to know him so intimately it was a need that rivaled the one I had for his body. But it would take time.

I frowned when that word repeated in my head: *time*.

'For how long?' I asked. 'You make a lot of demands, but give no end date. How long do you want me as your captive?'

'Captive . . .' he put his hands in his pockets and looked at the ceiling, a slight smile playing over his face. Damn that thing. I'd only seen one full-blown smile, and it was on the night we met. It was a vision. 'I like that. *Lana Case: My Captive.*' He looked back at me. 'Why don't we take this one day at a time?'

'So, you want all this commitment from me, and at any moment, you can discard me and—'

'I won't discard you. We're adults. We'll have a conversation if our relationship shifts.'

'Why does this feel like an arrangement more than a relationship?'

'It's both. I want to be clear with my brand of needs. Entering into any kind of relationship or arrangement without being up front would only give room for false expectations.'

'And you realized I'm not experienced with your brand of . . .'

'Fucking?'

'Yes.' God, did he have to sound so blasé and sexy all at the same time?

'Hence, my desire for you. You'll learn. And I'll teach you.'

'You said you don't share?'

He shook his head, a venomous look in his eyes. This was one thing I needed to bring up, needed to stick to my gut on, because the truth was, 'I don't either.'

'Good.'

'So, you won't be with anyone else?'

'While we're together, it will be just us.' He moved closer so that the cup he held pressed against my stomach.

'Okay.'

The look on his face was victorious and predatory. I hadn't just acknowledged his pledge, but this whole situation.

He was closing in, and I was already in over my head.

Chapter 9

'Get undressed and lay on the bed,' Jack said, walking past me into his massive master suite.

I stood in the doorway, taking in every single color and fixture. The bed was large, so large that it put a California king to shame, and it was centered in the middle of the room, with floor to ceiling windows on each side. We were on the second floor, and the city lights twinkled through like a backdrop of stars against the night sky.

I took another step in and peeked around the corner to where he had gone. A bathroom, I thought. Next to it was another door, perhaps a closet? I didn't waste much time thinking about it, because my eyes were back on the bed. Bright white sheets and pillows laid on the black four-poster bed that was against gray walls. It looked like a floating cloud amongst stormy skies.

The nightstands were black and on either side of the bed. Atop one was a box of condoms, as if awaiting my arrival. I swallowed hard and glanced around, looking at a large white chair nestled in the far corner, with a lamp on the opposite wall. It was simple, but clean and overwhelming.

Jack said my name in a deep tone that made my gaze snap from the bed to him. He stood near the foot of the bed, in nothing but black boxer briefs. 'I told you to do something.'

My neck tightened, attempting to swallow. Reminding myself

of my manners, I tried not to stare, but it was useless. The man was perfection. Tan skin that encased lean, cut muscles that made me want to lick his entire torso. The smallest trail of dark hair started just below his navel and disappeared behind the boxers.

His chest was strong, and broad shoulders led into chiseled biceps. Every ounce of him was hard and defined, and I suddenly felt lacking.

Sure, he'd seen me, well, parts of me, the other day in his office, but the confidence it took to stand nearly naked was something I didn't have, nor was it an experience I'd ever partaken in.

He took a step toward me, and I watched his powerful legs flex. His bare feet against the hardwood floors made the tiniest squeaking sound.

'You've had sex before, correct?' he asked.

My gaze met his. 'Yes.' Sort of. I didn't want to go into Brock and that experience, nor the failed attempts with my college boyfriend. *Yes*, was the technical and easiest answer for me to give. 'Why do you ask?'

'You've mentioned your lack of experience, but you're staring at me as if you've never looked at a man.'

That's because I really hadn't. Brock had snuck in and out of the shadows, my eyes squeezed shut the whole time. I'd blocked everything I could from that incident. And Andy was lights out and fumbling around, but no real sight or touching occurred.

But Jack?

I wanted to look, no, stare at him all night. Everything from his impressive body to the ridged bulge in his boxers was tantalizing.

'Sorry, I'll stop staring,' I said softly, and hung my head.

'Don't,' he snapped, making my neck do the same thing. His eyes zeroed in on mine. 'Don't hang your head, don't look away, and don't assume that what I just said was meant to make you cease what you were doing.'

He took another step. His voice softened an octave. 'I like your eyes on me.'

That one statement was stripped of the dark tone that usually marred his words and warmed my soul. He gave off a glimpse of his softer side. A side he said he didn't have. But I'd seen it. Felt it.

He'd considered my wellbeing, feelings, and comfort from moment one. It was why I held on. Why I let him push my limits, like now. Trying new things, especially with sex, should be terrifying. But Jack was with me. Would guide me. His rough words brought strength to my self-esteem, and whenever old habits of doubt and insecurity crept in, he was there to bat them away.

Yes, there was a raw softness to him. A protective instinct he had that I picked up on. I just had to concentrate to see it.

'You can look. But I still told you to do something. I expect you to do it. Unless,' he held his arm out and motioned to the door, 'you'd like to leave and we end this now.'

I shook my head quickly.

He crossed his arms over his chest, biceps bulging, and stomach flexing like he was some Greek god.

'Then,' he said slowly, his gaze raking over me, 'undress.'

Taking a deep breath, I stepped out of my heels, my bare feet hitting the cool hardwood.

His eyes watched me intently. 'You're a tiny thing.'

He took another step, and I realized that Jack was just about a whole foot taller than me. Something he realized as well. But tiny? No. I had wider hips, fuller breasts and bottom, and they weren't perfectly toned like the model at the bar slinging drinks or like his assistant.

And I was about to show all my flaws and shortcomings to a man who was likely used to such model types.

'Go on,' he said, coaxed.

There was a hint of gentleness that boosted my esteem just enough to reach behind me, unzip the back of my dress, and slide the straps down my arms.

'Keep your eyes on me,' he said, when I caught the fabric around my breasts.

I did. The dress fell to the floor and pooled at my feet.

His chest rose on a heavy breath, and his gaze ate me up. He looked from my feet to my chin, lingering on the triangle of white lace between my thighs and my matching bra. Thank goodness I'd went with the demi-cup. It shelved my breasts in a flattering way. Hopefully, I could keep it on.

While most may think a D cup was 'awesome,' it wasn't. My shoulders and waist were narrow, so keeping up with the weight of my chest was difficult, and standing without a bra, I worried the appeal would be lost.

I considered grabbing my dress and yanking it back up, but when I noticed Jack's eyes not only staying on me, but the bulge in his shorts growing, I pushed back the insecurity and tried to keep the hard proof in view that he liked what he was seeing. At least I thought so, since the hard proof was getting harder.

He unfolded his arms. 'The rest. Off. Now.'

Glancing down the front of me, I unclasped my bra. It was now or never. I shucked it quickly, then tore down my panties, stepped away from the heap of my clothes, and closed my eyes.

There. Done.

I was naked. Standing in plain view.

He cupped my neck and my eyes fluttered open to find him staring down at me. He was so much bigger than me in every way, and I felt engulfed by his presence.

'You know what I love the most about your body?'

I bit my lip and shook my head. Words were not coming out,

111

due to my nerves taking all my brain power to keep under control.

'This ...' He ran his big hands from my neck, down to my breasts, cupping them slightly only to encase my ribs. I thought he was going to lift me up, but his palms kept sliding down my sides. From my ribs, to my stomach, to my hips and finally, my outer thighs. 'I've never seen a more beautiful curve of a woman in my life.'

His voice was hoarse and it instilled a kind of confidence that was drugging.

He saw me. And made me feel not only beautiful, but unique.

'Thank you,' I whispered. 'I've never seen a man like you.'

'And?'

I frowned. 'And?'

The smallest grin threatened his lips. He grabbed my hand and placed it on his chest. His heart was like a steady drum, but picked up pace as he slowly slid my palm down his stomach until the tip of his cock brushed my fingers.

Feeling daring, I went a little lower, gently cupping the impressive length. Encased in his briefs, he was throbbing and straining and ... big.

'Just looking at you, this happens.' He looked at where I was currently touching. 'This is what you do to me. *And* I want to know what I do to you.' He glanced down the front of me. 'Hot or cold?'

'Hot,' I whispered.

'Show me.'

I took his hand and brought it to my center. I shivered when his first finger slid along my folds, which were already damp. This was another moment where he may wield control, but he let me choose. Let me go at my own pace. He could have reached out and touched me, instead, he asked me to show him. On my terms.

112

'Very hot,' I whispered. The anticipation was killing me. But he kept me in the moment. Demanding, but slow.

'Good. Now go lay on the bed, on your back.'

I nodded, and leaving his heat was like stepping into an icebox. But the bed was only a few feet away. I climbed up and laid as instructed. The downy sheets were cold and crisp against my skin. I looked up and—

'Mirrors,' I gasped. The entire ceiling was made of reflective glass.

'Yes,' he said, standing at the end of the bed and looking at me. 'Now, you have two options.'

He peeled off his boxer-briefs and, good Lord, I had been right in thinking he was big.

Attempting to keep my alarm at bay, I folded my lips together, and tried not to shake from anticipation, nervousness, both?

'You can either keep your eyes on me, or look up and watch. But never close them. Do you understand?'

'Yes,' I said.

He climbed on the bed, the way a lion may when stalking his prey. On his hands and knees, he kept his dark eyes on mine, and said, 'Open your legs, but keep them straight.'

When I hesitated, he bit my ankle, spurring me to obey. I did. A satisfied groan came from low in his throat as he continued to stalk up my body, trailing his lips up my calves.

'Oh . . .' I whispered. My body catching fire just from the slow, tortuous movement. And there was no escape.

Putting his arms under my thighs, he grabbed the sheets in his fists and yanked himself up my body, instantly hooking my knees over his shoulders and his mouth at my center.

'I've been craving you all day,' he said against my heated flesh. He didn't delve into me like last time.

No, this was different.

113

His lips skimmed and teased my clit, like he would if he were kissing my mouth. Tasting, playing.

My back arched, and when my gaze hit the ceiling, I saw us. It was the most erotic sight I'd ever witnessed.

Jack's dark head was between my thighs, my legs spread with invitation and draping around him like ivory curtains. I watched his strong shoulders bunch and flex as he moved, while also trying to focus on him eating at me like caramel from an apple. When he gently bit my clit, a hot flash of pleasure spread through my veins.

In the mirrors, I saw my breasts bounce subtly from the rocking motion of him thrusting his tongue in and out of my core. My nipples hardened to painful points, but they just kept swaying as he devoured me.

'You like what you see, don't you, baby?' he asked, laving at my clit again.

'Yes. Yes, so much.'

'I can tell, you're drenching my tongue. I knew you'd be like this.' He flicked his tongue rapidly against the little bundle of nerves, taking me to the edge of climax, only to stop before I spiraled out of control.

He continued his assent up my body. Licking my hip bone, then biting as he made his way to my chest.

I looked down at him, then at the ceiling, then down again. I wanted to see all of it. All of him. From every angle. His torso was now between my legs, his head at my breasts, and his rock hard ass in the mirror verses his perfect face were hard to choose between.

My issue of trying to decide where to look must have been obvious, because he said, 'Don't worry. I'll give you time to view both.'

He closed his lips around my nipple in a deep suck that was so hard it bordered on pain. But I liked it. It felt so good. As if I needed to walk the naughty edge of too much and not enough.

'You're sensitive here,' he said, biting the rosy peak, while swirling his finger around my breast.

'I suppose I am.'

'Mmmm,' he groaned, when he took the other in his mouth and suckled just as hard.

Each draw took more of my flesh into his mouth, causing more tingles to spread over my body. My hands flew to his head, my fingers threading in his hair.

'Yes.' I never knew how good this could feel.

Was this normal for women? To be so turned on by merely their breasts being licked? To be on the edge of internal combustion just from feeling skin against skin? Maybe it was Jack and his skill. Maybe I was sensitive. Whatever the reason, the fact remained that my body was not only turning on, but accelerating in a way I didn't know how to handle.

So much heat shot from my nipples to my core and back. I stared at the ceiling – at us. At Jack's beautiful skin covering mine. He told me once to do what felt natural. So I did. I rocked into him.

Praying his mouth stayed where it was, I ground my wet, aching clit against his torso. Over and over, rubbing myself along his hard stomach, while his mouth latched on to my breasts and sucked deeper.

Sparks ignited and increased this want – no – this *need* to feel him more. To give in to the fire that was taking over every cell of my being.

'You feel good,' he said. 'Getting a little eager. You want more, baby?'

'Yes.'

He reached one hand between us, and I thought he was going

115

to make me stop moving, but he didn't. Instead, he speared me with two fingers, and I gasped, my hands gripping his hair tighter.

'Jesus, you're tight.'

I stopped moving, stilling my hips as uncertainty engulfed me. Was that bad? Good? I didn't know what to do or how to respond.

His head snapped up and met my eyes. 'Did I tell you to stop?'

'N-no.'

'Then, why did you?' He twisted the fingers inside of me, then flicked a sensitive spot I didn't know existed, making me instantly arch and moan. 'I thought you wanted more.' He flicked again, and I begged for just that.

'I do. I'm sorry. I won't stop again.'

'Good.' Keeping his fingers deep, he returned to suck my nipples. He didn't move his hand though. He was waiting for *me* to move against *him*.

This was another moment of amazement. He kept a solid rein with control and guided the situation. He told me the position to lay in, but he was patient in letting me explore, not only him and his touch, but myself. He understood me and my needs. On a deeper level than I could explain. Amongst other wild emotions flaring through me, I was also grateful to have such an intuitive partner.

On a shaky breath, I watched our reflection and started moving. Slowly at first, grinding against his fingers and moving my hips up and down, then I tired swirling a little. Each movement hit a different spot inside.

Despite his blunt words and consuming touch, he was allowing me to figure out what I liked. How I moved. What I wanted. All while being the one to control my pleasure.

The feeling, the touch, the heat ... it was consuming.

'More,' I whispered, my chest feeling heavy for a different

116

reason altogether. I wanted to wrap myself around this man in every way. Feel all he was. Finally let go of everything, the past, my thoughts, and just focus on him.

'I decide when you get more,' he rasped, and took his fingers from me. Bringing them back to my breast, he spread the moisture from my arousal around my nipple, then sucked again. 'I'm not done tasting this sweet skin or this sweet cream.'

'Please,' I said, louder than I meant.

Something was happening to me. The fire was taking over. Demanding more. My body couldn't handle it. After feeling his hand against me – inside me – only to have it taken away, was torture. It sparked a want for much, much more.

Whatever woman I'd been up until that moment, the woman that laid dormant in fear, was rousing with wild passion. Needing it. Ready to fight to get it. It was a switch I didn't fully understand, but it had been flipped. Just like the first night I met Jack.

But he ignored me and continued to lick at my breasts. He had to be torturing me on purpose. The more I begged, the more he'd stay to his path.

But I needed him.

All of him.

I wanted the unleashed slave to pleasure, Jack the man, not Jack the machine. He'd turned my body into a livewire hopping and jumping with sparks like it was snapping with electricity on wet asphalt.

More.

It was all my brain suddenly understood.

Think. I had to think.

I reached over and felt around on the nightstand for the box of condoms, and quickly grabbed one. Ripping it open, I reached down between us in record time and tried to put it on him. But my lack of experience and his quick hands stopped me.

'I said,' he bit my nipple and I hissed, 'I wasn't done yet.' I had gotten the tip of the condom on, but Jacked rolled it all the way down. Not that he was anywhere close to giving me what I wanted. At least now I could try to coax him. I was on the brink of finally smothering all of the past memories – the nightmares – and replacing them with this moment. I needed that replacement. So much that I would do anything to have it.

'More,' I said more harshly, and raked my nails down his back. He groaned and unleashed my breast. I took the opportunity to wiggle down until I felt the tip of his erection at my opening.

He gripped my wrists and brought them over my head, his face laced with anger as he glared down at me, his nose almost touching mine. It was a battle of wills now.

'You're brave, I'll give you that, but you just made a big mistake, baby.' His teeth were clenched, his big body over mine and arms spread to hold my wrists locked above my head. All I could see were his dark eyes and bulging biceps in my peripheral vision.

'You know why I like control?' he said with venom in his voice. 'Because, without it, little girls like you would get scared off.'

'I'm not scared of you,' I breathed. 'I just want you. I want this moment.'

My answer seemed to both upset and fuel him. Because he moved to keep both wrists locked in one hand overhead, while he grabbed my chin in the other.

'You may regret that.'

He thrust hard inside of me and I yelled out.

It burned a little, the fit was tight, but the sudden feeling of fullness, of his heat warming me from the inside out, took over any discomfort.

With one hand still locked around my wrists, the other reached beneath me and hugged the small of my back, pulling himself deeper into me, while keeping me still.

'Oh, God!' The spot he'd touched inside was now being hammered over and over as he pumped in and out with such raw power that flames licked over my skin with an instant orgasm rising.

'Don't you fucking dare come yet,' he growled. 'You wanted this?' He thrust harder, my breasts bouncing between us. 'You wanted to challenge me?' He bent his head to snare my nipple with a quick suck, then bite, which only made me beg for more. 'Then you'll earn it.'

I watched the ceiling, watched him move over me, in me. He was all strength and fierceness. And I was caught beneath ... surrounding him. I locked my legs behind his back, the contrast of my light skin against his tan was beautiful. His body moved like a dream, as if built to move just like this ... built to take over another. Take over me.

I was his captive. And I liked it.

His hips and back continued to move, pounding in and out of me with purpose. With intent. I stared at the mirrors. Red welts marred his shoulders, and I realized they were track marks from my nails. The sight dialed my already raging need another degree hotter.

The roughness, the way he clung to me, made me feel, not like a victim, but like a woman who could bring a man, this man, to his desires, was empowering. He was strong, so I had to meet him halfway. And it was a good feeling.

He looked at my face, then looked up over his shoulder to view what I was viewing.

'You like me dominating you, don't you?'

'I don't know. I think so.'

With a growl, he bit my inner arm, my neck, then my breasts.

119

I moaned each time. He grinned and impaled himself to the hilt, stirring his hips to put constant friction on that spot inside, while his pelvis pressed against my clit.

'A part of you likes it rough. Likes the challenge.' He kissed my lips quickly.

'Yes,' I breathed. 'I can't wait. I'm going to ...'

'To what?' He pulled all the way out, only to thrust hard back inside. 'You're going *to what*? Say it.'

'I'm going to ... come,' I whispered the last word.

'And who is going to make this tight pussy come?'

'You, you are, Jack. Please.'

He surged deep, and did that stirring thing again, only slower this time. 'Beg me. Tell me you're sorry for trying to take control, and beg me to let you come.'

Slow.

So ... Slow ...

He kept me so close to the edge of falling into a wild orgasm it was almost painful.

'I'm sorry for trying to take control. Please.' The last word was a sob, I was so desperate. 'Please, please, allow me to come.'

There was that word again: allow.

It trigged something in both of us, because his body tensed and so did mine. He moved faster. Grinding down on my core and hitting every nerve perfectly, so that I spiraled over the edge as the most intense, earthshattering release overtook me.

'Fuck, Lana, I feel you. Keep going. You wanted more, didn't you?' His breaths were coming faster, harder. 'So do I. Keep coming. I want to feel you grip me.'

He pounded harder, but stayed deep, never retreated too far from my body. I cried out to the ceiling, and it was everything I could do to keep my eyes open, because I wanted to slide them shut and scream with ecstasy.

Instead, I looked at him. Lost myself in those deep dark eyes and pushed my body though another orgasm.

I whimpered. The intensity was too much for my sensitive flesh to bear, and it just kept going.

'Good,' he rasped and kissed me.

His cock shot harder and his whole body shivered, then tensed. I knew he had a condom on, but I felt the jolt of his release rock my entire body, just as it did his, carrying out wave after wave of pleasure.

He collapsed on top of me, the grip on my wrists loosening. His head lay on my breasts, as both our chests rose and fell on heavy breaths. I looked at the ceiling once more – at the picture that was Jack and I. Two tangled bodies lying on a cloud of sheets. I did the only thing that felt natural: I stroked his hair and wondered if I'd ever be the same again.

Chapter 10

As I made my way to my cubicle, I kept my head down, mostly because I was certain there was a blaring sign flashing across it that said: I had sex last night.

And technically, I had sex with the boss. Hot, wild crazy sex that I didn't even know I could handle, much less enjoy.

But I did.

I was a little sore, and understood why, but whenever I replayed last night, not a single part of it was negative. Maybe I could beat back the past with new experiences. Some kind of desperation came out in me last night. Maybe because I believed Jack when he said he wouldn't hurt me.

A part of me was uncertain, new to this experience, and was eager to talk about it with my best friend. But, once again, Harper's schedule conflicted with mine, and when I snuck in late last night, she was already in bed. I needed to talk to her badly. Because, while I didn't want anyone to know I was dating Jack, I didn't know how to process everything that had happened over the past couple of days, much less the past couple of weeks.

When I got to my desk, I saw a gigantic vase of gray flowers. Not gray as in dead, but the color gray. I'd never seen such flowers before. They reminded me of Jack's bedroom. Everything ranging from lilies to daisies to dahlias, were all gray. But in the middle of all those, was one perfect white rose.

'Gray flowers?' Edith said, walking up behind me, and chewing on a protein bar. 'Did someone die?'

'No,' I defended. 'It's unique and classic.' And the color of Jack's room. Not wanting to go into more detail about how incredible this actually was, I kept that last fact to myself. There was a small box next to the vase, and a card with my name on it.

'Ooooh! Who's it from?' Edith asked, all but clawing to get to the card.

'Can I have a moment please?'

She frowned and turned to go back to her desk, mumbling, 'Fine, be that way.'

I opened the card, and it was a single note that read:

Light within the storm.
~Jack

My breath caught. Four simple words that summed up last night and how he saw it. Light? He'd referred to me being naïve and innocent, but light? It made my heart beat heavier and happiness flooded me.

I tucked the card in my purse, then opened the box. There was a small tube of Ibuprofen, and thigh-high white stockings with lace trim. A small note said that the medicine was for the discomfort, and the stockings were for our next meeting. A surge of glee raced as I took the pills, but kept the stockings in the box, and stuffed it in my purse as well.

He cared about my comfort?

Not only that, but there would be a next time. I just didn't know when.

I'd never had a secret boyfriend-lover before. But what happened between us last night was intense. It wasn't lost on me that

Jack had sidestepped an entire conversation about Cal and what was said, but that was something I couldn't push. Not now. Not after agreeing to move forward.

Whatever was said between the two men was done now. And he knew where I stood with my job and keeping our affair low-key, since the staff finding out and being the center of gossip was not my idea of fun.

My cell rang, and I dug it out of my purse, smiling again when my fingers brushed the small glossy box that encased the stockings.

'Hey, Harper,' I answered.

'I feel like we keep missing each other.'

'I feel the same.'

'Well, I'm coming into Denver this afternoon, wanna grab lunch?'

'That would be great.' Since I had to talk to her and get some perspective.

'Okay, see you around noon.'

'Bye.'

With that, I put my phone back in my purse, pulled up my chair, and went to work. A hard task, since I kept stealing glances at the flowers on my desk and thinking of the storm that was Jack Powell.

A storm I couldn't help but think I'd awakened. Or maybe it was the storm he awakened in me.

'So, you're dating a shark?' Harper said with a smile, and took a bite of her pasta.

The little Italian place we met at was our favorite, and right down the street from my building.

I frowned, dipping my bread in olive oil. 'What?'

'Your neck, girlfriend. Got a little bite mark right below your ear.'

My hand flew to my neck, then I pulled all my hair over my shoulders, adjusting so it'd cover my neck.

'Relax, it's not that big of a deal.'

'What if someone at work saw it?'

'Who cares?' Harper said, with all the confidence in the world.

'I do. First the flowers, then this,' I motioned to my neck, 'someone will—'

'Hold up,' Harper said. 'He got you flowers?'

I nodded. 'They were on my desk this morning.'

'Nice. So, are you going to tell me who this guy is?'

'It's Jack.'

Harper frowned. 'The selfie guy from a couple weekends ago?'

'Yeah. He'd been out of the country. He's back, and . . . ' I took a bite of my bread, because I didn't know how to follow that up. Harper, however, had no problem pushing the topic.

'*And* you two had sex?'

'Yeah.' A huge smile lit my face, and I couldn't help it or care.

'Good for you!' Harper said, but her smile faded, and she leaned in and spoke softly. 'Did you handle it okay? Were you scared or . . . have bad memories or anything?'

She sighed, as if irritated with her own words, but I knew what she was trying to say. She was a great friend. She understood my struggle with sex and all the details, or lack thereof, when it came to my failed attempts in the past.

'Are you okay?'

'I really am,' I said, and reached for her hand. 'Thank you for being so wonderful. But last night was different. Jack is different.'

Harper raised a brow. 'Judging by the teeth marks, it wasn't standard missionary.'

A small laughed escaped. 'Actually, it was missionary, but there was nothing standard about it.'

'And, you were okay?' she asked again.

'Yeah,' I assured. 'Jack was intense and demanding, but he was also soft when I needed him to be ... and patient. It was like he could tap into my brain and turn the bad thoughts off. I just focused on him. Nothing else but him.'

'Wow, that's quite a feat.'

It really was. Jack had taken his time, let me feel out everything. Feel him. That was, until I shifted. When he took my pleasure to a point of no return and I clawed – literally – for more. More of him. More of the moment that wasn't terrifying, but fulfilling. I'd finally let go, given myself to someone of my own free will, and he'd taken me. With passion and so much ferocity it left me feeling strong and weak all at the same time.

'Sounds like your new boyfriend is off to a good start.'

Boyfriend? I liked the term. And while Jack said I was 'his,' we'd never discussed *terms* beyond that.

'I wouldn't say he's my boyfriend. Our relationship is tricky, and I'd rather not tell anyone else but you about it.'

'Why?'

'Because he owns the resorts I work for.'

'Oh,' Harper said around a mouthful, but she didn't looked as shocked as I'd thought she would. She shrugged. 'People date their bosses all the time.'

'He's technically not my boss. Well, not who I report to. Anyway, he's high up the food chain.'

'Yeah, pretty sure it doesn't get higher than the owner.'

'Which is why I'm going for discrete. Things like this get found out and it never ends well. I just want to do my job without gossip or misery, so I can save and go to grad school in a couple months.'

'I get it. Keeping your man on a secretive basis can be hot.' Harper winked.

There were lots of things about Jack that weren't for public

126

knowledge. Like his 'brand of fucking,' as he once put it. But last night didn't feel like that term matched it. It was more intense than I'd expected, but in a very good way. Yet, when I'd skyrocketed from turned on to nuclear meltdown, I had all but thrown a fit trying to get to him. Which meant I had acted without consideration of his needs. Including the need to control the situation. And I had a feeling I'd just chipped the iceberg last night.

Yes, it was clear he liked control. What that entailed, I was still learning. But when I fought him, begged for more, and interrupted his pace, he seemed both upset and turned on by it.

Logic would dictate not to push him like that again. Not because I was afraid he'd hurt me, but because pushing a man like Jack could lead to withdrawal. He could easily have countless other women filling his bed, doing his exact bidding at any moment. He didn't *need* me.

Yet, he chose me.

The flare in my gut made me wonder how far I'd overstepped last night, because while he might not need me, I was starting to need him. His power, warmth and strength brought out the fighter and the lover in me. This time, I was fighting for him, for myself, and for the passion I hadn't realized existed in me.

'Just promise me that this guy is a good thing. That you'll be careful.'

'He wouldn't hurt me,' I defended.

'I'm not saying that. I'm just saying to take it slow.' It was the same thing she'd said last weekend.

'I know it looks like things are progressing quickly. But for the first time, I feel healthier. Like I'm finally having experiences a normal woman would have. I'm finally moving on from the past.'

127

The weight I'd been carrying around was getting lighter. Jack was showing me that sex didn't have to be dirty or scary. It could connect you to something beyond yourself.

Harper nodded. 'And I think that's great, but there's another big thing you need to keep ahold of.'

'What?'

'Your heart.' She looked at me for a long moment, a kind of sadness in her eyes. 'Everything can go great, he can be great, but remember that in the end, people can always betray you. They can leave. They can lie. They can set you up. They can do nothing wrong at all, and for whatever reason, things just don't work out. Don't go into your first relationship blind to this.'

Okay, *that* sounded scary. One sexual experience, and I was naïve to the all the other stuff that came with a relationship. Like it ending at some point. But I couldn't tell her about that. Or that my relationship was more of an arrangement that was being taken 'one day at a time.' But there was mutual want and desire, right? That counted for something. Surely, I wasn't the only one feeling a connection. At least, I hoped not.

'Is everything okay with you?' I asked.

'Yeah.' She waved her hand like nothing was ever a big deal. 'Just working a lot.'

I went to ask her about the rumored firefighters that had a crush on her, but she motioned for the waiter and the check. 'Sorry I had to make this a quick lunch, but I have a meeting soon.'

'Okay, sure, no problem.'

She put money down on the table, got up, and hugged me. 'You finish your lunch and I'll see you at home tonight.'

'Okay.'

She hustled her designer heels out the door and into the Colorado summer afternoon.

128

I took another breath, as every memory from last night replayed in my mind once more. It would be smart to keep some kind of emotional distance. Especially since I had no idea of the final outcome, or much less the equation that made up Jack Powell.

Chapter 11

As I walked back to the office, I thought a lot about what Harper said. I thought even more about what Jack had done.

Everything about last night seemed to stretch this emptiness in my chest and warm it. Being careful, especially with emotions, was smart. But he was different, had been from the moment I met him. He'd been hard and rough, but slow and deep. Then he sent me flowers. A sweet gesture. One a man does for a woman he's interested in. A gesture that garnered a response.

I dug through my purse and pulled out my cell phone and the business card Jack had given me a few days ago, hoping he'd be at this number, and not at his house number. I may not be practiced in the correct relationship decorum, partly because this wasn't a standard relationship, and also because I was the one insisting on keeping it secret from most everyone but Harper.

I stood against the side of the building before my office around the corner and dialed Jack's office.

'Reign Resorts, Mr Powell's office?' the woman, who I assumed was Jack's secretary, answered.

'Hi, is Ja — ah, is Mr Powell available please?'

'Who's calling?' Though it was a question, it sounded more like a test. Who I was would determine whether Jack took the call. I knew about this game. My father had a 'take call' list. Only certain people got through.

I wasn't one of them.

Something I'd figured out by the third time I'd called his office, and was told he was busy, and to leave a message. It wasn't until I'd started working for him and overheard a discussion with his secretary about the 'take call' list that I'd understood. He'd wave conversations and people off. And, I realized I was one of those people. He never called back. So I stopped calling.

'This is Lana Case.'

There was not another sound, other than a faint click and then mute silence. I looked at my phone, wondering if she'd hung up on me. But the call still showed connected. Pressing my cell back against my ear, I waited. Anxiety rose. This was where Jack's secretary buzzed him, told him who was on the line, and he'd decide whether or not to take the call.

Another few seconds passed until ...

'Good afternoon.' Jack's deep voice made happy chills dance across my skin. I leaned against the building in relief.

'Hi.' I'd dialed him, and that was all I could think to say. My smile was too wide to get more words out at the moment. I was on his 'take call' list. And the idea of that made my chest hurry to keep up with the happy breaths I was taking.

'How are you?' he asked.

Still smiling like a goof, realizing that a simple acknowledgment was all it took to make my day, I said, 'I'm really good.'

'You sound like it. I can hear the smile in your voice.'

'Yeah, I've had a good day, and a good evening last night.'

'Have you?' There was a small smile in his voice that time. 'Tell me, what events of your day and previous evening have you so happy?'

'Well,' I sighed. 'There's this guy, and last night he showed me a delightful time, and today sent me the most beautiful flowers I've ever seen.'

131

'Interesting.'

'Yes, he is. He's also kind of intense, but there's a soft side to him I don't think he wants anyone to know about.'

'Is that right? You sure about this soft side of this mystery man of yours?'

'Pretty sure. He cared enough to think of my comfort after . . .'

'After?' His voice was thick and raspy, the way it was right before he put his mouth on me. The sound sent a shiver down my back.

'After we were together last night,' I said, a little softer. 'He sent me beautiful stockings and medicine in case I was . . . sore.' I hadn't spoken like this out loud, but this game was fun, and it was my own way of thanking Jack for the glimpse of his sweet side.

'And you think this man's actions are a symbol of softness?'

'Yes,' I smiled wider.

'Perhaps he sent you the medicine to ensure you'd be able to recover quickly and handle what he has planned next.'

I swallowed hard.

'And the stockings are all he's expecting you to wear at this next encounter.' He tsked. 'Instead of softness, sounds like he's a rather selfish man who has plans for you. And isn't willing to wait very long to carry them out.'

I bit my lip to keep from moaning? Gasping? I didn't know. Because everything in his voice was serious. And he always seemed to respond when I stood up and acknowledged him or his threats – or promises.

'Unless you say no, that is?'

He had told me before that I always had that option. Only 'no' was one of the last things I wanted to say when it came to Jack.

132

'I have no intention of saying such a word. Actually, I was wondering what these plans could be?'

'Well, that depends. Did you anger your mystery man?'

'Of course not.'

'You sure about that?'

The way he said it made wonder if I had. 'I'm pretty sure.'

'You weren't impatient? Impulsive? Exercised what *you* wanted *over* him?'

I thought back to last night and yes, that is what I had done. But he'd sent me flowers, which was a nice gesture. He'd said I had to be handled delicately. Weaving in the nice with the naughty, so as not to scare me off. Was that what was happening?

'He likes control,' I said in a hushed tone. 'He was doing things to me ... making me feel things ... I may have—'

'If I were you, I'd wonder what exactly this man of yours is going to do to you for being such a bad girl.'

I swallowed hard. 'W-what do you think he's going to do?' This was speeding up pretty quickly, and so was my pulse. I was already aching to touch Jack and nervous from the wicked glint in his voice.

'Smart money would be on your pretty ass being punished.'

I ran my fingertips along my lips. My nipples hardened, and a pulse of anticipation, uncertainty, and sheer excited fear of what to expect coursed through my veins.

'Don't look so surprised. I can tell by the way you're touching yourself that you're thinking about it, and they're not all bad thoughts.'

I stood straight up and glanced around. There was no one other than a few people here, and they were walking. But when I saw the tall building that Jack's office was in, I looked up. He could see me. Standing on the street this whole time.

My hand dropped from my mouth. I had been running my fingers over my lips, and he'd caught me.

Taking a deep breath, I stuck to my original notion. 'Whatever he has in store for me, I'm sure I can handle it.'

Though I couldn't see him, I looked up in the direction I knew he was.

'You think so?'

'Yes. Because, despite the stockings and medicine, he still sent the flowers. No other reason than pure desire and kindness.'

He didn't say anything to that. Which meant I was on to something. Jack may be hard and kept his control, but there was a soft side. Otherwise, I never would have fallen for him or been drawn to him the way I was.

'Have you considered that this man of yours, and his tastes, may be too bold for you? Perhaps he'll scare you off?'

I frowned. There was honesty in his voice that made me wonder if he was actually worried about this. After last night, I thought of a lot of things, but I didn't think about what Jack must be thinking. Was he worried about me? If he'd hurt me or if he'd gone too far?

I didn't want him thinking that, and I didn't want to give up what we had, because we'd just tapped into something amazing. Something I was dying to get another taste of. The heady line between lust, pain, need, and a deeper emotion I couldn't identify. It went beyond a mere fondness for someone. I didn't know where in the fall I was, but I knew I was falling. And it was for Jack Powell.

'He won't scare me off,' I said with confidence.

'What makes you know that?'

I smiled at the skyscraper, hoping he could see it. 'Because, I like that he's hard and rough. It brings out a different side of me I didn't know I had. He makes me feel strong. And I trust him to read me and know my limits. But—'

'But?'

'I may have pushed his beyond what *he* was comfortable with last night. I may have taken too much control. And I'm ready for the consequences of that.'

He took a heavy breath, but said nothing. So I tried to dig a little deeper.

'I just wonder why he needs the power the way he does.'

'If you don't know, then it's because he doesn't want you to know.'

That hit straight to my chest. It was no secret that Jack behaved a certain way, especially in the bedroom, with a certain power. The need to exercise his will was part of his instinct. Whatever had caused that need was something he wasn't sharing, and judging by what he'd just said, may never share.

Time.

My brain shuddered at the word. I wanted to know him. Bring out some kind of good feeling the way he brought them out in me. I wanted his trust in return. But, right then, I couldn't expect it implicitly. I had gone against what I'd said. I'd demanded, tried to take over. Not to mention, I had no intention of telling him all the gritty details of my past. So, for now, his secrets were his to keep, and mine were mine.

'I realize I overstepped last night. I only hope I get another chance to show him I can obey.'

I trusted him, at the very least, with my body. Problem was, I was staring to trust him with more than that.

'Have a good evening,' he said.

I was about to ask when I'd see him, but the line went dead. I looked up at the endless windows, not knowing which was his, and kept looking for a moment.

I didn't know if he could see me, or if he'd turned away, but I waited, and simply looked up.

Deep water was all I treaded when it came to Jack. I didn't

135

know what to expect, but I knew I wanted more. Whatever he'd give me: sex, punishment, attention, thought ... I wanted it all.

Maybe I was jumping in blind, but I had claws. A fact I clung to. And for now, I may have to use them to hang on for whatever ride he had in store.

Because all I wanted was for it to continue.

Chapter 12

I hadn't talked to Jack since yesterday afternoon. It was now Friday. I had no plans and hadn't heard from my kind-of boyfriend.

I looked at the flowers sitting on the coffee table. Apparently, I had sighed because Harper handed me a container of Indian takeout food, and said, 'What has you all mopey?'

She adjusted the rug by the door with her foot, making it perfectly even, before sitting down.

I opened my chicken tikka masala and shrugged.

'Oh no, don't go all shy and quiet on me. What's going on?'

I set the food down and looked at Harper, getting comfy on the couch in her sweats, perfectly happy to stay in tonight. Usually, I was the one who wanted to stay in our safe little home, far away from the city and any hope of being social.

'I want to be with him,' I said. 'It's crazy. I know it is. I just saw him a couple of days ago, and I already want to see him again. Not only that, I want to see him all the time. Then, there's thinking about him . . . which I seem to always be doing.'

Harper nodded. 'Yeah, this is the best part of a relationship, and the worst.' She looked at her food and took a bite. 'The beginning where all you can think about is more.'

Yes! That was exactly it. 'Will this feeling wear off?'

Harper scoffed and mumbled, 'If you're lucky.'

'Do you want to do something tonight?' I asked.

She shook her head. 'I'm just going to go to bed early. It's been a long week.'

I nodded. 'Okay.' I looked at my best friend. 'You know, I'm here. If you want to talk.'

She looked at me. 'I know. I'm good.' She smiled, but I knew her better than that. There was so much going on behind her eyes, and I wish she'd let me in. The dynamic we'd had since we were kids was that I was the broken one and Harper was the strong one. I loved her, but had no idea if she was hurting. Or upset. She finished her dinner, then hugged me.

'I love you,' she whispered.

'I love you too.'

She went to bed, and I sat in the living room, TV on in the background, and a half eaten plate of chicken in my lap. It was approaching nine, and I sat there, not dressed up and nowhere to go.

My phone buzzed, as if sensing my need for entertainment.

A text from Jack: Be ready in ten minutes

My heart leapt and hope skyrocketed as I ran to the bathroom and brushed my teeth and hair. Realizing my hair was a mess of big barrel curls I didn't have time to tame, I hustled to change out of my yoga pants and tank top when my phone buzzed again.

Jack: Out front. Now.

That couldn't have been ten minutes. But changing wasn't an option I had time for. He was waiting, and this was my chance to prove I could play by his rules. Wanted to.

Grabbing my purse, I looked out the front window and saw headlights in the driveway. Writing a quick note to Harper on the counter, I went outside, locking the door behind me.

When I approached the car, a man got out from the driver side and opened the back door. The large black car looked expensive, and Jack wasn't driving—

He was sitting in the back seat.

His dark eyes snapped to mine. 'Good evening.'

'Hi.'

I slid in next to him and put my purse on the floor. The driver shut the door, and we were on the road.

Jack's gaze roamed over me, and I felt a little self-conscious. 'I was going to change, but you said to come outside.'

'And you dropped everything and did what I asked?'

'Yes.'

He nodded, his mouth twitching to a satisfied grin. 'Good.' He looked at me again, pausing on my hips, then breasts. 'I like this outfit on you anyway. It molds to your body perfectly.'

I glanced down the front of me. I'd never thought of it that way. Just merely as casual wear, or what I wore the few times a month I popped the Pilates DVD in and gave it a whirl.

It was quiet, the road smooth beneath the wheels, as we sped away into the night. The privacy glass between the driver and us was up, and I realized quickly that I was in a relatively small space with Jack. Alone.

The smell of the leather seats mixed with his masculine scent made my knees weak and I was glad to be sitting.

'I hope you brought the stockings.'

I glanced at my purse. The little box was still in there. 'Yes.'

He nodded and looked out the window. 'Good. In the meantime, tell me how you've been the last couple days.'

I glanced at my hands. Should I go for honesty, even if it made me sound like an idiot?

There was a tug on my chin. Jack pulling me to look at him.

'Tell me.'

Honesty it was. 'I missed you.'

139

He let go of my chin, but ran the back of his fingers down my throat. 'Did you?'

I nodded. 'I'm in this constant state of uncertainty about what we are, what I mean to you, and when I'll see you next.'

'Haven't I told you?'

I kept my gaze on him. 'Yes, you said we're together, but the rest is foggy, and I'm not good at deciphering the rules or norms when it comes to relationships. Much less a relationship like ours.'

He nodded. 'We are what we want to be. The norms don't apply to us. We do what we want, as long as we feel good about it.' His eyes hit mine. 'Do you feel good about us?'

I smiled a little. 'I do. I'm just new to all this ... feeling stuff.'

'You mean *feeling stuff* that isn't fear or anxiety.'

It wasn't a question. I wanted to ask him how he knew that, but he finished with, 'That first night. Everything about you was frightened, uncomfortable, and contained.'

'I suppose so.'

'I meant it when I told you I don't want you to feel that way, especially with me.'

'And I don't when I'm with you. Just a little nervous at times.'

He smiled. A full-on Jack Powell smile that made my heart sing. 'Good.'

I looked at him for a long moment. He was in a suit, but the first two buttons of his white shirt were undone.

'Were you working late?'

'Yes.'

'Did you come straight from the office?'

'Yes.'

Now I smiled and clamped my hands between my knees to keep from reaching out for him in a maul of goofy smiles, kisses, and touches.

'You had that same look when we spoke on the phone yesterday,' he said. 'Like you're truly happy.'

'I am.'

'Why?'

'Because of what you do.'

He frowned. 'The flowers?'

'No, you showed up, and you answered my call.' I looked him in the eyes and all the giddiness was gone. 'That means a lot to me. More than I can explain.'

He raised a brow. 'My answering the phone means a lot to you?'

It was crazy that water collected behind my eyes, but the truth was, 'Yes, it really does.'

Softness flashed across his face, but it was accompanied by a fierce need that made my skin prick.

'We are on the way to my place. Once we get there, the dynamic between us will change.'

'My ... punishment you mean?'

He nodded once. 'You already test me in a way that is unusual. You make me want to give in to you.'

'Is that so bad?'

There was no humor on his face. 'Yes.'

He pulled on the cuffs of his shirt, beneath his jacket, and holy hell, my body went into overdrive. Just like the night he folded his shirt sleeves, something about the way he exercised his dominance in the most subtly intent manner had me trembling.

'However, we are not at my home yet, and I'm curious, if this moment were in your hands, your control, what would you do?'

My mind wanted to shout, 'Everything!' and instead, I tried to tamp down my excitement about this small gift he was giving me. Or maybe it was a test? Either way, I wanted to take it.

'I guess I would—'

'No,' he snapped quickly. 'I asked what you'd *do*, not how you'd explain it to me.'

A surge of heat raced up my spine. He was giving me free rein to show him what I'd do? In this moment? There was only one thing I could think of, and that was get closer.

Without saying anything, I moved toward him, slinging my leg over his lap, straddling him, and placing my hand on his chest, which rose on a heavy breath. I felt him hard between my legs, and looked down in shock. He flicked my chin once more to make my eyes meet his.

His voice was raspy. 'I haven't reached out since our phone call, not because I'm not thinking of you or I don't want to.' He shifted his hips just a fraction beneath me, to slide against the sensitive spot between my legs, and I gasped a little. 'It's *because* I want you.' His eyes stormed darker. 'Badly. All the time. Without provocation or reason.'

He wanted me. All the time. I'd been shocked that we hadn't even touched and he was already hard ... for me. I was now beyond happy that my yoga pants were made of thin material, because it just made me feel him more.

'If you want me like you say,' the challenge rising, but my tone staying soft, 'then why not take me? Why wait? Why not call? Come by sooner?'

He thrust a little and said, 'Control. You needed to heal from our last encounter.'

'You didn't break me.'

'Maybe not, but I felt you.' He reached between us and ran his thumb along my center. 'Felt how tight you were. I know you needed time. While I pride myself in control, I couldn't last longer than a day, so I hope you're ready.'

I nodded and ran my hands from his chest to his neck. 'I am.'

I leaned forward, showing him what I'd do in this moment,

142

and brushed my lips against his. A raspy groan came from deep in his throat, and his hands splayed over my backside, securing me to him, but he let me lead.

Parting my lips, I kissed his bottom one, then the top one. Exploring, learning, getting to know him at a slow pace. I didn't get a chance to touch him like this the other night – aside from clawing. This was my chance to be the one thing Jack said he wasn't: Soft.

Though he held me close, he didn't give me an inch. He made me work for his affection. I didn't know what to do or how an 'experienced woman' would go about seducing a man, so I went with what felt natural and what I wanted. Which was more of him.

A flash of boldness lit me up. He was allowing me access to him. I would take it.

I cupped his face. The soft scratch of his five o'clock shadow tickled my palms. I'd never touched his face before, we both knew it. I leaned back a little, the tips of our noses touching, and ran my thumbs along his cheekbones, then down to his mouth.

He caught my thumb between his teeth, and I gasped, loving the sting and the surprise of his bite. More than that, I was excited about his participation. I was wearing him down.

With my thumb locked between his teeth, I pushed down, he let me, his mouth opening just enough for me to swoop in, push my tongue inside, and kiss him hard.

That time, he really groaned. He sat up straighter, pulling me closer, and I wrapped my legs around his back and drove my fingers into his hair. I kissed him deep, but slow. Giving every sensation of his mouth on mine an extra second to sink in. I wanted to brand this to memory.

Trailing my lips from his, I kissed the corner of his mouth, then his jaw, the stubble scratching my lips in the most delicious

143

way. So, I did it again, and again, moving up his jaw to his earlobe.

The grip on my ass tightened further. Did he like this? Like the attention I was giving him? I sucked his earlobe, and yeah, he liked it. His hips jutted out to hit my sweet spot again. It felt good, but not as good as the idea that I was pleasing him.

My time was running out. He was letting me touch him, kiss him like this, but once we made it to his place, this would be over, and I would be at his mercy.

I fumbled with the buttons on his shirt, opening them as I tasted his neck, and felt his pulse beat against my mouth. Finally getting his shirt open, I scooted back on his lap so that I could bend enough to nip at his collarbone and lick the hollow of his throat.

His head didn't loll back the way mine would have, but he moved slightly, spurring me enough to keep going.

Running my mouth along his hard chest, I couldn't help but nip a little. His whole body tensed, his abs flexing. Even sitting, I could see his well-honed muscles cutting through his tan skin, and it made me want to devour him even more. But I hadn't gotten there yet.

Taking a few more open-mouthed kisses of his chest, I grabbed his belt in my hands, and sucked on his nipple.

'Fuck,' he groaned, and thrust up again, as if his cock was seeking my hands.

I flicked the little bud and sucked again, then trailed my tongue along the first flank of his six pack, but that was as low as I could go without scooting further back and falling off his lap.

I groaned loudly, annoyed with gravity and thought about how to reposition us so I could explore him more with my mouth. My destination was lower.

'You sound frustrated, baby?' he said in a gravelly tone.

144

'I am,' I whispered against his chest, moving to his other pec and delivering little kisses. 'I want to keep doing down, but I can't. There's not enough space.'

For a second, I thought he groaned at my response. Like the idea of me continuing my trip south sounded as good to him as it did to me. I had no idea what I'd do once I got there, but I'd figure it out.

Cupping my ass, he yanked me back against him, forcing me to give up the sweet taste of his skin and bringing me face to face with him. I could feel him throbbing between my legs once more, or maybe it was me who was throbbing?

He kissed me. One long, hard, consuming force of his mouth that took the breath from my lungs. Suddenly, I was weightless, then bouncing on leather.

I opened my eyes to find myself in my original seat, beside Jack, and him buttoning up his shirt.

I was instantly cold, and I wanted to climb back in his lap and kiss him more. But the car stopped, and Jack's house was right outside.

My time was up.

Fastening the last button on his shirt, he ran his hand through his hair, and looked every bit the controlled, kempt man he always appeared.

'I can honestly tell you that was the best car ride I've had yet.' His dark eyes glowed as he looked at me. My door opened, the driver waiting for me to exit. 'Are you ready to go upstairs now?'

I glanced out at the beautiful house and brightly lit porch. He was waiting for me to say no. But I was a few yards away from being in Jack's domain. While I didn't know what exactly to expect, there was no way I was turning back now.

'Yes,' I said, looking him straight in the eye. 'I'm ready.'

Chapter 13

I looked at myself in the mirror of the master bathroom and took a deep breath. Jack had given me specific instructions. Which was why I was naked, except for my stockings, and he was waiting in the bedroom.

This was my chance to prove to Jack I could give him what he gave me.

Control.

The more I was with him, the more I realized that there was a give with his take. I just didn't know how much he'd take. But I trusted him. Closing my eyes for a moment, I rested my palms against my thighs. The soft lace that lined them was like a brand. A statement that said I was ready and wouldn't challenge him. Not tonight. No matter what I wanted, how heated or needy or nervous he made me, tonight I was his. Truly and completely.

He'd told me, warned me from the beginning that his needs were different. Intense. I got a taste of that the other night. But I had a feeling tonight would go even beyond that. Beyond what I could imagine.

I could always say no. Not that I wanted to, or foresaw a problem. Jack wouldn't go too far, of that I was certain.

I opened the door and walked into the bedroom.

The lighting was low, like a soft glow of candles, yet none were present. The room looked true to its old architecture, yet the bed and walls gave a sinful, yet vibrant, vibe. Like I was stepping into a naughty dream.

Jack stood near the bed, completely dressed. Shadows played over his face, and I swallowed hard at the sight of this powerful man and his dark gaze on me.

'Look at you,' he said. 'Flushed skin.' He cocked his head to the side, examining me. 'Those pretty thighs trembling. Are you scared?'

I shook my head. 'No.' I was just nervous. Which was no surprise.

'You have an innocence,' he said, walking toward me. 'White lace and silk suits you.' He plucked my nipple and I gasped as goose bumps broke over my skin, 'But you're more than that.' He circled me, his chest brushing my back as he leaned in to whisper in my ear, 'Aren't you?'

'Yes.'

He trailed his fingers down my spine, and I tried to stay still. Tried to not arch into his every touch.

'Yes, you're more than this,' he reached around and ran his palm along my silk-clad thigh. 'More than the naïve girl trussed up in white. But how much more?'

'However much more you want of me,' I said breathlessly.

'Is that right?' he rasped in my ear, his fingers scratching from my thigh, up my stomach, leaving soft pink streaks in their wake. He walked around to face me once more, his dark eyes looking at the trail he'd left, seeming pleased.

I thought he'd touch me again – hoped he would. So much that my back arched of its own accord, pushing my breasts out, silently begging. He took off his jacket in a hard swoop, then started on his shirt.

'Go to the bed and bend over. I want your stomach flat against the mattress and your arms stretched out.'

I did as he said, trying not to shudder too badly. This was a vulnerable position. But Jack had seen me in vulnerable positions before.

Deep breath …

I bent over, the cold sheets hitting my breasts and stomach, as I laid my upper half flat and reached out overhead. The feel of the soft sheets against my palms was somehow a welcome comfort. I'd been on these sheets before. This bed. A heady notion that I belonged there pricked my mind and flooded my veins. As if laying out over my own bed, only better, because Jack was there.

He kicked my feet apart, and I moaned a little. Mostly in nervousness, because I was on display. For him. How he wanted.

'I like this view,' he said, and I felt him stand between my legs. His pants were still on, but his erection was pressing against my bottom. As soon as he came, he went. I could no longer feel him, but knew he was behind me.

'You are to stay just like that until I say otherwise. Do you understand?'

'Yes,' I said, the side of my face resting against the soft sheets.

A whirl of wind sounded, followed by a smack on my ass. A sizzle from the spank instantly surged and lit my blood on fire. I cried out.

It stung, but the heat spread quickly, and I was surprised to find that it felt … good.

'I told you I was going to punish this sweet ass of yours. You belong to me now. I make the rules, set the pace, don't I?'

'Yes.'

'And what did you do last time in this bed?'

'I tried to take over.'

He spanked my ass again, this time on the other cheek. I held my breath and clenched the sheets in my fists.

'Give me a number,' he growled, and spanked again.

'Nine,' I moaned. 'Nine, hot.' Because I was. So incredibly hot and so ready for him.

He may be exercising his will, his needs, but he was also considering mine. Because he didn't confine me. Didn't force me to do anything. He didn't even touch or hover over me. He spanked me. A fast whip of his hand was all the touch I got. But I was free. Could get away if I wanted. Run. Hide. Scream.

But I didn't want any of that. I wanted him. He made me feel alive. Feel like I could handle not only myself, but this situation and him. However he'd give himself to me. I wasn't scared the way I had been. Because in the past, I was restrained, used, terrified.

Not now. It was as if he understood an unsaid part of me. Everything, from how he spoke to how he positioned me, was calculated for my pleasure, as well as his.

'How do you do this?' he asked with a gravelly tone, palming my sensitive ass. His hands felt cold against the heated flesh. 'How do you look so fucking perfect? Smooth skin reddened with my hand. Like a naughty girl. But so innocent at the same time.'

He bent over me and bit my shoulder. At some point, he'd shucked his pants, because I felt his hard cock slide against the back of my thigh. The sound of latex crinkling. He was hard and ready.

Clamping the back of my knee, he bent it and placed it on the bed, then the other, scooting me forward until I was on top of the bed completely. I was still laying on my front, my face against the mattress, only now, my ass was in the air and Jack probed my opening.

'What kind of woman are you right now?'

I considered his words for a moment. What kind of woman was I? What kind of woman did he bring out in me? So many sides I could barely count them. He made me feel innocent, yet naughty. Passionate, but shy at times. Only one answer made sense: 'Yours.'

That was the only kind of woman I wanted to be.

He seemed to like that answer. He thrust hard inside of me, rocking me forward, my cheek sliding against the sheets. I kept my arms outstretched, and gripped the top cover as he withdrew and returned with another punishing thrust.

'Oh, God,' I moaned. When his hips hit my ass, the sting and heat he left only added to the sensation and made my blood pressure spike.

'You like this, baby?' He pumped, hard and fast. The sound of his skin slapping mine, echoing.

'Yes, yes, so much.'

Clutching my hips in both his hands, he drove in and out, pulling me against him as he surged inside, hitting deeper and deeper with every motion.

I bit the sheets to muffle my screams of ecstasy. Blood rushed to my ears.

He kept up his insistent pace until both of us glistened with a sheen of sweat. He was prolonging this, keeping us both on edge on purpose. While I wanted to come so desperately, I didn't want this moment to end.

'Touch yourself,' he said. I wasn't sure I heard him right, nor what that meant exactly. He picked up on that, because he clarified with, 'Rub your clit, while I fuck this tight little pussy. Now.'

I nodded and took one of my hands and reached to find my clit throbbing and wet. It was incredible that he could make me so wet that my pleasure couldn't be contained. I began rubbing slowly at first, then the amazing sensation was too much of a tease, so I picked up speed, moving faster and faster as he drove in and out.

'Good. I feel you tensing, drenching me. You're ready, aren't you? You want to come, don't you?'

'Yes,' I moaned. 'Yes, please let me. Please.'

Based on last time, I tried asking. Another thing he seemed to like. He slung one arm around my waist, burying himself to the hilt, and fisted my hair in the other hand and gently tugged.

I rose up until my back met his chest. With his hand in my hair, he yanked my head to the side and kissed me hard. I palmed his nape, drowning in his kiss, his body, reveling in the feeling of being totally still and totally connected.

'Feel me deep inside you?' he said against my lips.

'Y-yes.'

'Good. I'm going to stay just like this.'

I frowned. I was so close to coming, I was ready to sob. He grinned and kissed me quick, but kept his mouth against mine.

'Rub.' He unwove his hand from my hair, slid it down my body, and covered my hand that was against my clit. Together, we rubbed. He whispered something against my mouth. Like he promised, he kept still, but my pleasure climbed.

'I'm going to come,' I said.

'I want you to, baby.' He kissed me, just as my release engulfed my entire body.

A groan escaped his lips and vibrated off mine. He came right behind me. Amazement raced at the thought that just my core gripping him – clenching and releasing – was what pushed him over the edge. A sense of power and pride flooded me. He kissed me, hot and hard and slow, as we came together. Feeling each other. Getting lost.

So lost that I never wanted to be found.

The smell of freshly baked pastries had me groaning even before opening my eyes. After a long appreciative inhale, I lifted my

151

heavy lids to find myself engulfed in soft sheets, a massive down comforter, and piles of pillows. It was like sleeping in stuffing that smelled like Jack.

I sat up, realizing that I was completely naked.

The stockings were on the floor next to Jack's clothes from last night. I didn't remember taking them off. Maybe he took them off of me? All I remember was the most powerful orgasm I'd ever had, and going limp, satisfied and exhausted in Jack's arms.

I scooted to the edge of the bed. My backside didn't hurt, but a gentle sting throbbed from last night's foray, reminding me of how hot and amazing it was. And the thought made me smile.

I walked to the master bathroom. My clothes were still neatly folded like I'd left them next to my purse on the shelves by the door. The bathroom was monstrous. I splashed water on my face, and dressed. I tried to compose myself and get ready to face Jack, so I could say my goodbyes and do everything I could to make a calm, smooth exit.

I was pretty sure he was in the kitchen, though the idea of leaving made me cold and already missing him. But it was a new day, weekend or not, and time to head back to reality.

With my chin up, I hooked my purse over my shoulder, walked out of the room and headed toward the kitchen.

When I reached it, my mouth watered instantly, and it had nothing to with the croissants that were on the counter, it had to do with the man hovering near the stove.

He stood, his bare back facing me, and I could see every perfect muscle in his shoulders flex and work as he scraped a pan of what looked to be eggs. Those broad shoulders tapered to a narrow waist, where low-slung black pajama bottoms hung.

Lord have mercy, the man had a fine ass. I could also see the faintest remnants of scratch marks from a few days ago when I had clawed him. Something about seeing him this way: tousled hair, relaxed, with my marks on him, made me ...

Happy.

I cleared my throat.

He turned around, and my saliva glands went to double time, because the front, if possible, was better than the back.

'Good morning,' he said, then frowned hard at me. 'What are you doing?' He stared at my purse, looking me over like I was wearing an 'I support Satan' T-shirt.

'I was going to head out?' It was supposed to be a statement, but came out more like a question, because he was still looking at me like I was crazy.

'You'd like to leave?'

That was a loaded question. Would I *like* to leave? No. I'd *like* to crawl back into bed with the man in front of me and forget everything but his warmth. Instead, I went with, 'Isn't that protocol?'

'Protocol?' he stepped toward me. 'You insult me and yourself when you say that.'

'What?' I exhaled a heavy breath. 'I was just trying to give you space. Don't women usually leave after they stay the night? Or do the women you have over stay for breakfast? How am I supposed to know? I didn't want to assume anything, and just figured—'

'I don't have women stay over.'

That stopped my speech dead in its tracks. 'Really?'

'And I was hoping *you'd* stay for breakfast.' He looked me up and down again. 'Actually, I was hoping you'd walk out here naked and I'd eat you for breakfast.'

I swallowed hard. 'Sooo, not the protocol I was thinking.'

'No, baby,' he said, and turned back to take the eggs off the burner and put them on a plate. 'There's no protocol when it comes to us.'

153

Us. That word was even better than 'more.' Or 'boyfriend.' Or 'arrangement.'

Us.

I bit my bottom lip to keep from smiling. Jack turned and held two plates in his hands. Apparently, he'd been cooking longer than I realized.

'Lana,' he said in a raspy voice with just a hint of softness. 'Will you stay for breakfast?'

Nothing prepared me for that. Jack Powell just asked me to stay.

'I'd love to.'

He lifted his chin at the table behind me, but I didn't miss the grin that lined his face. 'Then, go sit.'

I put my purse on the counter and went to sit at the table.

'Wow,' I said, when I looked at the spread. Literally, everything imaginable you could think to spread on bread was in the middle of the table.

'I didn't know what you liked,' he muttered. He set my plate in front of me, then sat next to me. I looked at him for a long moment. He was incredibly thoughtful. This was the Jack that was ratcheting his way into my heart. Because, he may not think so, but it was the exact thing that made him more. In every way.

I looked at the plethora of options in the middle of the table. Everything from an assortment of jams to apple butter, to Nutella, to . . . was that jalapeno spread?

I'd never seen so many options. 'Did you have all this lying around?'

'No.'

I looked at him. 'You went and bought it?'

'Like I said, I didn't know what you'd like.'

'When?' I asked quickly.

154

'What?'

'When did you buy all this?'

'The day after I met you.'

I stalled for a moment. I didn't know what to think, or how to react, but shock seemed to be the typical reaction. He may not have given me his information, but he'd known after the night we'd met me that he wanted me, not just for a night, but for a morning?

Yet he didn't push it. He was patient. Controlled. But then sideswiped me with little details that showed his plan of seduction . . . or maybe it was wishful thinking? Either way, no one had ever taken an interest in me like he did. And no one had ever considered my comfort or desires like he did.

'What has you frowning?' he asked, glancing at the options on the table. 'Did I forget one?'

'No.' I smiled and scooted out of my chair, hitting my knees before him so I could be as close to eye level as possible. Resting my palms on his thighs I looked at him. 'You surprise me.'

He laughed! I'd never heard him laugh before, and it was so amazing that I wanted to record it and play it over and over. The deep chuckle was so sexy, and the way it made all those hard stomach muscles flex was an added bonus.

'You are the one who surprises me.'

He cupped my face and kissed me softly. Something very real, very scorching notched into place. Like a piece of my soul I'd lost that night so many years ago was mending. Being replaced and healed by the kindness and new experiences Jack was giving me.

He cared.

His methods kept me on my toes. His needs definitely had a story behind them, a story I wanted to know about. Jack was my single interest. But, at the end of the day, he thought of me, showed up, and cared.

155

And I found myself giving up a lot for that. Whether it was control, trust, or maybe more, I was giving it happily to him. Pushing past the walls that once held me like a vise was freeing. Trusting him to guide me through this next chapter of my life – show me what certain feelings meant – was wonderful. Feelings like appreciation. Warmth. Kindness. Heat. Lust.

It was all wrapped into a big ball that had my body flickering with the need to get my mouth on him however I could, while my chest ached to understand him. To know him.

'Jack?' I whispered against his lips. He leaned back and looked at me, his thumb brushing along the corner of my mouth.

'Yes?'

'Will you tell me something about yourself?'

His thumb stopped its gentle stroke. 'Like what?'

'Anything you're willing to share. A secret? A happy memory?'

He leaned back in his chair. I kept my hands on the tops of his thighs, and then it hit me, I was on my knees, asking him to indulge me. Asking for a piece of him.

And I waited, praying he'd give it. Because a piece was something I could work with. A sign that this was going somewhere on a deeper level than just sex. *We* were going somewhere.

'Okay,' he said with a long breath. 'Here's something: I love the sound of bare feet on hardwood floors. The way the wood creaks a little with each movement.' A smile played over his face when he said this, and he looked past me, as if recalling a happy moment. 'You know someone is coming for you when you hear a sound like that.'

I smiled back and rubbed his thighs a little with encouragement. I'd never thought about the sounds of footsteps on the floor before. But for Jack, it was obviously something good. Something I wanted to hear more about, because his usually hard, controlled façade was currently casual.

'Who do you hope is coming for you when you hear it?'

As soon as I asked, I steeled myself for his answer. He could say an ex-lover. The love of his life. A woman he once knew—

'My mother.' He placed one hand over mine. 'When I was young, we had this little house on the outskirts of Denver. Wasn't much – a one bedroom. We couldn't afford anything bigger. But she made it a home. She gave me the bedroom and slept on the couch.' He shook his head, a vicious look plaguing his face, like he was mad at himself for that. 'I would lay in bed and hear her walking around. Cleaning the house at night after she'd already worked a long shift. But I knew she was there. And the boards creaked and it was actually soothing to fall asleep to.'

He scoffed, then looked at me. 'Sorry you asked now, huh?'

'No, the opposite,' I said, overwhelmingly happy. That small glimpse of Jack was worth his weight in gold. He loved his mother and came from humble means. Certain pieces of this tricky puzzle started connecting.

I was going to ask more, but he leaned forward, the strong expression of master of dominance and control, was back in place. We were face to face. He looked me dead in the eye.

'Now, you tell me a secret,' he said in a gravelly tone. Whatever shifted in Jack, I didn't know. But heat buzzed from him, and I knew that happy-feeling time was over. Back was the sexy in-command man that looked at me like I was candy.

I didn't know why the shift. But I was caught in his spell.

'Um . . .' I bit my lip. I had a lot of secrets, most I didn't want to share, because it would just make them more real. I looked at him, trying to breathe in some of his buzzing energy, and get to the same place he was: humming.

I may be on my knees, but I could change the subject too. My hands were still on his thighs. Instead of my coaxing, supportive rub earlier, my path was slow, my target obvious.

157

'I was thinking that I wanted to try a few of the spreads you got.' I glanced at the table, then back at Jack.

'That's not a secret.'

'I know, but . . .' I wiggled between his knees even further and placed a kiss on his lower torso. His breath hissed. 'I'm hungry.' Another kiss. 'And I've never . . .'

With my face against his hard stomach, I felt, then saw his cock swelling in his thin pants. Just enough of a sign that maybe I could do this. Maybe he'd let me . . . or teach me.

'Lana.' He cupped my face and tilted it, so my chin brushed his belly button as he forced me to look up at him. 'Are you saying you've never sucked a man's cock?'

I closed my eyes. He turned my face gently, reminding me to keep them open and not look away, even when I was unsure. His words played through my mind from the first night I'd met him.

I held his dark stare. 'No. I've never done that.'

'Do you want to?'

His dick throbbed even harder in anticipation of my answer. I was nervous, but one thing was certain: 'Yes, I do. But I don't know, exactly . . . how. Will you teach me?' I asked.

'There's nothing to be taught. Like sex, you do what feels right. But understand that this act is no exception to what I told you about my preferences. I can be rough.'

I nodded. 'You haven't dished out anything I haven't liked so far,' I said honestly, because I'd handled a lot already. And he'd proven to be the man to show me how to take it. 'I trust you.'

I gave in to the truth of that. I did trust Jack. He had taken my body to its limits, and never pushed me past the point into fear. It was time I step up and be the woman I wanted to be. The woman he helped me be.

'But you need to understand something too,' I said, and

158

reached behind me, grabbing the peach jam off the table, 'I was serious when I said I was hungry.'

I could have sworn I saw Jack take a stutter swallow. Could I be getting to him? Tempting him past his restraint and keeping him in the moment? I tugged on his pants, and his cock sprang free. Thick and long, and this was the first time I'd had an up-close view.

I simply stared for a moment, which I knew I was doing. What I hadn't realized was that I was licking my lower lip while doing so.

'That's not very nice, baby,' he rasped. 'Flashing that pretty mouth right in front of me, teasing me.'

I looked up at him and smiled. 'Well, I'd never want to tease you. Surely there's no fun in that, right?'

His gaze narrowed and, yeah, he was getting a taste of his own medicine from when he kept me on edge.

I opened the jar of peach jam, took a little out with my finger and rubbed it along the crown. Going slow, I felt every ridge and the smoothness of him. I spread the jam all along the head, around and around, drawing small circles until the entire tip was covered. Then, I sucked my finger clean.

'Jesus, you're driving me crazy on purpose.'

I shook my head, my eyes riveted to his impressive length. 'No, just learning you.'

I leaned in, unsure what to do first. Simply lick? No, he'd used the word suck earlier. Had I ever *sucked* a man? I'm sure licking was involved, but I'd get to that.

Closing my mouth around the entire crown, I sucked, flicking my tongue to lick at the jam as I did.

'Fuck, baby,' he said on a strangled breath. He sounded pained.

I shot up immediately, his cock popping from my mouth. 'Oh, my God, I'm sorry. Did I do it wrong?'

'No.' he smiled, and ran his fingers through my hair. 'You have me on the brink already.'

'Really? But I haven't—'

'Just keep doing what you're doing. And it's the God damn teasing beforehand that's making it hard for me to hold out.'

I gave a sheepish smile. 'So, I suppose I should just . . .' I kept my eyes on his and licked the tip. His fingers tightened in my hair. 'Do something like that?' Another lick.

'There you go with that teasing again.'

I swirled my tongue around and around, pausing only to say, 'What happens when I tease you?' With innocent sarcasm, I looked up at him, daring him to show me. Because I wanted him to. Wanted him to lose himself to me. Just for a moment, the way I lost myself to him.

With one hand holding the majority of my hair at the back of my head, he cupped my chin in his free hand and coaxed my mouth to close around his cock.

'Keep your mouth on me,' he said. I nodded as he moved his hand from my chin to the chair he sat in. His muscles bulged as he levered himself off the seat enough to move his hips.

'You want this, baby?' he asked.

I nodded again.

He flexed his hips the way he did when he fucked me. The motion sent his cock deep into my mouth, then pulled it back. He flexed again. Rolling his hips slowly, pushing and retreating in and out. Every time, the suction I had intensified. Something he must have felt, because he groaned.

'Jesus fucking Christ,' he said between gritted teeth. His whole body was tense. Wetness pooled between my legs just watching him. The way he rolled his hips, the way his stomach flexed and his chest drew tight as he moved in and out of my mouth the way he would my core. It was incredible to witness his strong body moving.

160

'You like this? Me fucking this pretty mouth?'

I answered by flicking my tongue along his shaft. He grinned. 'I'll take that as a yes.'

He went slow, steady. Each time, going just a fraction deeper. He didn't shove or quicken his pace. He took his time, letting me adjust. I ran my hands up his thighs and to his hips. I wanted to feel what I was seeing. Feel him move.

'What are you doing to me?' he rasped, and I didn't know if he knew he'd said it out loud. But he was lost. The look of raw pleasure on his face was all it took to spark my need for him into overdrive. He took pleasure from me. And I gave it. Pride soared.

When he pumped inward again, he hit the back of my throat, and I swallowed in reaction.

'Ah, fuck!' he said, and hit that spot again, causing me to swallow around him once more. 'Yes, baby, just like that. You're so good. So fucking good.'

I realized that when I swallowed, my throat contracted around him, and that was something that seemed to drive him wild. So, I did it again and again. Grabbing his hips a little tighter, I went to try to take him deeper, but he pulled back.

'I'm going to come,' he said, and went to pull all the way out. Instinct took over, and my tight grip turned to claws, keeping him in my mouth.

I sucked hard, hoping he'd get the message that I wanted to experience this whole thing. Start to finish.

That dark heat came out and his eyes flickered with wicked lust.

'You want me to stay, huh?' he growled. He pumped deep into my throat. 'Then you're going to take all of me. Swallow me down.'

With that, he thrust deep, and a hot liquid splashed against the back of my throat. I watched his body shudder as lash after lash coated my tongue, and I did as he said and took it all.

161

He groaned. He slowly withdrew. I didn't have time to right myself before he ordered, 'Stand up.'

I did. He yanked my pants down and off, leaving me bare and him at eye level. He grabbed one of my legs and placed my foot on his thigh. I had to hold his head for balance.

'Are you wet, baby?' he asked, cupping my ass and bringing me to his mouth.

'Yes,' I sighed when his tongue hit my clit. He growled against me, the vibrations making me shudder.

'You're soaking. Just from sucking me off.'

'Yes,' I said again.

He licked madly at my clit, and thrust his tongue inside me. I threw my head back and screamed, because an instant orgasm took me over. I had no idea I was that close, but bringing Jack pleasure turned me on to the point of no return.

He licked at me until I was spent, then he stood. Keeping me in his grasp, he lifted me up, and I instantly wrapped my legs around his hips as he carried us toward the bedroom.

His cock was still semi-hard and prodded my entrance. I buried my face in his neck, and moaned at the feeling.

'I promise I'll feed you,' he said. 'But I just need a little more of you first. I may keep you captive for the whole weekend.'

I lifted my face to meet his eyes.

'Is it protocol to ask a woman to stay the whole weekend with you?' I teased, and nipped his chin.

He growled. 'It is now. So long as *you* are the woman.'

He tossed me on the bed, grabbed a condom from the bedside table, and was sheathed and covering me in record time. Kissing me hard and fast, that semi turned insistent real quick, and he thrust deep inside me. I wrapped my arms and legs around him, wanting to stay there a lot longer than a weekend.

Chapter 14

I rinsed the dishes from breakfast off and put them in the dishwasher. After Jack and I spent the morning wrapped around each other in bed, and the afternoon exploring each other in the shower, we finally made it back to the kitchen to find our eggs cold.

Which was why he ordered pizza.

The sounds of the front door opening and the instant smell of cheese and sauce wafted through the house as Jack walked in holding a large box.

'That smells so good,' I said, putting the last dish in the washer and drying my hands.

'You didn't need to do the dishes,' he said, setting the pizza on the table.

'I wanted to help,' I shrugged. Walking over, I sat where I had for breakfast, wondering if I could get through the second attempt at eating today without ripping his clothes off.

My stomach growled.

'Sounds like you need to eat,' he said.

'Yeah, I've been putting it off. There's been a pressing matter I've been attending to that makes me forgo food.'

He raised his brow and set out napkins in front of us. 'Oh?'

I sighed dramatically. 'Yes, it's true. But I can't seem to think straight.'

I glanced at him, and my eyes wandered down his impressive

chest, which was encased in a black tee that matched his hair and eyes, and down to the most amazing pair of jeans I'd ever seen on a man. Or maybe it was just Jack. When he moved and reached to take a slice of pizza and put it on the napkin in front of me, I caught sight of the silver clasp of his belt glinting, and just a hint of tan skin.

'I seem to have a one track mind lately,' I said.

He stared at me, did his own foray of my body, and said, 'I understand that notion completely. It seems I'm struggling with the same.'

I smiled and glanced down at myself. Same tank and yoga pants. Though the shower helped, the scent of Jack's spicy soap lingered on my skin, making me want to groan with desire. I'd ditched the panties, and realized I needed to ask him about what he'd said.

'You said earlier about me staying the weekend?'

He sat down and took a bite of pizza. 'Yes.'

'Is that . . . something you meant?'

'I don't say things I don't mean.' He frowned and looked at me. 'Unless you'd like to leave?'

I shook my head quickly, cursing that I'd just taken a bite and my mouth was full. After a few chews and a swallow, I finally was able to say, 'I don't want to leave, but I think I'll need to. To get a change of clothes, toothbrush, things like that.'

I'd done my best with the toothpaste and mouthwash in Jack's bathroom, but would love to actually brush.

'I'll launder your clothes, and you can wear something of mine in the meantime. There's a spare toothbrush in the bathroom in the second drawer.'

I paused. He kept a spare? He said he didn't have women over, so why would he keep a spare? Whatever he saw on my face made him say, 'It's brand new, and in the package still.'

'That's not what I was worried about.'

'Then what?'

'Why do you have a spare?'

'For you.'

That made my chest still. It was the same as the variations of jams he'd gotten.

'You bought me a toothbrush?'

He nodded. 'After our first night together, I thought it would be a good thing to have on hand. I like to be prepared.'

'So, you've planned this? Seducing me into staying at your house?'

A wicked gleam laced his face. 'Yes. But to be fair, you're not free of guilt in this.'

'What have I done?' I asked in shock.

'You,' he leaned in, 'are a seductress yourself.'

He kissed me quickly on the lips, then took another bite of pizza. I ate mine, marveling at how natural this seemed. He was calm, yet still in control. Always. But it was simple, easy to be with him. Not just the sex, which was amazing, but spending time with him and hearing his voice was nice.

Still, how set up was this? He'd thought ahead, knew what he wanted, and if that was me, he had taken steps to see to my comforts. It wasn't like he was giving me his house key or sectioning off a drawer in a dresser for my stuff. He'd thought ahead enough to know he wanted me to stay the night at some point.

Despite all I was learning, I now knew he'd wanted me from the beginning.

'I have some T-shirts you can wear, boxer shorts, or nothing, if you prefer.' He took a bite of his pizza, then glanced at me. 'My vote is for the third option.'

I smiled. This was fun. Teasing with Jack. The idea that he wanted me to stay around. It was a chance to get to really know him. See him better in the light of day, where we were comfortable and happy.

'So, no plans for today other than lounging?'

'We can do whatever you'd like,' he said.

I glanced out the massive windows. For a summer day, it was a bit foggy, and the idea of staying in, getting lost in Jack, sounded perfect.

'I hear there's a *Godfather* marathon on TV today.'

He nodded. 'Excellent.'

A flare of guilt caught me, though. 'I don't want to take up your whole weekend. If you wanted to see your friends or your mom maybe?'

'My mother is dead, and Cal is out of town, as you know.' He didn't spare me a glance that time, but there was a low, dangerous timbre in his voice.

'I'm so sorry,' I said. 'I hadn't realized about your mom.' He didn't say anything, so I gently pushed for a little more detail. 'Can I ask what happened?'

He looked at me, as if deciding whether or not to tell me. I didn't want to kill the mood, but any insight I could get into him was like a beacon of hope I clung to that maybe we could be more. That we were heading in that direction at least. Something beyond sex and lust and taking the need I had for him to another level. Because I was already heading there, and I really wanted him to head there with me.

'She was in a car accident and died when I was eight.'

I reached out and grabbed is hand. 'That's terrible. Did your dad—'

'My father died last year.'

'So, after your mother passed, what happened to you?'

'My father showed up to claim me. I'd never met him before. But my mother had life insurance, and I was underage, so he

166

jumped at that opportunity.' So much hate marred Jack's voice, I thought he could bend steel just from the scary sound of it. 'He lived down the street from Cal, which is how we met. Been friends ever since.'

'I'm glad you met Cal and still have him in your life,' I whispered. 'That must have been hard.'

He scoffed. 'It's fine. It was a long time ago.'

I nodded. I was afraid to press the subject, but the need for him to keep going was too heavy. 'Brothers,' I said, repeating Cal's words from when I'd been between them both in the bar. 'Cal said you two were like brothers.'

'Yes, close as brothers.'

'Did your dad—'

'My father is not a man I want to discuss.' Something very dark laced Jack's face. 'Why don't you tell me about yourself?'

I sat back in my chair, and stared at my crust for a minute. He put another piece of pizza on my napkin, and waited for me to say something. It was only fair. I was asking a lot of him. Though nothing I could come up with seemed really great. But he was interested in me, so that made a happy heat rise in my chest.

'My mother is not around, hasn't been for a long time,' I said. 'She left my dad when I was young, and I haven't seen her since. She's in Florida somewhere. We've had a couple calls and a few cards over the years, but that's it.'

'So your dad raised you?'

'Until he married my step-mother.'

He nodded. 'Ah, the infamous step-brother from the first night I met you.'

'Yeah. Brock.'

'You said you don't like him?'

There was way more to it than that, but I was trying to push those memories out, not rehash them.

167

'No, I don't.'

'He's a VanBuren. Of Case-VanBuren,' he stated.

'Yeah, that's my dad's company.'

He looked at me for a long moment. It was no surprise he knew of it. It wasn't a big time investment firm, but it was decently well known.

'What's your stake in the company?' he asked, as if it was a totally normal question.

'I don't have one. I don't even work there.' I shook my head, realizing how much had changed in the past couple of weeks. I still wanted to work there, because it would make me a part of my father's world. Someone he believed in and supported. But Jack had been an amazing gift that allowed me to focus on other things, instead of getting consumed with this need of approval. Which, if I were honest, was still very much present. Another thing I was working on. 'I'm just gearing up to be a grad student.'

It was all I was at the moment. Maybe, one day, things could be different, but my father made it clear that I provided little value to him, especially when dealing with the company.

'You should be proud.'

I shrugged. 'I am, my dad has a name, and his company, and—'

'I'm talking about you. You should be proud of *yourself*.'

I stared at him, and could see he was serious. 'You work hard, manage expectations from others, and yourself, and chase your goals. That's strength.'

The way he said it, tied with the way he looked at me, made my whole body ache. Like I was desperate for his arms, his chest. For him to wrap me up, so I could cling to him.

For all my shortcomings, my baggage and damage – some he didn't even know about – he seemed to see me, not only that, he encouraged me.

'Eat,' he said, motioning to my second piece of pizza he'd placed before me. 'You're going to need that strength, baby,' he gave a teasing smile, and it made the heaviness of the conversation a little lighter. 'We have an afternoon of the *Godfather*. Though I hope you weren't expecting to focus too much on it, seeing as how you'll be naked on the couch.'

I stood in the bathroom doorway, looking at Jack sleeping.

Dark hair and tan skin amongst a sea of eggshell white cotton was like looking into a dream. Or upon a dream man.

It had been a long day, and night. Saturdays had never felt so good. Only now it was past two in the morning, and it was officially Sunday.

And he asked me to stay the weekend.

I wrapped my arms around myself, the feel of his button-up shirt the only thing against my skin, and I hugged it closer. With the soft glow of the light from the bathroom behind me, I simply stood there, watching him.

He looked so perfect, so handsome. His chest rose and fell steadily. His thick lashes rested against his cheeks and his brow was relaxed. The man that wove so much control in his world was naked, with nothing but a sheet covering him, stretched out in bed with one arm thrown over his head, and the other resting on his chest.

I smiled, thinking maybe I had worn the CEO out. He definitely had me in desperate need of a protein shake, a shot of B12, and some Gatorade to keep up with him.

The thought of doing just that made my whole body buzz, as if picking up on the sexy memories I was replaying from today.

As I made my way toward the bed, my shoulder caught the bathroom door on the way out, causing the hinges to whine.

Jack's eyes shot open.

169

I stopped instantly. Staring at him.

I'd never seen anything like it. I didn't know if he was awake, but suddenly, those dark eyes were instantly seared in my direction. He made no movement other than his eyes. Staring at me.

What concerned me was the emotion behind them. Jack looked terrified.

'Jack?' I whispered.

His eyes just stayed locked on me. It was eerie, as if he was looking right through me.

'The door,' he growled, low with sleep and anger in his voice. The look of fear left his face, and now he scowled.

I glanced behind me. 'I'm sorry, I didn't mean to wake you.' I hadn't realized he was such a light sleeper.

'The. Door,' he said again, and sat up. I had no idea what to say. He seemed so angry.

'I'm really sorry,' I tried again. 'I didn't mean to—'

Jack threw the sheet away, and stomped out of the bedroom. So fast I didn't know if the blur I witnessed was of him or something I imagined. I heard rustling coming from down the hall. Cabinets banging, drawers being opened and closed. Finally, he was back with ... was that WD40?

'What are you doing?' I asked quietly, but he just passed me and knelt by the bathroom door.

I read once to never disturb a sleepwalker or scare them.

'Jack?' I said quietly, coming into his line of vision. I realized he not only had the WD40, but a screwdriver and paper towels. 'Are you awake?'

He wiggled the door back and forth, frowning at the bottom hinge, realizing it was the one that was squeaking.

'Of course I'm awake.'

I took a deep breath. Okay, that was a start. He sprayed the

WD40 and tightened one of the screws in the hinge, then wiggled the door again.

'What are you doing?'

He frowned and looked up at me. 'I'm fixing the door.'

'I can see that, but why?'

That frown turned into something darker. Something beyond anger, fear and terror. It was haunted.

'Because I don't like squeaky doors.'

'I'm sorry,' I tried again.

'It's not your fault,' he said, giving the door a final tug. No more squeak. He went into the bathroom and washed his hands, leaving the items where they were, as if not caring about a thing in the world, as long as the door didn't squeak anymore.

He came out and cupped my face. 'Let's go to bed.'

I nodded and followed him. But everything in my body was screaming that this was bizarre. More than bizarre. I'd never seen Jack look so lost. So terrified. For a brief moment, when he first awoke, that was the look I saw. I recognized that look. Had had the same one: fear.

Fear of what's coming through the door.

'Jack?' I whispered, as he sat on the bed and I stood before him. 'Why does the sound of squeaking doors bother you so much?'

His stare stayed on my stomach, he unbuttoned his shirt I was wearing, and threw it to the floor.

'They just do.' He kissed my hip, my side, my stomach, then tugged me into bed with him.

'You can talk to me,' I said, but he just rolled us over, so my back was to him and his arms were wrapped around me, spooning me.

'Not about that.' He buried his face in my neck.

'I want to know you.' It was clear there was an issue. Something maybe I could help, at the very least, identify with what he

171

was going through. Whatever fear that gripped him when he thought someone was coming through the door, I couldn't shake. 'Maybe I can help. Or just listen.'

'Don't ask me again,' he said, very calm, but very stern.

I nodded, and he hugged me closer. Funny thing, he was right there, yet felt so far away.

Chapter 15

'Have you enjoyed yourself?' Jack asked from across the little table.

We were eating a late lunch on Sunday afternoon in the sunshine of downtown Denver. The little café had a dining section outside, and people passed us, strolling and window shopping, as Jack and I sat there, like nothing was missing between us.

All I could think about was what happened only twelve hours earlier in the early hours of the morning.

'It's been a wonderful weekend.'

I took a sip of my water. My clothes had been cleaned and waiting for me this morning. I didn't know when Jack had washed them, or perhaps he had a housekeeper that possessed ninja qualities. That was the least of my worries at the moment. Sure, sitting across from him looking perfect in his jeans and button-up, while I was in glorified loungewear was difficult on the self-esteem. Though he kept himself casual, the blue shirt rolled at the sleeves, I still felt sloppy in comparison.

'Something on your mind?'

I nodded.

He waited.

He told me once to say what was on my mind. Lord knew he had no problem speaking his thoughts. My only hesitation was fear of pushing too far and having him shut me out. Only way to know …

'I'm confused about last night,' I started.

He stared hard at me. 'There's nothing confusing about it.'

'It was odd,' I said quickly.

He sat back in his chair, as if gearing up for a verbal brawl. 'Perhaps it is odd.'

'Then why won't you talk to me about it?'

'Talk to you about what? There's nothing to say. I was awoken, took care of the problem that awoke me, and went back to bed.'

'There's more to it than that. I saw more than that.'

'Really? Enlighten me then. What more is it you saw?'

'I saw fear,' I said quietly. 'In your eyes. You were terrified when you heard the door squeak.'

I knew what it felt like to have someone come through the door. Someone you didn't want to see. Everything in my body was reaching out for him, identifying with him, with whatever incident he'd survived that put that look on his face. I didn't know the details, but I recognized what a shattered past looked like. And Jack was a master at hiding his past.

He sat, his face like stone, his body even stiller. It was like staring down a snake, waiting to see if he'd strike. A heartbeat passed, then another. He said nothing, but I felt him pulling away. Felt the air between us turn colder, and my own fear swept me up, nervous that I was losing him.

'Jack,' I whispered, and leaned into him, snagging his gaze with mine. 'That night we met, you said you saw fear in my eyes. Do you remember?'

'Vividly.'

'And you reacted. That's the same thing I'm doing. Reacting.'

'Why?'

I swallowed hard. 'Because I care. Very much. About you.'

His jaw ticked, his brows sliced down, as if he were trying to determine the truth in my words. What had happened to this

174

man? This amazing, strong, powerful, puzzle of a man. Last night, I'd caught my first glimpse of vulnerability in him. I wanted to help. To comfort, anything I could do.

'Pumpkin!' I jerked upright, surprised to hear my father's voice booming right next to me. 'I thought that was you.'

'Dad?' I looked up to find him and Brock, in suits even though it was a Sunday, standing on the other side of the rope that kept the café seating from the general walking area of downtown.

He opened his arms, as if awaiting a hug. Now I was really confused. But I stood, and he hugged me. It felt frigid and staged. My father wasn't an affectionate man, not to mention the fact that last time we spoke, it ended with me quitting.

Jack stood, and my father finally let go of me. Brock reached out his hand and shook Jack's.

'Brock VanBuren,' he shook continuously. 'With Case-VanBuren Investing.'

'We've met,' Jack said in a calm voice. Brock, being the slithering liar that he was, nodded.

'That's right.' He plastered on a fake smile. 'Good to see you again.'

'Jack, this is my father, Carter Case.'

Jack reached out and shook my dad's hand next. 'Mr Case, very nice to meet you.'

'And you, Mr Powell. I didn't realize you knew my daughter.'

Jack looked at me, and whatever internal button he pressed to turn on the corporate charm, he did it then. All traces of the emotion behind what'd we just been talking about were gone. But he looked at me with admiration, kindness, and interest.

Part of me loved that. That one look made me feel seen by him. His presence also made me feel, like for the first time, I wouldn't get sick being this close to Brock. I was feeling stronger. And it was because of him.

175

But one thing terrified me in this skill of Jack's. He had the ability to shift from business to personal to social, then back to business. One moment he could be saying the sweetest things, or on the brink of discussing something personal, the next he wore a mask of indifference. What was even more terrifying was that trait he harbored was the same as my father. He knew when to turn it on, and who was watching. Like right now.

My dad hadn't reached out to me since I'd shown up at his house and quit. But now I was in the presence of a millionaire who owned resorts, and suddenly I was back to being 'Pumpkin' and on his radar.

My heart hurt a little. Yet the kind gesture and hug from my father still made my pathetic chest tighten, and the desire for him to notice me – love me – persist.

Yeah ... pathetic.

'Lana and I met a few weeks ago. I've had a hard time letting her out of my sight since.' Jack glanced at Brock, then back at my father.

His words warmed me and eased the ache rising from this encounter and just how deep in the Case-VanBuren game I was. False niceties, passive aggressiveness, and hidden agendas were swirling so thick it was suffocating.

'Oh!' my father said, pleased. 'That's wonderful. You two should come to the house for dinner then.'

'No,' I said quickly. Jack's eyes landed on me, but I just smiled at my father. I could play this game too. With my best smile and 'there's nothing wrong' attitude, I sweetly said, 'We can't make dinner tonight.'

'Why?' Brock asked in a challenging tone that was laced with just enough sugar to make it not sound threatening. But it was meant to threaten. The mere sound of his voice made my skin crawl.

176

'Because we're calling it an early night. Work tomorrow and all,' I said, not looking at Brock, rather at Jack, who I was trying to syphon some kind of invisible energy from to get through this chat. It was all I could do to keep from shaking because the dread from this 'casual run-in' was building.

'Oh, responsible, Lana.' Brock put his hands in his pockets and rocked on his heels, then looked at Jack. 'She's always been this way, responsible and sensible.'

'She's a good girl,' my father said, and suddenly I had no idea what the hell was happening. Brock was trying to see how long I could stand in his presence before the anxiety got the better of me, and my father was being condescending on purpose.

Jack just stood, his gaze on me.

'Another time then?' my father offered, looking at Jack. 'When is good for you?'

'You'll have to talk to Lana,' he said, rubbing his hand along the small of my back. 'She's the boss. I'm on her schedule.'

Stupid tears threatened to make an appearance, but I urged them down before anyone noticed.

Jack was not the kind of man to be on anyone's schedule but his own. But he just gave me the power, in front of Brock and my dad, and the surge of strength made me stand taller.

Both Brock and my father were clearly surprised by Jack's admission, but Jack simply sat down, as if he were done with them, and said, 'Good to meet you both.'

'Yes,' my father said, confusion riddling his voice. 'I'll call you later, Pumpkin.'

They left, Brock sparing me a gross smile and equally chilling glare.

Once they were gone, Jack looked at me from across the table.

'Tell me about that.'

'About what? My father?'

177

He nodded. 'And your step-brother. Clearly there's animosity there, and everything else was a big show.'

'It was that obvious, huh?'

I looked at my plate, which was half eaten, and shook my head. 'I can't remember the last time my father hugged me.' Then I scoffed because it sounded so silly. 'I'm not a part of their world.'

'They don't deserve you in their world then.'

I looked up at him. 'Do you think it's stupid that part of me misses the way my father used to be before—?'

I bit my lip, but Jack urged me on.

'Before what?'

Before he married Anita. Before Brock snuck into my room and not only wrecked certain parts of my psyche, but drove a wedge between my father and me. Before I suddenly didn't matter to my mother, or father, or anyone else. Before I merely existed.

'Before the divorce,' I said instead, keeping it as surface as possible, because tears were lining my throat.

'Nothing about what you want or how you feel is stupid.' He reached across the table and cupped my cheek.

'I want you,' I whispered. 'I want to know you. Want more every day.'

He stilled and took a deep breath. 'I want more of you every day too.' He ran his thumb along my bottom lip. 'I asked you to trust me. I'm asking again.'

I nodded. 'I do trust you.'

'Then hear me when I tell you that there are certain things I won't talk about. My past is not a place I want to revisit. You're astute and yes, perhaps you saw something last night, perhaps you care, but,' his voice was soft, not commanding or dominating or threating. It almost sounded like he was begging. 'Please, don't ask me about it again.'

My heart broke for this man. For all the weight he carried and everything he kept hidden.

'How can I get to know you more if you won't tell me anything? It's not my goal to upset you or bring up unwanted memories . . .' I knew how that felt, and I could understand that. Far too well. 'How can we move forward when there isn't an exchange? When I'm the only one who seems vulnerable.'

'You're not the only one, Lana. I have a significant vulnerability, and it's only getting worse.'

'Then tell me, please.'

He looked me dead in the eye. 'It's you.'

My breath caught, and he leaned back in his chair, the warmth of his hand leaving my face.

'I'll give you as much as I can,' he said.

The chill that crept over my skin was breaking me more than I realized. Not just breaking me of fear, but breaking me wide open with the need to understand him. It hit me then: I'm falling in love with a man who will never fully open up to me.

'Would you like to come in?' I asked Jack as we sat in my driveway.

He glanced in the rearview window, seeing the reflection of the fire station behind us and across the street. Stillness washed over him. Learning Jack was like figuring out how to dance around a sleeping bear. In one breath, his body could go from tense, to calm, to still. Scary still. I'd never met his equal when it came to the kind of intense presences that radiated from him. Everything was always on another level with him. Just when I thought he couldn't be more dominant, more perfect, he surprised me with yet another layer of his personality and demeanor.

'Jack?' His gaze snapped from the mirror to my face. Whatever thoughts he'd been having were consuming. 'Do you miss Cal?'

It was obvious he wanted to laugh that off, but instead, he adjusted to face me slightly.

'Miss?'

'Yes, *miss*. It's an okay emotion to feel, you know.'

'I never said it wasn't.'

'But you balk at the word.'

'Cal and I have a tricky friendship. We spent a lot of time together growing up, protecting each other. I know he'll be back. But when he's gone ...'

I leaned in a little, excited for another tiny fact about the closed off man beside me.

'When he's gone,' I prompted, but got nothing, so I tried to fill in the blank myself. 'It's like a disturbance in the force?'

Jack smiled. 'Something like that.'

I smiled back, and grabbed his hand. He was opening up! He clearly had a tight bond with Cal, but whatever they went through as kids forged something unbreakable.

'True friends are hard to find, and even harder to keep. I'm glad you have someone you trust.'

Jack looked at me. 'I trust him with everything in my world, including my life itself, and he's come through on that.'

There was a dark undertone to the last part of that statement. So much shaped the man that Jack was, and I didn't even understand a fraction of it. Sitting in my driveway, with the firehouse behind us, and him talking, I wanted to know more.

'You said you protected each other. From what?'

'From our lives,' he said, and opened his door to exit the car.

A thick tremor slowly crept up my spine at his words.

What kind of lives did they have? What life did Jack have? What made it so bad that his seemingly only friend in the world was more like a comrade-in-arms?

Jack walked around the car and helped me out, taking my arm

as he walked me to the front door. His stance and silence shutting down the minimal conversation we'd barely scraped the surface of.

Pulling the keys from my purse, I unlocked the dead bolt, and we walked in.

He cupped my hips, pulled me into him. 'Thank you for staying with me this weekend.'

I brushed his biceps, my palms trailing up, as his went lower to the small of my back. 'I feel the sudden urge to throw a fit and demand that you stay,' I whispered, my mouth hovering over his.

He raised a brow. 'Demand?'

He squeezed my ass hard, pulling me even closer against him, until I felt his cock nudging my stomach. 'You have me walking around like a damn teenager. Hard and ready to take you at any time.'

'Is that such a bad thing?' I said, and swayed my hips, just enough to brush against his swelling length.

'You tease me.'

'Maybe you should do something about that then?' That time I was really challenging him.

He nipped my bottom lip. 'I see your brazenness is coming out. Tempting me now? You know what happens when you tempt me.'

I wrapped my arms around him, stood on my tip toes and whispered in his ear. 'I liked it. All of it. You take me over. And I love it when you do.'

His hard chest rose and fell on a deep breath, the action causing his sculpted torso to brush along my nipples, which only made the inner heat pooling low in my belly rise.

'I slapped your ass,' he said quietly.

'Yes, and I liked it.'

That seemed to please him, but when I leaned back to look in

181

his eyes, they were conflicted. His hold on me was tight, like letting me go, giving me space, was something he wasn't willing to do.

'You liked it,' he repeated. Not as a question, but almost a statement of proof he needed for himself that everything worked out. I wanted to ease whatever was weighing on his mind.

'I've seen you,' I said, repeating his words from the first time he *saw* me in his office. 'I've felt you. There's no reason to worry anymore about what I can handle.'

'Hot or cold?' he asked. 'I need to know if the other night was too much. If the spanking was—'

'Hot. The only time I start to feel cold is when you pull away.'

That seemed to take him off guard. Whatever internal battles he fought, it was clear on his face that they were raging. He was confident, sure of himself, but over the past weekend, I'd caught glimpses of a man beneath that I didn't understand. But wanted to desperately. Because all signs pointed to him caring about me.

'You've been with women,' I started.

'Yes,' he said with a faintest 'duh' in his voice.

'I feel like you worry about me a significant amount. Did you worry about the others like this?'

'No, I didn't worry about them the way I do you.'

'Is something about me different than the others?'

'Yes. Why do you ask?'

'You don't strike me as a man that asks for much. Yet you've gone out of your way to make sure I'm comfortable.'

He looked at me like I'd just took a hammer to a mirror and shattered his prized possession.

'The other women were all masochists.'

'They enjoyed pain?'

'Yes, they took pleasure in it.'

'I liked the spanking,' I restated, hoping he believed me this

182

time. 'And you're intense, but never too rough with me, and you don't scare me or hurt me.'

'It's not the same.'

'I don't understand why. Why are they masochists and I'm not? You worry about me, but not them? Do you think I'm weak and can't handle things?' That was the exact opposite of what I was going for. I wanted to show Jack, and myself, I was more. That I didn't need constant worry. 'I've enjoyed everything we've done.'

'Every woman I've been with, I've found based on their self-proclamation of being passive and masochistic. It's a lifestyle they live and breathe. You are not a part of that lifestyle. You like a spanking, but there's way more to it than that.'

I swallowed hard. 'So, if this is a lifestyle, and they enjoy receiving pain, does that mean you enjoy inflicting it?' My voice was soft, and I held my breath awaiting his answer.

He stared at me for a long moment.

'Good-bye, Lana.'

He pulled away, opened the door, and walked out.

'Wait!' I went after him. 'You can't just cut me out like that.'

He spun on his heel, kissed me quickly, then went back to walking away. There was pain behind his movements, his eyes. He opened his car door.

'I'm standing right in front of you, just trying to understand. I wouldn't judge you.'

He shook his head. 'Of course you wouldn't. Because you're better than that.' He wasn't condescending, actually, he sounded wounded.

'Please,' I said, as he sat in the driver seat and shut the door. His window was down, and I bent to face him. 'Please don't leave.'

'I need to.'

He reversed, pulled out on the road, and left within seconds.

The walls around Jack were chipping, but the more pieces that fell, the more he pulled away. I was walking a fine line between understanding him and shoving him away.

I had no idea how to help. How to feel. How to reach him. But there I stood, standing and watching him drive away. While I waited. Waited for an answer that may never come, and a man that may never return.

'God damn it!' Harper yelled at the TV. 'Top of the eighth inning and our pitcher gives up a home run.' She huffed, and sat back on the couch. She got heated whenever watching baseball.

After Jack left, Harper came home and started dinner, while I did some chores around the house. It was nice to be in the same room with my best friend, relaxing with no agenda, and enjoying the evening.

Yet, my mind drifted to the conversation I'd had with Jack.

I'd asked him if he enjoyed inflicting pain, and he didn't answer. The look on his face was one of disgust. Disgust with himself? The women he'd been with? Me? I had no idea. But if he liked giving pain, what did that mean for us? Because he was right, a spanking and some rough sex was different than some of the stuff I'd spent the past hour Googling.

If he was deep into this kind of lifestyle, what did that make him? A sadist?

If so, could I handle the next step?

Based on what I read, and what he said about it being a lifestyle, I didn't know. Of course consent was always involved, but the reason I loved being with him so much was because he made me feel empowered. Even when he was exercising his dominance, I always consented and felt taken care of while giving up my control.

These women from his past were different than me. He'd made

184

that clear. But maybe that was a good thing. Maybe he cared on a different level then? Or maybe I was looking at angles that didn't exist and grasping at explanations without proper facts. One such thing that worried me was whether my difference from his past interactions with women was a bad thing. If I wasn't a masochist, perhaps he wasn't getting his needs fully met?

Jesus, I had no idea! The man shut down every time I broached a topic he didn't like.

'What's up with you?' Harper asked, looking at me from across the room. A commercial was on, which meant her attention was momentarily taken away from the game.

'Men are confusing. That's all,' I said.

As if the universe could hear me, my phone rang. I reached for it on the coffee table.

'It's my dad,' I said, reading the caller I.D.

Harper frowned at the phone like it was the anti-Christ calling. 'I'll give you some privacy.' She aimed the remote at the TV, and paused the game. 'Yell when you're done.'

She walked to her room, and I answered. 'Hi, Dad.'

The man barely returned my texts and hadn't taken my calls in the past. For him to be calling after seven o' clock at night, when he would usually be at home with his wife, was odd.

'Hi, Pumpkin. How are you?'

'Ah, fine.' I was wondering what he was doing suddenly calling me, but my politeness won out. 'How are you?'

'Well . . . I'm alright, I suppose.' The tone of his voice followed by a long sigh made a familiar sting in my chest rise.

Guilt.

Confusion.

Sadness.

My dad knew which strings to pull, and he could do it with a single inflection of his vowels. That was all it took for my mind

185

to race, thinking he needed me. Thinking I could somehow help whatever was bothering him. Thinking we were still on the same team.

We aren't, I reminded myself. We hadn't been on the same team for a long time. But old habits were impossible to break, so I asked, 'You sure everything is okay?'

'Yes. Seeing you today was just a reminder of how much I'm missing out on. You looked so pretty. Happy.'

My eyes suddenly ached and strained to keep tears behind them.

'Thank you,' I whispered. His words were so kind. It melted a piece of my heart that had been continually freezing for the past ten years. 'I am happy.'

'Is it that man that makes you so happy? Jack, right?'

'Yes. It's still new, but—'

'He likes you, I can tell.'

I hoped so.

'I've been doing a lot of thinking since you quit. I was rash in dismissing you. I think you'd do great at Case-VanBuren.'

My heart wanted to ask why, but my head picked up on the slight altering of his voice, which made me realize that this wasn't him calling to fix things between us. This was a sales pitch.

He was putting on the professional hat.

'I appreciate that, but I have a job for the summer now.'

'Of course, and I wouldn't want to get in the way of that. Perhaps we can do something off the books to get you cemented in the company, then you can work while going to school, maybe oversee a single account, just to get your feet wet.'

'Are you serious? You want me to take over an account on my own?'

'Well, you'd have to land it first, but yes.'

'Wait, land it?'

186

And there was the second sigh. 'I wasn't lying when I said before that the Denver branch is struggling. We need a new client with substantial investment means to get Denver performing at the same level as New York.'

And the dots connected.

My entire body deflated like a balloon that had just been stabbed with a steak knife.

'You want me to get Jack to invest in your company, don't you?'

'I'm giving you the opportunity you said you wanted. You wanted to work for me. Be an associate.'

Actually, I wanted to be a Finance Analyst. Something I'd told him several times over the years, yet he still didn't seem to know.

I shook my head. 'Here, I thought you actually called because you cared.'

'I do. I care about your future and I want you at Case-VanBuren.'

'Because you think I can benefit you somehow now. You had no problem letting me walk out, telling me Brock was taking over, and kicking me to the curb.'

'You're being dramatic, Lana.'

Those words stuck to my stomach like day-old liquor in a burning gut. Only instead of day-old, it was more like ten years. It was always me being dramatic. Not the truth. Not the truth then, and not the truth now.

'I can't help you.'

'Just talk to Jack. Set up a meeting for us to discuss business.'

By 'business,' my father meant trying to sway Jack into entrusting his money to them on some level.

'No,' I said sharply. I wouldn't use Jack like that, and I wouldn't turn a blind eye to my father obviously using me.

187

He huffed like he had a right to be frustrated with me. 'I told you, I'd make you an associate. You can help with an investment strategy for his funds. This is something you could actually put on your resumé.'

'No,' I said again, calmly this time.

'If Denver gets a client like Jack Powell, there would be no need for Brock to be here. He could go back to New York.'

My heart stopped. My dad was pulling out the big guns of persuasion now. Using my fear and unease of Brock being in the same city against me. I hated that Brock was so close. That his encounters caught me off guard and put me on a higher anxiety level, knowing he was near. But I still couldn't do that to Jack.

'What do your wife and Brock say about this grand plan of yours?'

There was a long pause, and I heard my father shuffle like he did when he was nervous. 'Brock will play ball. And Anita wants what's best for both Brock and the company.'

Uh-huh. Everything in my body was sick with disgust and realization that this was what my father and my relationship had descended to.

'I can't help you,' I said. 'If you want Jack Powell's business, you'll have to acquire it without me.'

'We'd have to woo him.'

Which was why he was coming to me. But I wasn't going to help with this.

'Well, good luck with that.'

My father scoffed. 'You talk about your dislike of Brock. I give you an opportunity to work for me, gain distance from Brock, and you refuse. Stands to reason that your issues with him are more in your mind than reality.'

Knock. Out.

In a verbal left hook, my father managed to call me a liar,

188

defend Brock, insult me, and blame this entire mess and the lack of a client on me in one fell swoop. All while maintaining the passive aggressive approach and using words like 'issues.' And it hurt worse than anything he'd ever said.

'Good bye,' was all I managed to get out before the tears spilled over. I tossed my phone on the couch and caught the water before it could skate further down my cheeks. I wouldn't cry over this. Reality was too much to handle, but crying would only prove to myself that I gave weight to his words. And I wouldn't.

Maybe there really was nothing left of the man I once knew as my father. Because all I could see was manipulation.

I called for Harper to let her know I was off the phone.

'Everything okay?' she asked, resuming her seat.

'Yes and no.' I needed to tackle one thing at a time. Since I wouldn't help my father with his scheme of 'wooing' my boyfriend for his professional gain, I'd stick to the more important issue: understanding Jack.

'What was your dad calling about?'

'He's just trying to suck up to get something out of me.'

'Dick,' Harper mumbled.

'Yeah,' I agreed. 'But there's more than that going on.'

'With Jack?'

'Yes. Whenever I try to get any kind of personal details out of him, he gives me a little, then totally shuts down.'

'Just enough to drive you crazy, huh?'

'Exactly!' I threw my hands up. 'And now I'm sitting here wondering what to do. Trying to plan some kind of solution based on what may or may not even be relevant.'

'Slow down,' Harper said. 'First, you start with what you know for sure.'

I took a deep breath and mentally calculated all the tiny tidbits of Jack I'd gathered over the length of our relationship.

'He controls his world. He's intense.'

'Duh,' Harper agreed.

'He doesn't think so himself, but he's thoughtful and kind. He makes me feel strong, and he's ...'

Harper raised her brows, waiting for me to finish.

'Let's just say his intensity carries into the bedroom.'

'Ah.' She nodded. 'And you are comfortable with everything he does, in and out of that bedroom, right?'

'Yes. Jack is very considerate of me. He pushes my limits, but in a good way. I've never been scared, and he's never restrained me.'

'Has he done anything else?'

I took a deep breath. 'He's spanked me.' The words were barely audible.

She stared at me for a moment. When she didn't say anything, I moved quickly past that little fact and went on.

'He's close with Cal, they're like brothers. Grew up together, and he said they protected each other, which makes me think something happened.'

'Okay, there's the speculation. You have to be careful with that.'

'He came from meager means. He speaks fondly of his mother, and hardly at all about his father, yet he's the one who raised him after his mother died.'

She pursed her lips and tapped her chin. 'So, based on the facts, the guy you're dating has a shit ton of layers.'

'It would seem so.'

The first night I met him, he stepped in and protected me. I'd also seen the look of sheer terror on his face. Heard him talk about Cal. Felt his control and experienced his brand of love-making. There was a lot going on behind the face of Jack Powell

'I think that if you want to continue this relationship and have any kind of growth, you have to get to know each other on these different levels. So, now, after having gone through the facts, you have to decide what you want and what your limits are. What are the things you're willing to concede on?'

'I want things with us to work.'

'But if he's not being honest with you, and you aren't being honest with him, you have to realize that could come back to bite you in the ass.'

'How am I not being honest?'

A look of pity laced her face. 'Have you told him about Brock? What he did to you?'

'No,' I shot out quickly.

'Do you have any intention of telling him?'

I opened my mouth to reply, then shut it, because reality hit. 'No,' I whispered. 'Because it's shaming. I don't want to remember it. I'm trying to move past it.'

Harper nodded. 'I know. Your past comes with demons I wouldn't want to remember either. But you never know what demons line Jack's closet. If *you* aren't willing to share yours . . .'

'I can't expect him to share his,' I finished.

I closed my eyes, because what I'd thought was a storm brewing between us, was turning into to a massive hurricane. There was a lot to think about. Like how to proceed with Jack. If I told him about Brock, would he look at me differently? Pity me? Think I'm tainted or damaged beyond repair?

Jack was the one man who looked at me and treated me like I was beyond some ruined little girl. And I didn't want to lose that. But I wanted him. So much. In every way. Harper was right. It would have to be a give and take. Question was, what would I allow myself to give?

191

Chapter 16

I pounded on Jack's front door. It was just after eight o'clock and I'd only seen him a few hours ago, when he dropped me off, but this couldn't wait.

'Lana?' he opened the door. He was still wearing his jeans and button-up. As if the idea of relaxing escaped him.

'I'm sorry for just showing up.' The whole half-hour drive to his place, I'd spent thinking about why what I was about to do was a bad idea. Yet, I still showed up.

'Are you okay?' he asked fiercely, like he may just go kick some ass if I asked him to. The notion made me happy. The truth was, no, I wasn't okay.

'Can we talk for a second?'

He opened the door and led me in to the living room. 'Can I get you something to drink or eat?'

'No, thank you,' I said, and paced in his living room, my fingers threading and unthreading. 'I just need to talk to you.'

'Okay,' he stood tall and still and crossed his arms. Waiting. I, however, continued to pace in front of the fireplace like a fidgety wreck.

Deep breath.

'I . . . I want to tell you about something that happened to me.'

He lifted his chin, his brows gathering slightly with questions. If I didn't get this out now, I never would.

Another deep breath . . .

'I was raped when I was thirteen.'

The words held so much weight, that the moment they slipped out of my mouth, I felt lighter, and instantly sick. As if purging this secret was like purging part of my being.

'I'm telling you this because it's not fair for me to ask for so much from you and give you nothing in return. I trust you, that's why I'm telling you. I just . . .'

I shook my head, unable to look at him, for fear of what I'd see. 'I don't want to talk about it. Because it's terrible. I understand the idea of not wanting to share something because it's so bad. But you,' I met his eyes for a moment, which looked like they were forged of black fire, 'You changed all that.'

I took a step toward him. 'I hate this,' I whispered. 'This secret . . . this feeling . . . it's been buried and a part of me for so long, I don't know who I am without it. Then, I met you, and you made me feel alive. Make me feel like there's more to life than the past. You're helping me move past it.'

His chest slowly rose on a long inhale. 'Jesus.' He ran a hand through his hair, but didn't move. I had no idea what to expect. What to say.

My body started shaking slightly and he cupped my shoulders and looked me over. 'What's happening?' he asked.

I could barely hear him. Blood was rushing to my ears, my mind was fogging, and my vision was wavering. I couldn't breathe, so I tried harder, but it only made it worse.

'P-panic . . .' I said, but it sounded like a muffled sound in my eardrums. I hadn't had an attack in so long, but I couldn't stop it this time. My legs lost their stability, and before I hit the ground, Jack caught me. The last thing I felt was his big arms surrounding me, as my entire body went numb, and my mind went black.

*

'Lana . . .'

Jack was calling me. I looked around to find him, but it was foggy.

'There you go, baby. Open your eyes.'

I blinked several times. Finally, the haze cleared, and Jack was looking down at me. I was laying on the couch.

'Oh no,' I whispered. 'I passed out, didn't I?'

He stroked the back of his fingers along my cheek. 'Is this a recurring thing for you?'

'Not for a while.' By that, I meant not since Brock had moved to New York and away. Harper was the only person who knew and believed me about Brock and the incident. I'd never said it out loud before to another person since that night. Between my father calling earlier, and admitting this dark secret to Jack, my anxiety got the better of me and I tapped out.

'How long was I out?'

'Thirty-four seconds,' Jack said. I couldn't help but smile. He'd actually counted. 'I was going to call an ambulance, but you were mumbling, your eyes fluttering, and you were breathing. Your heart was racing, though.'

'There's no need for an ambulance. I'm fine.' I looked up at him. Concern laced his face. 'Thanks for catching me.'

He cupped my face in both hands and kissed my forehead along my hairline several times. The gesture was so sincere, so sweet, like he cherished me.

'I didn't mean to come here and be dramatic and—'

'You just said something out loud that, judging by the effect on you, you haven't spoken of much. Don't you dare be sorry or think that's dramatic. That's brave.'

'I pretend like it's not a big deal, but, it still haunts me. I just wanted to tell you because you make me feel better. Make me feel stronger and happier.' Though I left the part out about who the

194

person was, I'd still told him the one thing I'd never told anyone outside of Harper. Of course, I'd told my father, but he didn't believe or support me.

'Does this change things between us?'

He nodded. 'Yes.'

I folded my lips together. It was what I was afraid of. He'd think I was dirty or ruined—

'I've never respected anyone more in my life,' he said, and my pulse skipped. 'But this is the first time where I'm fighting my instinct on what to do.'

'What do you mean?'

He shook his head. 'I want to make this better ... yet, I feel like all I've done is make it worse. Played on a bad moment of your life.'

'You haven't. That's why I told you. Because of how much I do trust you and how much I love our time together. All of it.'

He shook his head. 'There's something dark in me.'

'You can tell me,' I whispered.

His eyes smoldered as they fastened on my face. 'You're tapping on fractured glass.'

I reached and held his hand, brought it to my mouth, and kissed his palm. I wouldn't push. That wasn't the point of me telling him. I did it because Harper was right, there was give and take. I gave what I could. I gave the truth, omitting one detail. Which was the who. It was up to Jack if he'd take it and give back.

'You're the only one who makes me feel out of control. And it terrifies me,' he said in a low tone. 'You say you *love* our time together? I don't know how to *love* correctly.' His jaw tightened. 'I could be the worst thing for you, and yet I can't give you up.'

'I don't want you to,' I said.

'There will come a time where I can't keep you.'

'Are you still worried I can't handle you?'

195

'Yes,' he said in a gruff tone. 'But in a very different way than I imagined.'

My lips parted on a silent gasp. Jack's secrets ran deep. Whatever waters we were treading were dark ones. He stood up and looked down at me.

'I don't want you driving home. I'll call Harper to come get you.'

'Wait.' I rose to face him. 'I'm fine. Please, can we finish a single conversation?'

'It's not a good idea.'

'Why?'

'Because!' he faced me, so close that I felt his warmth dance from him, heating my own skin, and he wasn't even touching me. 'What I want to do right now is ...'

'Is what?'

'It's sick.'

'What do you want to do?'

He stepped toward me. 'I want to fuck you.' He scoffed. 'How disgusting is that? You bare your soul, and you know what instinct drives me? Taking you. Feeling you. Surrounding you. Anything to take away the pain you felt. But all I'm doing is adding to it.'

'You're not! Don't you understand? It's the connection we have that I need. I want you too. So much. Because you're my goodness. From my memories to my experiences ... everything good is from you.'

He shook his head, and took another step toward me, then another.

'Push me away, Lana.'

'No,' I whispered.

He took another step. 'Push. Me. Away.'

'No,' I said more firmly.

196

'You asked me if I enjoy inflicting pain?' Another step. 'The answer is no. I don't. I know what it feels like to be beaten, marred, cut, and broken. Throughout every moment, as it happened, I thought that pain was part of love. Because nothing else made sense.'

My heart broke open for the man before me. 'It was your dad, wasn't it? That hurt you?'

'Until the day I outgrew him.' Another step. 'I would have killed him. I almost did. Cal stopped me. He's the reason my father didn't die years ago by my hand.'

My eyes shot wide, and the tears I'd been fighting lined them. 'Is that what you want me to share? How I'm a monster? That pain translates into some kind of fucked-up notion of love? Or caring?'

'Yes.' Because that was Jack. His scars and all. And he was trusting them to me. Just like I trusted him.

'Every day, I worry I'm him. Will become him. Because, while I hate pain, a twisted part of me loves watching your pretty skin turn pink from my hand. The feel of your ass warm and red, the snapping sound of my hand coming down.' His eyes darkened another degree. 'They're conflicting emotions. I hate it and love it. It's a part of me. And all I can think of is getting lost to that part. Because with you, that's what happens.' He was right against me, mouth brushing mine. 'I lose myself to you.'

My back met the wall, and he surrounded me. 'Now you know the fucked-up piece of my brain. So, I'll tell you one more time: Push me away.'

I swallowed hard. 'No.'

His mouth crashed down on mine. I kissed him back. Crazed and ready for him. Wanting to lose myself right back.

I breathed his name. 'Thank you.' I kissed him hard, clung to him, clawed at his clothes. 'Thank you,' I repeated. I wanted to know him. To understand, to feel him on every level he'd let me, and he finally let me in. Give and take.

Now I wanted him to take me. In every way. Because when I was with him, a part of him, I felt better. Was better.

I tore at his shirt and pants, and my clothes were off in seconds. He lifted me, our mouths never breaking, as I wrapped my legs around his hips and he walked us to the plush rug in front of the fireplace. He grabbed a condom quickly and was back on top of me.

There was no power play, no exchange of control, no rules. Just us.

Laying on the rug, his forearms rested on either side of my face. I kissed his biceps, his shoulders, his chest. He gripped the rug and surged inside of me.

He growled my name and thrust again, and again. Each time, I lost more of myself to him, letting him take whatever he needed, allowing myself to let go.

Hooking my ankles around him, I pulled him as close as I could. All of his weight rested on top of me, and it was the heaviest, most wonderful feeling in the word. Every inch of our skin was smashed together as he rocked in and out, kissing me deep and thoroughly until I didn't care if I ever caught my breath again. Because I had Jack. Right there with me, the only oxygen I needed.

My body lit up and his dark eyes fastened on mine for only a moment. He was gentle, but hard. Slow and urgent at the same time. Littering kisses along my face and neck, he said nothing, but I felt his intentions. With every glide, every kiss, every sweep of his hands, he was taking it away. Taking the nightmares, the weight of the past and the shame.

He was taking it all.

I'd never felt like I had a true partner until that moment.

Unburdening this onto him, he was choosing to stay and deal with this with me.

'Thank you,' I whispered, hugging him with every fiber of my strength.

'I'm here,' was all he said.

Burying my face in his neck, I breathed in every single atom that made up this incredible man. I was surprised when my body lit up with release instantly. Between the emotion, connection, and pleasure, it was almost too much. But I rode the wave, and he was right there with me.

The only thing I wondered was: How will I ever live without this man?

After several long kisses and dawn finally breaking, I reluctantly headed out of Jack's home and back to my car. It was Monday, and work started in a couple of hours. I still had to drive back home to change and shower.

I sat in my car for a moment, replaying all the ground we'd covered last night. I felt like I finally understood where Jack came from. I didn't have all the details, but there was truth between us. Trust on a new level, and that was exciting.

Putting the key in the ignition, I adjusted my seat to reach the pedals, and—

I looked down.

I'd driven to Jack's house last night. My car was out front the whole time. There was no reason to adjust my seat, unless someone had messed with it.

I looked around, a buzz of panic racing through me. The car was quiet, clean, nothing out of place. I rummaged through the few papers on the back seat. Everything was as I had left it, yet everything felt like it'd been touched.

Maybe I was being paranoid. Maybe I had adjusted my seat last night before going in. In the past, when I'd been in a panic-induced mode, I forgot things.

Or maybe the icky feeling was legitimate.

I pulled onto the road, and headed back toward Golden. In one night, I'd gone from anguish and hurt, to fear and anxiety, to finally a little peace and lots of pleasure. My body was exhausted from the emotional rollercoaster.

A major hurdle was crossed. But, as I sped down the highway, I glanced around my car, and couldn't help but feel that somehow, not everything was as it seemed.

Chapter 17

'Hey, Lana, there's an older guy here to see you,' Edith said, as she rounded toward my cubicle. It was midweek, and my money was on the UPS guy, since it had become my job to sign for all the packages lately.

I looked up to find my dad near the entrance, searching me out. It had been a couple days since I talked to him on the phone.

I got up and headed him off by the break room.

'What are you doing here?'

'Thought I'd take you to lunch.'

'I meant what I said. I'm not helping you lure Jack in to your company.'

'Can't a father just take his daughter to lunch?'

My father has several masks he put on, and I knew them all well. Today, he was going for logical. He may be changing tactics, but his mission was the same.

'I have plans already.'

'Oh? With Jack?'

'With some co-workers.' Jack had been super busy the last couple days. Word around the office buzzed about a new resort opening in Great Britain. He'd warned me he'd be busy, but this weekend would be ours to look forward to together. And I was looking forward to it.

'I was hoping we could chat. I came off a bit harsh the other day, and I wanted to clear the air.'

'Do you still want me to help you with Jack?'

'My offer stands. It would be a meeting, something you could set up, and could end with you benefiting and Brock leaving, since that seems to be important to you. But I could be wrong. Maybe him being closer will give you two a chance to bond.'

The hint of threat in my father's voice was something I'd never heard before. A chilling fear crept up my throat. He was playing dirty, and I was trying to stay strong, especially with everything that had happened recently.

No matter how hard I tried, I couldn't stomach the idea of Brock, much less the sight of him. Getting him as far away as possible was appealing. Part of me was finding strength, while the other part had regressed three years in the past few weeks. I hadn't had paranoia or a single panic attack in a long time. Now with Brock being back, I only prayed the nightmares didn't start up again too.

I looked at my father. The one man in a girl's life she should always be able to count on, and for the first time, I had no idea to what level he'd stoop to get what he wanted.

'I can't do lunch today,' I said.

The smirk he unleashed was paired with renewed anger. His ears were turning red from the inner rage he was fighting. 'Some other time then,' he said through gritted teeth.

He turned and walked out. Whatever kind of trouble he was in, or Case-VanBuren was in, I didn't know. But what was clear was that I wasn't free from whatever shadows were following my father. Problem was, he was casting his own shadow over me as well, and the sickness in my gut twisted.

How much trouble was he in?

*

My phone lit up with a text from Jack: Meet me downstairs now.

I glanced around my cubicle. It was four o'clock, still another hour or so to go before work was over. My floor manager was nowhere in sight, though.

'Hey, Edith?' I said, looking over her wall.

'Yeah?'

'I can't find Devin, will you let him know I'm taking my last break?'

'Sure,' she said.

I locked my purse in my desk, and hustled down to the lobby. I had ten minutes, fifteen if no one noticed. Jack was nowhere to be found. Then I saw his town car across the street. At least, I was pretty sure it was his. The windows were so tinted, they looked black, and I couldn't see who was inside.

Taking my chances, I walked over and the back door opened.

Jack was inside. I slid in, and he locked the doors. The partition was up, giving us privacy from the driver. Jack's mouth was on my mine in record time.

'Well, hello to you too,' I said between kisses. He undid the first few buttons of my blouse, enough to tug my bra down and expose my breasts. He latched on immediately.

I gasped and threaded my fingers in his hair. Outside the car, a few people passed, never the wiser as to what we were doing, thanks to the tinted windows. It was thrilling, though. Rounding second with only a pane of glass between us and the real world. But that's how Jack affected me, he simply took me to *our* world.

'It's a busy week,' he rasped, and sucked hard on my nipple. 'Meetings,' nip, 'calls,' lick, 'but I needed a taste of you.'

We only had minutes. Between my break and Jack's obviously busy schedule, I loved that he made time for me. That he seemed addicted to me the way I was to him.

'How about more than a taste?' I said breathlessly and fumbled with his belt. I shoved his pants down, his cock springing free. He pulled a condom from his pocket and handed it to me without taking his eyes or his mouth from my body. My skin was buzzing, my core drenched just from his mouth on my breasts.

As I sheathed him in the condom, he hiked up my skirt to my waist, and peeled my panties off. When I went to straddle him, he stopped me.

'We need to do this carefully, baby, unless you want everyone to see the car rocking?'

I bit my lip and shook my head. 'Probably not a good idea.' I was the one who'd have to climb out of the car afterward.

'Then, once I have you in position, you are going to stay still, do you understand?'

'Yes.'

Jack adjusted so he was sitting in the middle of the seat. Thank God for spacious cars. With his cock out, yet clothed otherwise, he spread his arms along the back of the headrests, and stared at me. He looked like some kind of corporate sex god, and I was ready to go to my knees to please him.

'Come here,' he said. 'I want you to sit on me, take my cock deep in one slide, and stay just like that.'

I nodded and moved to do as instructed.

'But,' he said, with a wicked glint in his eye, 'I want your back against my chest.'

I frowned for a moment, then the position he wanted was clear, and I did as he asked.

With my back facing him, I moved to sit on his lap. With his legs between mine, his outer thighs brushing my inner thighs, I straddled him. The heels I wore today gave an extra four inches, which I needed so my feet could touch the floor. I thought I'd heard Harper refer to this position once as reverse cowgirl.

204

He peppered kisses along my nape and shoulders, and I reached down to position his hard cock at my entrance.

'Good,' he said, when the tip nudged my opening. 'Now, sink all the way down, and watch as you do it.'

I did. The leather seat squeaking as I wiggled, adjusting to accommodate him. I groaned at the full feeling of him impaling me.

'Fuck, you feel good,' he rasped. 'Now, relax, baby.'

I leaned back against him, my head resting on his shoulder and my face nuzzling in his neck. I kissed along his throat, his ear, his jaw. I sat there with him deep inside me, taking a moment to appreciate the connectedness.

'Stay still,' he reminded me.

'Okay.'

With that, he cupped my sides in both hands, and thrust deeply.

My eyes widened, but I remained still. Jack pistoned in and out of me so fast and hard that I almost came instantly. We'd gone from being slow and still, me within his vise grip, motionless, as he fucked me with fervor.

With just his hips working up and down, the car made little movement. He clamped one arm around my waist, while the other slid down and rubbed my clit.

'Oh, God.' I laid against him, helpless to do anything else but stay still while he conquered my body. My thigh muscles burned from holding the position. Still. I would do as he said. It was a drugging feeling, being totally taken over and pleasured while I sat there, allowing it. Letting him. Feeling nothing but him.

'Come for me, baby.' He fucked me harder, rubbed faster.

My body responded immediately, shuddering violently, coating his cock with my release so that he slipped even faster and easier in and out.

'That's it,' he rasped, his hold tightening on me as he followed me over the edge of bliss.

He languidly rubbed my clit, drawing out every ounce of pleasure until I couldn't sit still. He slowly pulled out of me. He trailed his lips from my neck to my arm as I moved and sat next to him. I adjusted my clothes as he took care of the condom.

He zipped up his pants and refastened his belt.

I reached for my panties on the floor, but he snagged them before I could.

'I'm keeping these,' he said, and put the lacy undergarment in the inside pocket of his jacket.

'You can't expect me to walk around with nothing beneath my skirt for the rest of the day.'

'That's exactly what I expect. Because I'll be walking around with the scent and smell of you on me for the rest of the day.'

I kissed him. Long and deep and hot. Jack did things to me that I couldn't explain. He made me feel like a wanton. This may have been quick, but it left me feeling whole, not cheap. We stole moments where we could.

'Thanks for making time for me,' I said quietly.

'I always have time for my priorities,' he said.

I opened the door and made sure he caught a glimpse of my ass before climbing out of the car and adjusting my skirt.

'You're a wicked tease,' he said.

I looked at him through the open door, loving the sight of him just pleasured. By me. Pride and so much happiness flooded through me.

'Maybe. Guess you'll have to visit me on my next break to see how bad of a tease I really can be.'

'Sounds like an enticing invitation.'

I shrugged and smiled. 'Enjoy the rest of your day, Mr Powell.'

*

The week dragged on, mostly because I didn't get to see Jack much. A few calls and texts were better than nothing. After our quickie a few days ago, he made a point of staying in touch. Yesterday, he stopped by again, but it was so brief, I got one amazing kiss in before he had to go.

It was torture and I missed him.

After our breakthrough last Sunday night, I was feeling better about the direction of our relationship. And that we officially had one. A weight had been lifted from both of us, and we were moving on. Together.

'You think the big boss man will take you to the UK with him?' Edith said, hovering, as usual, over my cubicle.

'Excuse me?'

Her judgmental gaze could have melted flesh. 'I know what's going on. The way you sneak out of here. I saw you get out of Jack Powell's car the other day, looking . . . ' she gave a disgusted expression, 'tousled.'

Heat lit my face and embarrassment took over. This was one thing I wanted to avoid. But the details of what she said made another emotion rise: anger.

'Did you follow me?'

'You left in such a hurry, it was obvious.'

'No, you said you saw me get out of Jack's car. So you would have to have followed me down to the lobby and watched where I went.'

'Don't flatter yourself. You've been acting weird, and it shows in your work.'

'You aren't my superior.'

'Clearly. You treat your superiors much differently.'

That made bile rise in my throat. I was defending Jack and our relationship. But I was done being pushed around.

'You know what? My personal life is none of your business.'

She scoffed and mumbled a less than flattering name for me, as she walked back to her cubicle.

'He's leaving the country to open the new resort, you know.'

I stared at Edith. I did know that a new one was opening, and figured Jack would be traveling, but surely nothing long term. Whatever Edith's problem was, I didn't want a part in it. It was clear from day one that she had a thing for Jack. I had a short time left of this job and summer to get through, then this would all be behind me and focus shifted back to where it should be. Moving forward with my life, in every sense of the word.

With Jack.

My father, Edith, or a busy schedule wouldn't get in the way of that.

Chapter 18

I jammed my key into my front door and unlocked it. It had been a long week, and thank God it was Friday. Maybe Jack and I could spend the weekend together.

I set my purse down, tossed my keys on the table, and stalled.

I glanced around my little house. It was dark. Harper wasn't home, but a chill raced up my spine, because everything looked off.

'Hello?' I called out, staying by the doorway. No answer.

I took a deep breath and looked around. Paranoia was getting the better of me. But there were subtle things that weren't right. My home felt like it'd had company, yet no outward signs would show that. Except for the rug by the door. Normally straight, thanks to Harper's allergies to crooked things, it was off. Like someone had walked along it after we left this morning. The accent pillows on the couch didn't look right either. I could have sworn the yellow one was on the left this morning.

'Hey,' Harper said, walking up behind me, and I jumped and screamed a little. 'Whoa, sorry, didn't mean to scare you.' She looked at me, then at the dark house. 'Were you going to stand in the doorway all night?'

'Does the house feel off to you?'

Harper frowned and took several steps in, turning on the lights. 'No. Why?'

I shook my head. 'I feel like someone has been here.'

'Was the door locked?'

'Yeah.'

Harper quickly checked the windows, no break in, nothing stolen. 'Everything looks fine to me.'

I took a deep breath. 'I just feel like I'm being watched, or someone is messing with my life.'

Harper faced me and cupped my shoulders. 'How long has it being going on this time?' she asked gently.

'What do you mean?'

'The paranoia, Lana. It's getting worse. Are you having nightmares or panic attacks too?'

'No,' I cut myself off. 'Well, a small attack recently, but there was a lot going on.' I had told Jack something personal, tied with my father and his annoying nonsense. 'I'm just not feeling great. But, maybe I am a little paranoid.'

'Which you have every right to be. Brock is back in town. I'd feel shitty too. The guy is creepy, and with everything going on, I'm not surprised.'

'Maybe you're right.' Maybe I was just being paranoid because Brock was so close and I knew it. I also knew things with my dad and the company were not going super great. But I still couldn't shake this feeling that someone was messing with me on purpose. Subtly leaving a trail that I wasn't invisible and I was on their radar.

'I'm sorry, I'm not trying to discredit your feelings,' Harper said, and took out a pot to boil water for dinner. 'Have you noticed anyone snooping around? Brock hasn't shown up anywhere near you, right?'

'Only by accident, it would seem.'

'Maybe that's it. He's in the same city now, works for your dad for Christ sake. Maybe it's that feeling like you could bump into him at any moment, and your lack of control in the situation is making you nervous.'

That did make sense. 'Yeah, I'm sure that's it.'

'I'll just pay better attention to things,' I said softly. This kind of unease could drive a person crazy. 'Why can't he just go back to where he came from?'

Harper shrugged. 'Hopefully, he will. Your dad only needs him here until they land a new client, right?'

'Yeah.' Could I last that long? Already, my mind was playing tricks on me, making me feel increasingly worried and scared. I hated this so much. It was the same terror that I had battled as a kid. Lying in bed and waiting. Wondering if he was going to sneak into my room again. Wondering if he'd show up out of nowhere and wreck my life. Just waiting to be destroyed.

I felt instantly sick. It was the shadows, not the darkness, that terrified me. Because you never knew what or when such things would emerge.

There was one thing I could do to speed Brock's departure from Denver along. But that involved setting Jack up with my father's company and giving in to the notion that I was letting myself be used. And using Jack for my own gain. Which I'd never do.

I just wanted Brock gone.

I was tired of second-guessing everything in my life, waiting for the bad stuff to happen.

'How can I help?' I asked Harper, and headed into the kitchen, determined to get these thoughts out of my mind.

'You want to cut up some veggies for the salad?'

'Sure.' I got all the stuff from the fridge and started putting together the salad on the bar, while Harper manned the pasta and sauce at the stove.

'Aren't you leaving for your week off tonight?'

211

'Yeah, I was going to pack and eat, then take off. I'm excited to get away from this town for a bit.'

I nodded.

'So, how are things going with Jack?' she asked.

'Good,' I said. 'I feel like a teenager most of time, all giggly and checking my phone to see if he called.'

Harper nodded. 'Yeah, the honeymoon stage is the best. You seem happier.'

'I am. This last week has been different. Like we finally opened up enough to each other and are moving forward together.'

'Wow, sounds like you're getting serious about the boss man.' She smiled.

I nodded, and the truth hit me. I froze mid-cut into a carrot. 'I think I'm falling in love with him.'

Harper faced me. 'Be careful.'

'Why would you say that?'

'Because a man like Jack doesn't look like the long-term kind.'

'You don't even know him.'

'I know his type.'

'I'm sick of this. You tell me all the time what's wrong with me, what and who is bad for me, and you don't even know him.'

'I'm just trying to help. I worry, and don't want you to get hurt.'

'I'm a grown woman. And I care about Jack.'

'I know you do, but all the bad habits are starting up again.' I stilled, and so did Harper. 'You think someone is messing with you. You're getting paranoid and had a panic attack.'

'So, you think I'm making this up?' Hurt stuck in my lungs. 'Do you think my mind is getting the better of me?'

'I just think that you're under a lot of stress with Brock being back and, yes, it can mess with your mind.'

My chest felt tight and wanted to fold in on itself. 'I don't have proof, but I really think something isn't right. Someone is messing with me.'

Harper just looked at me with that pity expression, and it tore my soul in two. She was discrediting me.

'Just be careful,' she finally said. 'You are going down a path you worked really hard to get off of, and now you're dating a guy that requires a lot of emotional stamina. He has a world that is different from ours.'

'What does that mean? Because he has money and owns resorts?'

'That's part of it. Jack has a reputation and persona that comes with success and money. Other people, including women, will sniff that out, and you are . . .'

'Naïve.' I finished for her.

'It's smart to question what someone stands to gain from you. And trust?' She scoffed. 'You don't just hand that out.'

'I don't.'

'You did with Jack. Hell, you even cozied up to Cal at the beginning of summer.' That stung. Just in how she said it.

'Who I trust is my decision,' I said, and put the contents of the salad in the bowl, grabbed my purse and keys, and headed toward the door.

'Where are you going? Aren't you going to have dinner?'

I looked at my best friend. 'I'm not that hungry anymore. And I'm not losing my mind or making things up. Yes, Brock being back has affected me.' When all the other elements were peeled away, the truth was clear. 'I don't feel safe,' I admitted. 'Except when I'm with Jack.'

'I want you to feel safe, too. I'm not trying to push you away,' she said softly with hurt behind her eyes.

'I know. But that is what you're doing by not taking me seriously.'

*

213

After drinking my dinner at the little café two blocks down, I walked back to my house with a belly full of vodka and orange juice and tried to sort out what was going on in my world.

Everything felt like there was an underlying scheme. Like my father and his interest in Jack and me. Harper wasn't acting herself, and while Jack and I had made progress, there was so much more to come if this was to be a relationship of growth.

'Plus, I may be going crazy.'

Maybe Harper was right and I was being paranoid because Brock was just closer than usual. I walked up to the house, which was dark. Harper's car was gone. I felt terrible, walking out like that. She must have left for Aspen, and I hadn't said goodbye. I had reached my max on hearing the reasons I was struggling, failing, and naïve. I dug my keys out of my purse and stopped when I saw my car.

'Oh, my God . . .' I looked for a long moment, making sure it wasn't my vision wavering, but what I was seeing was real: All four of my tires had been slashed.

So much for thinking this was just my imagination. Which meant, if this was happening, someone had been in my house. And inside my car last week.

I looked around, feeling very exposed on a dark street. I felt violated. Worse, I didn't know who was behind it this time.

'Hey,' Jack said, opening the door to his house. While he was still dressed in semi-casual business attire, he was in bare feet. It was a good look for him. 'You must have read my mind, because I was just finishing up some business and was going to call you.'

I forced a smile the best I could. I didn't want to go into details about tonight until I was sure who was behind this mind fuck. So, I'd taken a cab to Jack's.

'I hate to invite myself, but do you mind if I stay with you this weekend?'

'I'd like nothing more than that.'

He let me in, and I picked up the small bag I'd packed. He raised a brow. 'Prepared, I see.'

I felt embarrassed. I wasn't trying to be a pushy girlfriend, I just couldn't step foot in my home. I'd literally sprinted through the house to gather a few things, then waited for the cab outside. And I couldn't handle this idea of someone lurking in the shadows. I needed evidence about who it was. So many times before, I'd been questioned. My gut told me maybe Brock had found out about my father trying to hire me and he was behind this.

I needed Brock gone.

'Lana,' he cupped my face and looked at me. 'What's wrong?'

I blinked away the scary thoughts. 'Just a tough week.'

'Have you been drinking?'

'Yes.'

He nodded. His hands skating from my neck to my shoulders. 'You're tense.' He looked over my body. 'Something happened. What?'

I shook my head quickly. There was no easy way to explain without explaining everything. And I didn't want to get into that tonight.

'Just a stressful week. Edith found out about us and was giving me a hard time. Then some asshole slashed my tires.' There, truth. Just not what was the key to my tension.

'What? Are you okay?'

'Yeah, I'm fine. It happened tonight. I'll get new tires tomorrow; I just didn't want to stay there.'

'Of course. Do you know who would do that, or do you think this is just random?' He took my bag and then my hand, and led me upstairs.

215

'I honestly don't know.' Not the whole truth, but the closest I'd ever come to lying to Jack. I was sure someone was behind all these little taunts. But that wasn't a clean story to dive into. More questions would arise, and I'd have to think about how to answer them. Questions like: why do you think Brock would do this? Yeah, not a question I wanted to answer. 'Is it okay if I just want to escape for a while?'

'That can be arranged.'

'Oh, yeah?'

He glanced at me as we walked into the master bathroom. 'I have some ideas.'

Turning on the bath, hot water filled up the claw-foot tub and steam rose.

Jack slowly took my clothes off, until I stood before him naked. He helped me into the warm water, and I laid back.

'You're not joining me?'

He knelt and rolled up the sleeves of his white button-up. 'This is for you to relax.'

Threading his fingers through my hair, he combed the locks up into a pile on my head and fastened it with the band I had on my wrist. The feel of his fingers along my scalp, brushing my hair away from my face, was soothing. Then, he reached into the tub and got a massive sponge and put soap on it. His soap. I loved the spicy smell.

'Sit up,' he said, and I did. He ran the sponge down my back, washing away the tension, seeming content to just see to me. It was a nice feeling ... being taken care of.

I hugged my knees to my chest, and he continued to massage my back and shoulders. I looked at him.

'Do you ever wish you could control life? Turn back time and make things go how you want them to go?'

'Every day.' He focused on his task and said, 'But, things

216

happen that we can't control. No sense in dwelling on that part. Simply take control of what you can now.'

If that didn't show the kind of man Jack was, nothing did. It made sense now. His mother's death, his father's treatment of him, all of it happened out of Jack's control. Which is why he looked for ways to control his world now.

'Is that why you have hardwood floors throughout the house? Because of your mother?'

A small smile tugged his mouth. 'The sound makes me think of good memories, before everything went to hell. It's amazing how one moment can change your entire world and course of fate.'

'I understand what you mean.' For Jack it was his mother's death. For me, it was the night Brock snuck into my room.

'Will you tell me about the squeaking door?'

He glared at the water, watching it run down my back, and continued to sponge my skin.

'All the doors in my father's house squeaked to high hell. When he stumbled through them, drunk usually, I knew what was coming.'

'He hurt you.' I didn't ask, rather stated.

'Usually, I was just in the way. But a few times, it got bad. I was eleven the first time I tried to defend myself, and he choked me until I passed out.'

'Oh, my God.' I grabbed his free hand.

'That was when I really understood that my own life was in someone else's hands, and I hated it. He thought he'd killed me. When I came to, he hugged me. Cried. Swore he'd never hurt me again. It was the one time I believed he gave a shit,' Jack scoffed. 'But his promise didn't last long.'

Tears danced along my eyes, and I unwove his fingers from mine, skimming them along my lower lashes. 'Don't cry for me.

217

I don't want it and I don't need it. I'm telling you this because you asked, and because I trust you.'

That made me want to cry for a different reason. Jack was so strong and intense. It made sense how growing up in that situation causes confusion and guilt and anguish. He couldn't control what happened to him any more than I could. Yet, somehow, we'd found solace in each other.

'I'm sorry for what you went through,' I whispered.

'I'm sorry for what you went through too, baby.'

'It's getting better,' I said with a soft smile. 'You make it better.'

'I'm glad. I just ... worry.'

I was hearing that word a lot lately. Coming from him, it made my chest hurt.

'What do you worry about?'

'You,' he said. 'If I'm what's best for you.'

'You are.'

He grinned and ran his thumb along my lower lip. 'I'm glad you think so.'

'You don't?'

'Not always.'

I sat up further, leaning over the side of the tub to face him. 'Why? I know there's a lot to work through. I know there are details and pasts that we both have that we haven't shared. But I want to get there. I'm tired of being afraid. I'm tired of worrying, and I'm tired of you worrying. I just want to be happy. With you.'

The truth rushed my brain. I couldn't really let go and be happy while being so close to Brock. I wouldn't run, but he needed to go. Because Jack was what I wanted. A future where I had pride and wasn't scared of who was haunting me was what I wanted.

'There's so much between us. Said and unsaid. But can you just believe me when I tell you that I ...'

218

He frowned. 'You what?'

With a heavy breath, I said the one truth I could, 'I love you.'

His face flashed with shock. I'd never seen Jack so caught off guard. But then sadness washed over him.

'You shouldn't.'

My ribs tightened. 'Well, I do.' I rose to my knees to meet him face on. 'I love you. And you can't tell me otherwise this time. Do *you* understand *me*?'

Something dark unleashed behind those smoky eyes, and he kissed me hard. My wet breasts rubbed against his crisp white shirt and tingles pricked over my skin. He devoured me, drinking me in with hard, deep swipes of his tongue.

I wrapped my arms around him, pressing my entire body against his. He maneuvered me back into the massive tub, not caring that he was fully clothed.

'Say it again,' he growled against my mouth.

'I love you,' I whispered.

Reclining against the tub with Jack on top of me, he wedged himself between my thighs and ate up my skin like he would an ice cream cone, licking and sucking from my neck to my breasts. Plucking my nipples with his teeth, then suckling them like a starving man.

There was something so hot about him being clothed, sopping wet in the tub with me while I writhed naked beneath him.

Reaching between us, I unclasped his pants and shoved them down enough for his hard cock to spring free, which was difficult because the wet material didn't cooperate well. But his white shirt was see-through now, sticking to every hard ridge and muscle of his stomach and chest.

'Make love to me,' I begged, and twisted my hips so that his cock nudged my entrance.

'I want to, baby,' he sucked my breasts, pulling so much flesh into his mouth that I couldn't breathe, the pleasure was so intense. 'Let's get out and I will.'

'Please.' I pulled him close, terrified of losing this connection. This moment. 'Please, just take me.'

'I can't. I don't have a condom.'

I cupped his face and met his eyes. 'I'm on the pill, and I'm clean.'

His brows sliced down, taking in my words and pondering them for a moment.

'I haven't been with anyone but you since I was checked last, and I'm clean too.'

I nodded. 'Okay.'

He wrapped one arm around me, and the other held the edge of the tub by my head. 'You sure?'

'Yes. So sure.'

He look at my face, into the depths of my soul, and thrust inside of me.

My eyes widened and Jack watched every expression I gave as he retreated, then thrust again.

'Lana . . .' he said my name with awe and pleasure that made me want to burst from the tenderness of it.

Long, slow, and hard was the pace he kept as he penetrated me over and over. His wet clothing scraped against my skin. He kept his eyes on me as he buried himself, each time deeper than the last. I clung to him. The water sloshed around us, tickling my skin as he took me with every ounce of power he had.

He growled with frustration because his pants were restricting his movement. I used my feet to push them down, and finally off his legs. He reached back and threw them out of the tub.

I whispered his name and sat up. He let me. He didn't seem pleased leaving my body, but once I had him sitting, I straddled his lap. His cock bobbed between us. I rocked my hips, sliding my clit along his length, but never penetrating. The fire of pleasure crackled further.

'You're teasing me again,' he rasped, and cupped my waist. I continued my foray of his body. Using it to tease us both a little as I removed his shirt and tossed it to the floor.

'I don't want to take your control,' I said. 'That's why I'm asking if you'll allow me to have you.'

His expression was fierce and soft at the same time. With his face at my breasts, he looked up at me.

'Yes,' he said.

I reached down and gripped his cock. I'd never had this much control before. I was the one who took over, who would join our bodies and set the pace. And he let me.

I positioned him at my entrance, then sank down, slowly. The feel of him, all of him, was incredible. There were no barriers between us. Just our world, there inside a tub, surrounded only by hot water and each other's skin.

'You're perfect,' he said, kissing my breasts like he would my mouth. He tasted my skin, and his hands explored, as if trying to feel every inch of me while I slowly rose, then sank down again.

I could tell he was fighting the urge to hug me tight, pull me close and take over, but he let me lead. Trusted me enough to let go of a little of his control.

I took him as far as I could. All the way to the hilt and stopped there. He cupped my neck and rained kisses over my mouth, my face, and my breasts. I'd never felt so . . .

Loved.

He didn't say it. But the way he held me was like he was silently worshiping my body, my whole being, and it brought tears to my eyes. I didn't want to rise up and pull away. I wanted to stay right there, with him deep.

So, that's what I did. I rocked back and forth, slowly circling my hips in his lap, but refusing to pull away. He hit every nerve ending deep inside, and I clung to him as I grinded harder. Wanting more.

'Baby, I'm there.'

'Me too.'

Fire built low in my belly, and I wrapped my arms around him and kissed the top of his head as my release took me over, my body gently shaking and convulsing.

He hugged me back, wrapping me up in those strong arms, his mouth at my breast as he trembled with his own release. I felt him, hot and strong, coming inside me. It was so powerful, it made my already sensitive body light up with another round of tremors.

Jack seemed to have felt it, because he sucked my nipple deeper, eating at my skin until there was not even a breath of space between us.

There was nowhere to go. Nowhere I wanted to go. Because right there, in Jack's arms, was the only world I wanted to be a part of.

222

Chapter 19

A low buzzing noise woke me from my sleep. A wonderful sleep spent in Jack's arms. I slowly got up, careful not to wake him. My phone was going nuts on the bedside table. It was seven in the morning on Saturday, and already I had nine missed calls and several texts. One from Harper, letting me know she made it to Aspen, the rest from my father.

Putting on my shirt and pants, I walked downstairs, leaving Jack sleeping in bed, and called my father back.

'There you are!' he said, with happiness in his voice.

'What is it? Is there an emergency?'

'No, not really . . .' he did that sigh thing I was starting to hate so much. 'I drove by your place last night and saw your car out front.'

'Really?' That awful feeling I'd been having? Just doubled. My father never sought me out like this. Much less randomly drove by my house. This seemed convenient. Too convenient. But would my father stoop to this kind of level? I'd expect creepy behavior like this from Brock, but my dad?

The world felt like it was spinning faster, and I couldn't gain footing. Playing on my fear would be a new low for my dad, but just the fact that I questioned him, thought of him as a foe before a friend, broke a final piece of my heart and hope that things could ever be different between us.

'Yes, everything okay? Do you need some new tires?' he asked.

'You're offering to buy me tires?'

'I worry about you.'

That was the last thing I wanted to hear from him. He hadn't *worried* when I needed him to. This was all a ploy.

I was making headway with Jack, at least, I thought so. Sure, he hadn't said he loved me back, but I was determined to continue to move forward. I needed to handle my life to prove to myself that fear would not dictate my world.

I couldn't deal with my dad, and I couldn't be in the same city as Brock. Maybe I was being paranoid about my father possibly having a hand in this, but I'd never wished for anything as hard in my life as I did in that moment: Please just let Brock go back to New York.

'Funny, you stop by my house the night my tires are slashed.'

'Lana, I need to be honest with you.'

'By all means,' I said sarcastically.

'It's Brock. There's something not right about him. I told him about the plan for you to bring in Powell—'

'I agreed to no such thing.'

'—and he's been acting strange ever since. I thought he'd like to go back to New York. Maybe it's best that way.'

'I'd like for him to go back to New York too.' Further, if it were possible. 'But, what are you saying? You think Brock is the one who slashed my tires?'

'I think Brock is capable of a lot of things,' he said lowly. 'But I can't get him out of here until the Denver branch is secure. I need a new client, Pumpkin. Believe me, I want him gone as much as you.'

'Then do that. You're the boss.'

He scoffed, and we both knew that the real boss was his wife.

224

'Most of the big fish we need around here are already taken, and we aren't big enough to get their attention, let alone sway them to our firm. I wouldn't ask if I wasn't desperate. Please. I don't want Brock near you any more than you do.'

My stomach knotted. All of my emotions were torn. I didn't think my father magically woke up and decided to be a decent parent out of the blue. No, he wanted something, and that was Jack's business. But maybe he wasn't in on this scaring me scheme like I thought. If he was worried about Brock? Tied with the fact that if it was him breaking into my car and house . . .

I choked on the thought.

I was back to square one. Wondering and worrying when he'd come after me.

I couldn't live like that. In constant fear. Especially with how hard it had been to move past it. If I had my dad on my side this time, and he saw that Brock had problems, maybe this could work.

'If you get this account, Brock will be gone?' I asked.

'Yes,' my father said, with way too much hope in his voice.

I took a deep breath. Here, last night, I had felt safe, able to breathe for the first time in what felt like a lifetime without the weight of fear pressing down, but I couldn't stay at Jack's forever – even though that was just what I wanted. No, if I wanted a real chance with Jack, a chance to see where this could go, I needed to get Brock out of town as quickly as possible. Otherwise, I'd never know if Jack wanted me with him because he was protecting me, or because he loved me.

'If I set up a meeting, it doesn't mean he'll invest with you.'

'Of course, I just need the meeting, Pumpkin.'

'*If,*' I said clearly, 'I can get him to agree to sit down with you, and he still doesn't invest, I still want Brock gone. Back to New York, no matter the outcome with Jack's company.'

225

He was silent. Not a good sign. I was gambling with something I valued very much, and that was Jack's trust. But there was no other way. If I told him it was Brock who hurt me, he'd never sit down with them. Worse, he'd likely do something that only made Brock angrier and give him more of a reason to keep harassing me.

Brock was a sociopath to his bones, and that's what terrified me the most. Common sense didn't dictate his actions. If I could get him gone, then I could finally move on, with Jack. I wanted my strength back. Strength Jack helped me find. Strength I'd fight for.

'Those are my terms, Dad. One meeting. Regardless of the outcome, Brock leaves Denver.'

'Okay,' he said finally.

'You swear to me?'

'Yes,' he snapped. 'I swear.'

'I'll see what I can do.'

I quietly walked back into Jack's bedroom, to find him sitting up and awake.

'I don't like that,' he said, those steely dark eyes fastened to my every move.

'Don't like what?'

He put an arm behind his head, stretching those amazing muscles from his abs to his biceps, and I checked the urge to pounce on him.

'I went to bed with this warm woman, and woke up to a cold, empty bed. I don't like that.'

'Forgive me,' I said, and shimmied a little with my walk toward him. 'I didn't mean to displease you.'

'Where did you go?'

'Harper texted to let me know she made it to Aspen, and my dad called several times.'

'Everything okay?'

'Yeah, Harper's just taking a week vacation. My dad actually keeps talking to me about you.' I wiggled my eyebrows.

'He's not my type.'

'Oh, my God!' I put my hand to my chest in mock surprise. 'Did you ... did you just make a joke?'

'No, that can't be right.'

I nodded and smiled wide. 'You totally just made a joke!'

I hopped on the bed and pinched his side, getting a smile to come out. 'And you're ticklish! This is the best day ever.'

'Damn it, woman, you've gotten through my defenses,' he said with a chuckle, and finally won the battle, pinning me down with all his delicious weight on top of me.

With the morning sun coming through the windows I couldn't help but get lost in Jack's handsome face. He seemed lighter today. Last night, we'd shared something. An honest exchange of trust, and he looked happier.

'You were saying?' he asked. 'About your dad?'

'Oh, right.'

My stomach hurt just bringing this up, but it was the best way to get over this issue. I wasn't going to lie to Jack. I just wasn't going to tell him the details about the possibility that Brock was stalking me and wrecking my stuff, leaving me in a state of panic and terror.

'He wants me to try to convince you to meet with him and his company about investing.'

'That so?'

I nodded.

He looked at me for a long moment, then finally, a playful grin split his face. 'And how would you go about *convincing* me?'

I raised a brow and shrugged. 'Well, several things crossed my mind. The first of which was oral persuasion.'

'I'm listening,' he said.

'Then, I don't know, present the best possible outcome.' I shifted my hips. Sliding my center along his hardening cock.

'You seem to make a good case.' He kissed me quickly, then with seriousness asked, 'Is it important to you? That I meet with them?'

The way he asked me that tugged on my heart. Was it important to me? It was important that Brock moved back to New York, and stayed far away. But I didn't care about my father's business. I was beyond hoping that would ever work out with me in the future. I was actually excited about grad school, and looking at the world from a different angle. An angle free from the past and all the negativity that went with it. But first, Brock needed to go away.

'I would really appreciate it. I know they're a smaller company, but if you just had one meeting, I would be grateful.'

'Okay.'

'That's it?'

'Is there something else you'd prefer me to say?'

'I just thought that would come across weird or . . .'

He kissed me again, his nose brushing mine briefly. 'It's a meeting, and you asked.'

'Yeah, but you're busy.'

'You asked,' he said again, like this explained everything away. The look in his eyes was so tender it made me reach out and hold tight.

'You said Harper is gone for the week?'

I nodded.

He tucked a lock of hair behind my ear. 'How would you feel about staying with me for the week then?'

'Really?'

This made my anxiety lessen, because honestly, the thought of going back to the house, especially empty, was terrifying.

'We can go pick up some of your stuff.'

'I brought that small bag, it will last me a couple of days.'

'Well, we'll figure out the details later then.'

Jack kissed me, and I got lost. Content to stay in our world just a little while longer.

Between school starting up in fifteen days, my job winding down, and staying at Jack's the past week, life was moving quickly. I'd taken half the day off to go get my textbooks and run a few errands. When I had shown up to my house a couple days ago, I saw my car, parked where I'd left it, with brand new tires on it.

My hope was that it was my dad, but the sight just redoubled the notion that the VanBuren clan, which now included my father, no matter that his last name was Case, was one I wanted to stay away from.

My life was under a microscope when it came to them. Now that my father got what he wanted, hopefully, things could get back to normal. Only this time, I was moving past everything, including him.

Jack was set to meet with my dad – I glanced at my watch – right now. Opening my front door, I put my books down and unloaded some of the groceries. I had been staying at Jack's, but the weekend was approaching. Harper would be home, and if my father stuck to his word, Brock would be packing up and heading back to New York.

Time to get this arranged.

'Isn't this charming?' A staunch voice came from the front porch. I spun around to find my step-mother hovering in the entryway. It was daylight out, but I hadn't gotten back to shut the door all the way, with my hands being full. Something I was really regretting now.

'Is there a reason you're here, Anita?'

She pursed her lips in a venomous smile. 'Just to check in on you. Your father said something about you running into some bad luck with local vandals. Thank goodness no one broke into your home or anything like that. Frightening thought.'

My stomach dropped. Anita just stared at me, her thin lips and beady glare masked by money and pure evil.

'I know what's going on. You think your father is noble? Brock isn't going anywhere, and he never was.'

'I spoke with my father, and—'

'Yes, and he made you promises. But I didn't think you were foolish enough to believe him. Who do you think told him about you and Jack Powell? Pushed him to lean on you?'

'Why are you so awful?' I asked. Nothing else seemed to make sense other than that.

'Going around accusing someone's son of heinous things can do that to a woman.'

'I understand he's your son, and it's hard for you to believe, but it happened.' I tried to stand tall and hold my ground. 'I don't need you or my father to believe me anymore. I just want Brock to stay away from me.'

'Oh? And where has all this fire come from? Surely not the man you've been seeing and set up to meet with your father? If so, that may prove difficult.'

'What do you mean?'

'I had a lovely chat with Mr Powell today. Wanted to thank him on behalf of the company for meeting with us.'

My stomach lurched.

'I also thought he should know that one of his employees lies about rape, and was using him for professional gain. Perhaps not someone to trust, much less continue to employ.'

'I didn't lie,' I said, the words shredding my throat.

230

'I'm not the one you have to convince of that anymore. But Jack seemed a bit upset when he learned that you stood to take over his account if he signed with Case-VanBuren.'

'My father offered that to me, and I declined. I only wanted Brock gone.'

'Yes, well, good luck with that endeavor. But you'd be wise to keep your mouth shut about my son.' She hit me with a glare. 'Have a good day, dear.'

With that, she left, and my stomach dropped to the floor. I had to get to Jack.

I raced into Jack's office, bypassing his secretary, and barged in. He sat behind his desk, everything about him calm, aside from the look in his eyes.

'You just missed your father and step-brother,' he said.

'Jack, I have to talk to you. Anita VanBuren came by, and said—'

'Yes, she had plenty to say earlier today.'

I stepped toward him, and he stood, walking around his desk to face me.

'I can explain,' I started.

'Oh? Then please do. And start by telling me that you didn't just lie to my face.'

'I told the truth, just evaded some details.'

His eyes narrowed. 'And which details are those? How about the one where you were going to work for your father's company, handling my assets, if you landed me as a client?'

'My father offered me that, but he lied. I didn't accept it anyway.'

'But you pushed for this meeting.'

'Because it was the only way to get rid of Brock. Someone has broken into my home, my car, slashed my tires—'

231

'And it's Brock?'

'I think so. I'm not certain, though.'

'What about the rest?' he growled and stepped toward me.

'The rest what?' I whispered, looking down. I knew what he meant, but I hoped to God he wouldn't make me say it.

'You said you were raped.' The word had a power that stung. 'Who did it?'

I shook my head.

'Tell me, Lana. Tell me what that woman said to me isn't true. Tell me you didn't have me sit down and talk business with the man that violated you!'

Tears gathered, and all I could do was stare at the floor.

'Jesus fucking Christ! That's sick. After everything you begged of me. You kept this piece from me?'

'I just wanted him gone.'

'You could have told me.'

'I didn't know if you'd believe me.' Because no one, except Harper, ever has. But my words looked like they slapped Jack in the face.

'I've been on your side from day one,' he growled. 'The fact that you'd rather have me ignorantly sit down with a criminal man, shake his fucking hand, then tell me, is . . . ' he looked disgusted with me. 'You played the naïve card well.'

'I wasn't playing anything. I love you.'

'And I'm supposed to believe that? You let me sit down with a man that assaulted you, threatens you, and you wanted me to invest with him? Who are you? You plead for my secrets? Want me to bare all, and you're the biggest liar of them all.'

That broke my heart into two brittle pieces.

'No one believed me with Brock before. I didn't think they would now—'

'I would have.'

232

I looked up, and his eyes cut through me. The mixture of rage and sadness tore at my heart.

'I wanted to help you from the beginning. The moment I saw that look in your eyes at the bar that first night, I had to make you mine. Make you safe. Because that fucking look haunts me.'

'What do you mean the beginning?'

His eyes stayed on mine. 'I made sure you got the payroll job for the resort.'

'That's impossible. I went to a temp agency Harper told me about.' He didn't say any more, just let my mind run with that bit of information. Which it did. 'The night I met you, I texted Harper. You got her number didn't you? Reached out to her and told her to tell me about the job?'

'Yes.'

My entire chest was going to explode. It explained why Harper kept trying to warn me about Jack not being long-term and his possible ulterior motives.

'And when I asked you about it being a coincidence, you made me feel like a fool.' I shook my head 'And you call me the liar?'

'I put you in my path. The means are irrelevant.'

'Everything we had was a set up. A manipulation from the beginning.' I'd known about certain things, like the jam and the toothbrush, and I thought it was him being thoughtful. Thought it was romantic even that he wanted me. Just me. But he had an agenda from the start.

'Maybe it's better this way,' he said. A face of stone would have shown more care than what I saw on Jack's face. Gone was the man that smiled, touched me with gentle or rough hands. Gone was every emotion from his face.

'What's better? Nothing about this is better. It's falling apart.' I placed my hands on his chest. '*We* are falling apart.'

He covered my hands, then pushed them away.

233

'I'm going to London to oversee the new resort.'

'When?' I breathed, but it was difficult.

'Monday.'

I frowned and stepped back. That was a few days away. 'You weren't going to tell me?'

'I was going to do a lot of things.'

His words cut every ounce of hope I had. Every sign that we were more, moving forward, was shattering before me, along with the trust we built. Trust we never had. Because I stood there, realizing I was a pawn to him. Just like I was to everyone else, and he was convinced I used him.

'How long will you be gone?'

'Long enough for us to end this now.'

Tears spilled over, and there was nothing I could do. My ribs split in half and the pressure of this moment, of losing Jack and realizing that we were doomed from the start, was too much.

'I just wanted to be strong on my own,' I whispered. Something he had wanted to help me with. Something he *did* help me with. Yet, I stood there, crushed beneath the weight of what was slipping away. I just wanted Brock gone. I wanted a fresh start with my life. And I wanted that with Jack. Yet, all the emotions we'd shared were frosting over.

'You promised you'd never hurt me.' I looked him in the eye, and he had the decency to at least show some anguish. 'You should have clarified that you meant only physically.' Though, in that moment, my entire body ached.

'Lana,' he whispered my name, and the faintest touch of his hand brushed mine.

'Ten,' I said and stepped back. We both knew ten was my limit. He didn't have to ask for the last part, but I gave it anyway. 'Ten: Cold.'

His brows sliced down, and his hands balled into fists at his sides, as if wanting to punch the wall, or maybe keep from touching me. Either way, I couldn't stay. Couldn't handle the look on his face any longer.

I turned and walked out, his presence as always, engulfing. And it was swallowing me whole. Leaving nothing left of the woman I was, or could have hoped to be.

Chapter 20

I sat on my couch, which had been my spot over the last couple days, and took a break from crying, only to fall asleep and wake up to find my life was the mess I'd left it in. It was Sunday. Tomorrow, Harper would come back, and Jack would leave.

'I can come home today,' Harper said. I pressed my cell against my ear.

'No, you stay. You've earned every day of your vacation. I'm fine.'

'When Jack got ahold of me to offer you the job, I didn't think of it as a manipulation. I thought I was helping.'

'I know.' And I did. She was looking out for me, like she always did. Only this time, she'd lied to me too, and suddenly I felt as though I had been betrayed by every last person I'd ever known.

'He's right on one thing though,' I whispered, fighting back the tears for the millionth time. 'I messed up. I should have told him it was Brock. I never meant to use him. I *wouldn't* use him.'

'You were trying to get rid of an asshole,' Harper said. 'You were handling it the best way you knew how. The situation was fucked up. You were being used by your dad and that bitch wife of his. It's over now. You're still strong.'

'That was because of Jack, and he's gone.'

'No,' Harper said. 'From the beginning, I told you—'

'Please, God, spare me the "I told you so" speech. I can't handle it.'

'I was going to say, *I told you* that he was the catalyst for your strength. He helped you find your spark. But you're the one that's maintained it. You should be proud of yourself. Don't go backwards now. Go forward. With or without him.'

I nodded. But the without part hurt to think about.

'Thanks. Have fun, okay?'

'You sure you don't want me to come home?'

'No, I promised myself this is my last day of wallowing.' Because tomorrow, Jack would be on a plane, and out of my life.

The sun was setting, and I'd never experienced a longer Monday than today. Harper had just left to get some dinner, and I was getting ready to get into pajamas early, when a knock came at the door.

I opened it.

'Jack.' His name on my lips both stung and overjoyed my entire body.

He stood tall, in a black suit, looking pressed and perfect with his town car and driver idling in the driveway.

'I thought you left?'

He nodded. 'I'm heading to the airport now.'

I crossed my arms. There was so much I wanted to say. So much I wanted him to say.

'I tried to stay away,' he rasped. 'But I couldn't leave without seeing you one more time.'

Just when I thought my heart couldn't break further, it did. This was my chance, maybe my only chance to say what I needed to say, so I could at least sleep at night, knowing all my cards were on the table.

237

'I'm sorry. I'm sorry for a lot of things. I should have told you the whole truth. My reasons seem flawed now, but they came from a place of logic. I wanted to be strong, wanted to live a new life, one that didn't include this nightmare that has been following me around since I was a kid. But I want you to understand that I would never use you. I just wanted to be the kind of woman you could be proud of.' I met his eyes and my throat closed up a little. 'I wanted to be the kind of woman I could be proud of.'

His brows sliced down, and a look of pain crossed his face. A single tear escaped my eye.

'I love you, Jack. And it hurts so much, but I'll never be sorry for that.'

His jaw clenched so hard I thought his teeth would snap. His whole body looked like it was humming. His hands flew out so fast I didn't see them coming. He cupped my face and pulled me in for a searing kiss. I felt all the pain and tension thrum through him. I squeezed my eyes tighter, more tears coming, and wetting his cheeks as well as mine.

He pulled away quicker than he'd come and stepped back.

'I am proud of you,' he said, gravel lining his words. His cheeks were wet from my tears, but it was then I noticed the slightest bit of moisture coating his own eyes. 'You are strong, and it's time you realize that ... without me.'

'We can work through this, can't we?'

A sad smile lined his face. 'Maybe someday. But not today. I'll be busy in London for the foreseeable future.'

'Then, we make it work.'

'All of my focus needs to be on the project,' he said quietly. 'Timing is everything, Lana. And our time is up.'

He turned and walked toward his car. Tears rolled down my face. Part of me wanted to cling to the notion that maybe he loved

238

me. Maybe he loved me so much that he was leaving so I could find myself, for myself. He was giving me what I wanted.

The other part of me watched his back as he walked away, and my entire world crumble. Because walking away was something you don't do to people you love. I stood there and fought for him, and he turned his back on me.

'You knew about London from the beginning. So, was this timeline something you set up from the start?' I called after him. 'From the moment you chose to put me in your path,' I used his words back on him, 'was this whole thing just a countdown to now? To you leaving? Were we doomed to have an end date?'

'Yes.'

That single word shattered the final pieces of hope I held to that Jack and I could bounce back from this. But he'd set the clock from the start, and the alarm went off. Time for me to go back to the real world. And it devastated my entire being.

'Lana?' he said before getting into the car. I met his gaze. 'I believe you. About everything.'

I cupped my hand over my mouth to keep from retching.

He believed me.

Despite the nasty things Anita said, the way the meeting went down, and even about Brock. He believed me.

But it didn't change the fact that he was leaving, and we were over.

With a final look of his dark eyes skating over me, he got into his car and drove off.

Taking half of my soul with him.

Epilogue

'One week from today you start school,' Harper said. 'Here's to fresh starts.' She clinked my glass and took a sip.

It was a beautiful afternoon, and we sat on the porch drinking spiked lemonade. And as I promised, I gave myself a week to be a devastated wreck about Jack, and I was done now. Well, I was trying.

'Are you glad to be done with work?'

I nodded. 'Yeah, it will be a good break, and I can really prep.'

'Only you would prep for school before it even starts.'

I had this whole week ahead of me to really clear my mind and focus on grad school. I'd saved enough money for living expenses for a little while. I would have had more, but I used a chunk to have a security system put in on the house, which helped me sleep at night. Especially since Brock wasn't moving anywhere.

I'd probably have to find another temp job around the holidays, but I'd deal with that later. My focus was on grad school. That's it.

'Have you heard from your dad?' Harper asked with caution.

'No.' The only thing I had heard was that Brock was very much around, living at my dad and Anita's place and 'working'

241

on building back up the Denver branch, since Jack had basically told them to fuck off. 'I'm enemy number one to a lot of people at the moment.'

'Well, fuck them. I'm here. We'll get to spend way more time together, and everything will settle,' Harper said.

I looked at my lemonade. I could always leave, except my life, Harper, and school were here. And leaving because I was scared of Brock was not going to happen. He'd messed up my life when I was young. I wouldn't let him chase me from this one.

I just hoped the 'issues' of feeling watched and my things being messed with would stop.

I have the alarm on the house now. Everything will be fine, I reminded myself.

Except for this gaping hole in my chest that Jack used to fill in. I missed him. His heat and commanding control. The way he made me feel like I was his alone, made me feel like I was strong and alive and a woman. I didn't have him anymore, but I took Harper's advice and clung to the strength he'd helped me find. I just would have to cling really, really hard to keep it.

Just when tears started to line my eyes, as they did every time I thought of Jack, a loud honking sounded from down the street. A few trucks rolled up to the firehouse. Several guys got out, and were met by men at the fire station.

'Looks like the wild fighters are home,' Harper said.

I glanced across the street. One of the firemen stood out in particular: Cal.

He was at least an inch taller than most of the men, and he was as strong and large as I remembered. From his chest to his shoulders, there wasn't a small or un-honed part of him.

'Be right back,' Harper said, and headed across the street.

I didn't get any words out, because she walked across, drink in

242

hand, and started chatting with one of the firemen. One of the same ones from the night we'd gone to the barbeque at the park, I thought.

Cal appeared to say something to Harper. She chatted with him for a minute, then he looked my way and hustled over.

Crap.

I wasn't in the best mood, and between my lack of makeup and crying all week, I wasn't feeling overly self-confident. Not to mention that the cutoff shorts and old T-shirt I'd donned were hardly cute.

Not that I was trying to look cute for Cal, but he was Jack's best friend, and the last thing I wanted was a report back to him on how destroyed I was. I continued sitting on my porch, trying to appear calm, and smiled.

'Hey, Kitten,' Cal said. 'Told you I'd be back.'

'Looks like you keep your promises.' I had meant that to be nice, but it came out bitter, and I quickly took a sip of my drink. Cal, however, didn't miss it.

'Something wrong?'

I shrugged. 'You haven't talked to Jack?'

He put his hands in his pockets and rocked on his heels. 'I know enough.'

Great. Just great.

'Got room for one more?' he asked, tilting his chin at the spot next to me on the porch.

'Yeah.'

He sat, his long legs bent, and his elbows resting on his knees. 'You want to talk about it?'

I looked at him. Blue eyes boring into mine, big muscles encased in a white T-shirt and jeans. He was so casual. His presence actually calmed me, and part of me did want to talk about it. But the other part of me thought better of it.

'Things didn't work out with Jack and me,' was all I said.

He nodded. 'Jack can be a tough guy to crack. But I know he cares about you. A lot.'

I laughed. 'Yeah, which is why he left, didn't tell me for how long – could be an eternity – and set our whole interaction between us up from the beginning.'

'Well, if you don't count those few small things . . .'

I laughed again, only this time it came from a place of humor. Cal was making me do one thing I hadn't done in days: Laugh.

'Are things always so easy with you?'

He shrugged. 'Everybody has baggage. Jack's is heavy. I'm not claiming to be any better. I just chose to outrun mine. When that fails, I run faster, when that fails, I run even faster, and usually toward a fire.'

'Sounds like you either have a lot of baggage or are an adrenaline junky.'

'I like the workout. Also, I'm not convinced about this whole gravity craze. One of these days, when I jump down from a tree, I'll just start floating. I'm sure of it.'

I laughed again. He was so good at taking my mind from . . . well . . . everything.

'Not sold on gravity, huh?'

'Nah. In my experience, it's way more fun when your feet are off the ground.'

'Well, good luck disproving gravity.' I smiled.

He nudged my shoulder with his. 'If it means anything, I know Jack better than I know myself. There's always more going on with him than he lets on. But, he's a good guy. Just deals with things poorly sometimes.'

'You don't have to defend him,' I whispered. Because I messed up a little too. My intentions were clean. I never wanted to hurt

Jack, or have him think for a second I was using him. I just wanted Brock gone. Wanted to handle things in my world, so that I knew when he invited me into his it was for the right reasons.

Not that it mattered anymore. It was set up to be this way from the beginning. The only kink in his plan had been Cal. Who, ironically, was now sitting next to me.

I looked at the impressive firefighter. 'Are you okay? No burns or lung damage or anything?'

He smiled and stretched a little. 'Nah, that wildfire had nothing on me and my boys.'

'Course not.'

'Harper was saying you start school next week?'

'Yeah.'

'Okay, so I'll see you around then? Hang out sometime?'

I frowned. 'Um, maybe. I don't think I'm going to be up for much of doing anything.'

'Well, then I'll help you through a pity party. I'll bring the booze and karaoke machine. Can you cover mixers and snacks?'

I smiled, then frowned, because he looked serious. 'Are you out of your mind?'

'A little,' he winked. 'But you look like you could use some fun. You have a week before school. I'm not trying to swoop in and get into your panties, I'm just asking if you'll spend some of that time you have with me.'

I looked at him for a moment. Between the dimples, blue eyes, and casual demeanor, part of me really wanted to escape the pity party I was throwing myself.

'Fine,' he threw his hands up when I didn't say anything. 'Your silence is unbearable, and you've broken me. The truth is, I do have motives.'

I scowled at him. Of course he did!

Before I could curse him out, he said, 'I have water motives. I'm giving you fair warning going into this. I'm going to try to hydrate the hell out of you.'

That made me bust up laughing. My memory flashed to the first night I met him.

'Well, at least you're upfront with your intentions.'

'Yeah, this woman I met a couple months ago told me that she likes it when intentions are clearly stated.'

'Oh, yeah?'

Cal nodded. 'Yeah, she was really smart, and a hottie, so I figured she knew what she was talking about.'

I shook my head and grinned.

'There you go. Smiling is a good look for you, Kitten. You should do more of it.'

I met his eyes, and realized I hadn't done much of that lately. Even before Jack and I broke up. It was funny how these two men were the best of friends, and yet seemed like night and day in personality.

'Maybe we can hang out,' I finally said.

Cal slapped his hands together and rubbed them. 'Awesome, be prepared to sing. I need a duet partner for *Endless Love*.'

'Oh, God . . .'

But Cal was already standing and calling across the street to the guys outside still chatting. 'Hey, karaoke party this weekend! And, Simpson, you've been replaced. I have a new singing partner!'

A guy, who must be Simpson, threw his arms in the air. 'Ouch, bro. What ever happened to the *Endless* in *Endless Love*?'

Everyone laughed.

My cheeks heated a little. Cal faced me, bent, and brushed his fingertip along my cheek and winked. 'Everything will be okay.'

246

He was serious and sincere, and somehow, I believed him. He turned and walked back across the street. There was so much that had happened. So much that hadn't. This path I was on had been set from day one. While the outcome was already in motion, one thing still tumbled through the back of my mind.

'Cal?' I called after him, and he stopped and faced me. 'Remember when you said that you and Jack were both at the bar that first night?'

He nodded.

'Where were you?'

His blue eyes locked on mine. 'I was throwing an asshole out the door.'

My breath caught, as my memory stretched to recall that night. When the fight broke out, a large man in a white T-shirt interfered before the bouncer even got there.

'That was you?'

His smile was all the confirmation he gave before he turned and headed back toward the firehouse. Jack may have come in to be my wall, but Cal had thrown himself into the fray before anyone got too close to me in the first place.

I took several swallows of my drink. My chest was still throbbing from the battle it'd undergone with Jack the past couple months. But, somehow, I didn't feel destroyed beyond repair.

Which was hopeful.